The Mummy's Quest

by
Robin Bailes

oo

Prologue - The Tomb

There is no light here. There is no sound. There is no movement. And there has not been for over four thousand years.

What there is - if there is anything in this still, silent darkness - is patience. It would be too much even to call it anticipation, nothing so vital could exist here. But patience, the oppressiveness of waiting for something. Patience like this you can almost feel - it has substance, it has weight. And now, that patience is about to be rewarded. The wait is almost over. Somewhere, just at the edge of sensation, there is the merest suggestion of something that at some point in the future might be considered a sound.

The tomb's sole inhabitant had long since lost any concept of what 'sound' might mean. But perhaps, inasmuch as they understood anything in their current condition (that condition being dead), they understood that their long sleep was coming to an end.

That understanding was felt here, but it was also felt across the sea, many hundreds of miles away, in a land which the people who built the tomb had never heard of, in a place they could not have imagined. Here, the lights were hard and unforgiving, the noise was hushed but constant, and the movement continual. By day, at least. By night you might have said that this place across the seas was as silent as a tomb, except that nothing could be as silent as that tomb.

Here too was one who had been waiting, one whose wait was coming to an end, one who had no concept of the journey that now lay ahead. But for him the experience was different, it was sudden and brutal. One minute he was nothing, the next, with a jolting rush of reality, he was alive and possessed of only one thought: the need to go home, to her. In the dim vagueness of his mind he was aware that he had once possessed such things as desires and personality. Perhaps those things would return with time, but for now he was animated only by the single driving force of that one need. It pulled at him, fierce and unrelenting, it would brook no disobedience and admit no delay, it defined him.

He thrust his arms upwards shattering the clear case that surrounded him. Unsteady, testing long-unused muscles, he pulled himself out of the remains of the case and felt a light on his face that cut sharply through the darkness of the room. At the far end of the shaft of light stood a man in strange clothes, staring with his mouth

4

hung open, his face blanched to white, his eyes wide. He seemed to be rooted to the spot, as he did not even try to run when the creature from the glass case lurched angrily towards him, grabbed him by the throat and squeezed.

The man's torch dropped to the ground, followed moments later by his body. Neither was working any more.

The creature looked about once again. That was when it saw the cat.

Chapter 1 - The Priest With Turquoise Eyes

Amelia Evans could trace her interest in Ancient Egypt back to a film she had seen on TV one Sunday afternoon when she was a child. It had been one of those huge spectacles that Hollywood was keen on making in the 1950s to prove that film was better than TV, and which latter-day TV schedulers love to put on because they fill a good 3 hours at a time when no one is watching anyway. The plot had passed young Amelia by, but the place made an indelible impression. She had sat cross-legged, barely a foot from the screen, goggling at pyramids, sphinxes and temples, wondering at the glamour of the Egyptian women and the passion of the Egyptian men. She was old enough to know that not everything you saw on TV was real, and such a world as this surely could not actually exist. She mentally filed it alongside *Star Wars* and Ralph Bakshi's *Lord of the Rings*. Even when her father told her that Egypt was a real place where Pharaohs had ruled long ago, she still refused to believe it - her father was not above playing games with his daughters. So her parents took Amelia, and her younger sister Zita, to the British Museum, and Amelia's jaw hit the floor. If her nascent interest in Egypt had been established by Hollywood's paint and papier-mâché recreation of it, then her interest in Egyptology was forged that afternoon in central London. She goggled at the massive statue of Rameses II, she peered with ghoulish fascination at the mummies, and frowned with intense concentration at the hieroglyphics carved into the base of a statue. At first her parents thought it a childish phase, but as their daughter consumed book after book on the subject - books written for far older readers - they began to wonder.

The phase never passed, the interest never died, and it was interesting to contemplate now, nearly twenty five years later, that a journey which ended up in the Fitzwilliam Museum Cambridge, had begun cross-legged on the floor in front of a Sunday matinee. The enthusiastic young girl had grown up (not as high as she would have liked) dark-haired and quietly serious, introspective and bookish. All of which are considered *de rigueur* for experts in dead languages, specialising in Ancient Egyptian. Every now and then Amelia wondered if, had *Ben Hur* been on instead, she would have ended up in a different career. She always concluded not. She and Ancient Egypt had been destined to find each other, if not this way, then some other.

To be clear, Amelia did not work in The Fitz (as it was called by those in the know), she was a research fellow at Cambridge University, but the Museum was where she spent much of her time, owing principally to the Egyptian gallery's star exhibit; The Priest with Turquoise Eyes.

The mummy of the Priest had been discovered in the 1920s in so grand a tomb that he had initially been identified as a Pharaoh, and even now his exact identity remained a mystery. The tomb had been plundered by thieves in antiquity, as had so many ancient tombs, but the stone sarcophagus itself and the coffin of the mummy within had remained unmolested. This was unusual, and researchers hypothesised that there was something about this man that had made the tomb robbers think twice. Certainly he was an arresting sight; most notably, two pieces of turquoise, carefully carved into the shape of eyes, had been placed into his own vacant sockets, delicately tucked into the bandages, to stare out at any who disturbed his rest. Popular legend had it that Professor Petrie, who had first opened the case, had wet himself with shock on seeing the mummy staring back at him.

That the mummy was that of a priest had been determined by the few funerary goods which had survived the robbers. Plus, a tomb this opulent for someone not royal strongly suggested a religious leader. Little more than this had been gleaned because, although the sarcophagus was liberally inscribed with hieroglyphics, they dated from a period known as the Lost Dynasty. During this sketchy and historically vague period, Egypt's capital was believed to have moved, there was vast social upheaval, and a new way of writing was adopted (perhaps even a whole new language spoken). Amongst Egyptologists this alternative hieroglyphic alphabet was officially referred to as cryptoglyphics, and privately referred to as a pain in the arse which was preventing them from learning about one of the most intriguing periods of Egyptian history. They were infuriatingly difficult to crack - only one man had ever come close and he had left the job half done. What was needed was an enterprising young expert in ancient languages to come along and make her name by deciphering them.

Or at least, that was what Amelia hoped.

"Here again?" The elderly custodian smiled down at Amelia as she sat cross-legged (a habit she had never got out of) copying a section of the sarcophagus inscription down into one of her notebooks. Amelia lived out of her notebooks.

"Hi Mr Pearson. How are you?" It was impossible to spend as much time here as Amelia did without getting to know the custodians, and Mr Pearson was one of those who always stopped for a chat.

"Got the night shift again," Mr Pearson grumbled. He presumably had a first name but was of a generation that saved such familiarities for family and close friends, and Amelia had never had the courage to enquire. "Third time this month. It's all politics. You've got company, you know."

Amelia looked up to see Valerie, the museum's cat, looking down at her, seated in a stately pose on top of the glass case that housed both sarcophagus and mummy. She gave an erudite meow.

Amelia forced a smile. She was not really a cat person - the one aspect of Ancient Egyptian life that left her cold - they always seemed to be quietly plotting to kill you in your sleep just to watch you die.

"What are you up to there?" Mr. Pearson asked. He asked the same thing most days.

"Just copying them out," replied Amelia, indicating the cryptoglyphs.

"Surely you've done that already?"

Amelia nodded. "Couple of times. But you can't get into the head of the writer unless you write too."

The old man nodded sagely, not quite disguising the fact that he thought this theory to be so much cobblers. "Enjoy yourself."

"Thanks, Mr Pearson."

The theory had been strongly advocated by Professor Joseph Muller, the afore-mentioned only man to make any headway deciphering cryptoglyphics, despite being widely thought to be barking mad. The idea was that you could not understand a written language unless you wrote it yourself, and Amelia could see the sense in this. Letters in the roman alphabet we use today have changed over time through usage - it made sense that the cryptoglyphs were the same, so writing those letters helped you to understand how they had become what they were and maybe where they had come from. Which was one reason that, despite clever

8

computer programmes which allowed researchers to transpose hieroglyphs, Amelia still preferred to copy them by hand. Another reason was that she just preferred the individuality of the written word to the uniformity of the typed. And she didn't really trust computers - what were they doing with all that information anyway? But, on a deeper level, she liked the idea that she was writing something that had first been written so long ago. It felt like a physical connection to the person who had written it. For all that she was a serious researcher, the sense of childlike wonder that had first attracted her to Ancient Egypt had never left Amelia Evans.

Was any of this paying off in the interpretation that had eluded scholars and academics for decades and beyond? Well... maybe. What Amelia had not told Mr Pearson was that she was making progress. Not because she thought the old man might blab, but because she was afraid to say it out loud for fear of tempting fate. Even thinking it made her nervous. She glanced back over the line of characters she had just copied down: *'When the tomb of the Queen is violated...'*

It made sense. There was no getting around that fact that it made sense. And the odds against it making sense if she had gotten it wrong were long to say the least. She *was* making progress. Probably. It seemed likely. Or at least not impossible. All signs indicated that she was going in the right direction. Touch wood.

That night, Amelia sat alone in her 2nd floor flat, just off Trumpington Road, and pored through her notes; *'...to the city of the dead where her slaves still lie.'*. It still made sense. You couldn't deny it. Sure, a person with a good imagination can think they've translated something when in fact they are just imposing onto it what they've already decided it should say, without even realising they're doing it. That had happened to people before. But Amelia didn't credit herself with that much imagination. The bottom line was, if you could translate as much as two sentences and it all made sense then... well that could hardly be an accident could it? She had the key. It would still take work to decipher it all, but it was not like Amelia had anything else to do with her time.

Almost unwillingly her eyes crossed the room to the chair on the other side of the fireplace, the leather creased and dented to fit the shape of the person who had sat in it, and no longer did.

"What have *you* done recently?" she asked, accusingly.

"Actually, don't answer that. I don't want to know."

When Amelia had moved here - the first place she had ever bought, or co-bought - it had been with a man. A partner (you couldn't use the word 'boyfriend' to describe someone you lived with). His name was Frank Jenson and he was a lecturer in Classics at the University, which gave him and Amelia a certain amount of crossover. They could stay up late into the night debating the merits of Beowulf or discussing Virgil's treatment of Dido in a feminist context. It had been nice to find someone like Frank (although God knows, Cambridge is the place to find such men), someone who enjoyed quiet evenings in with a book, who understood what made a good cup of tea great, someone soft-spoken who seemed almost embarrassed by his own fierce intelligence, someone quiet and simple and sweet and lovely. It had come as a serious shock to discover that he had been sleeping with one of his students.

The news had been broken to Amelia by a tear-stained, redheaded girl who had turned up on her doorstep one afternoon. The girl had been so distraught to discover that the lecturer she was dating was in a long-term relationship with another woman, that Amelia had actually felt sorry for her. She invited the redhead in and made a cup of tea while the girl sobbed out a mixture of heartbreak and guilt. Taking care of the girl (whose name, it emerged between sobs, was Isobel - Izzy for short) distracted Amelia from having an emotional reaction of her own. She found herself analysing the situation rather than reacting to it. It slightly baffled her. Once Izzy had stopped crying and wiped the tear streaks from her face, it became obvious that she was a very beautiful girl. And not just in the conventional way; Izzy was one of those girls who seem wilfully more beautiful than those around them - as if they are doing it deliberately. She was stunning in every respect, and while Amelia obviously found Frank attractive, it was still hard to imagine how he had scored Izzy. Amelia wondered if it was polite to ask what Izzy was doing with a Classics lecturer, more than ten years her senior, who collected antique writing ephemera. She decided that it would just make a weird situation weirder

"I'm so sorry!" Izzy blurted out for what had to be the twentieth time.

"It's not your fault," said Amelia, more because she didn't want the girl to start crying again than because she actually believed it.

10

Didn't girls these days check? A girl who looked like Izzy was bound to encounter this issue - were there no precautions she could take?

"If I'd know he had..."

"I know."

"I never would have..."

"I understand."

"I mean," Izzy continued, "I'd heard the stories, but he just seemed so nice and quiet."

Amelia nodded. Frank did indeed seem so nice and quiet. Who knew that that was an aphrodisiac to female students who were sick of being hit on by their male contemporaries, whose idea of a good night out was a game of beer pong. Perhaps it was not so very strange that... Amelia's train of thought ground to an unscheduled stop as she reanalysed Izzy's last sentence.

"I'm sorry; stories?"

The fact that quiet, simple, lovely Frank had been sleeping with one of his students had come as a shock to Amelia. The fact that he had been sleeping with several of them took the top of her head off. Apparently, Izzy had not been the only girl looking for an alternative to the beer and boob obsessed males who infested the student union bars (even in Cambridge). Quiet, simple, lovely Frank had discovered that he was 'in demand', and he had taken advantage.

His best excuse, when confronted, was that he was weak, and what he had with these girls was 'nothing compared to what we have, Amelia, what we have is special'. And what Amelia wanted more than anything else during this speech was to throw something at his head and then throw his belongings out the window.

Actually that was sadly untrue. What she wanted more than anything else was to accept his apology and go back to how things had been. It was appallingly weak she knew, but she had been happy, and that was a hard thing to let go. But everything had changed; there was no going back. Frank was out by the end of the day. There were no histrionics, nothing flung, few shouted words. It was a very civilised parting, and Amelia felt like a traitor to her gender and to everything she believed for letting him off so lightly.

The whole affair left Amelia with a bad taste in her mouth, with a flat that she would otherwise not have been able to afford (the least Frank could do), and with an unexpected new friend. It was

11

inconceivable that Izzy had been the only one of Frank's student girlfriends to find out that he had a partner, but she had been the only one who sought Amelia out. That sense of duty had endeared Izzy to Amelia, and while they had little in common, they found that they got on rather well. The studious older woman enjoyed going on a night out with the socially precocious teenager. Watching Izzy, men swarming around her, brushing them off with practiced ease, Amelia wondered about her own life. Not so much about men - they had never been a huge concern - but about independence. Izzy was her own woman through and through. Amelia wondered if, outside of her career, she had ever done anything that was for herself.

The chair by the fire remained empty for as long as she stared at it and Amelia redirected her attention to the notes in front of her. But the cryptoglyphs swam before her eyes, crossing the page and getting to know each other in unhelpful ways. She put the notebook to one side and headed for bed.

Whether as a result of this train of thought or due to the heat and early morning light of the season, Amelia slept only fitfully and woke early.

"Damn it," she muttered to herself, staring accusingly at the faded red curtains which were maliciously letting in bright summer daylight.

With sleep not being an option, Amelia rose, showered, dressed, ate a light breakfast with heavy coffee, and set out. The Fitz was not open to the public at this time of the morning, but she knew all the security guards and they were always happy to let her in early when she knocked at the side door. Ignoring the grand main entrance, she went through a nondescript iron gate and headed down the paved path to the museum's employee entrance, just next to the security guard's break room. There was a skip in her step as she walked; it hadn't been a fun night but now the sun was up, she had a good day's work ahead of her and that work had never seemed more optimistic. Today she might not just be copying inscriptions, she could be reading them. Touch wood. She rang the bell.

Inevitably, given the size of the museum, it took the guards a while to reach the door, and of course they might be busy doing other things. But after about fifteen minutes, Amelia realised that no one was coming. That was odd. She tried peering through the window but could make out nothing unusual in the little kitchen.

12

With no other obvious course of action, she went for a wander around the building, glancing up at the high windows and down through the basement ones, but everything was closed up for the night.

The first impression she had of anything being wrong was the sound of a crunch beneath her feet. She looked down to see broken glass on the cobbles, then up to see the broken window.

Instantly Amelia pulled out her phone, fumbling in her haste, then she paused. Was this really a case for 999? It didn't constitute an emergency yet, did it? What if it had been an accident and all they needed was a good glazier? As she was pondering the right course of action, she noticed something else amiss. The rear door that led to the service elevator was ajar. Amelia dialled 99, so she was ready in case of actual emergency, then pushed the door open and went in.

The museum was always quiet at this time of day, but this morning it seemed so much quieter, even with the sound of Amelia's heartbeat banging like a snare drum in her ears. Her footsteps too sounded abnormally loud, the scuffed sneakers squeaking and slapping against the cold stone floors. On autopilot, she made her way through the darkened rooms towards the Egyptology section in the basement. By the time she reached the familiar staircase, lined by Assyrian statues, her heart was thumping loud enough to wake the dead, banging insistently against the inside of her chest. Her mouth was dry and she had to keep reminding herself to breath. Her skin was clammy, an icy chill had claimed her, yet she was sweating enough that a strand of dark hair stuck to her forehead. She peered through the doorway into the Egyptian gallery and caught her breath, clapping a hand over her mouth to stop herself from squealing and, potentially, to stop her heart from leaping out.

There, lying on the floor in a crumpled mass, was the body of a man, clearly dead, a broken torch on the ground beside him. Amelia felt the bile rising in her throat - Mr Pearson had been on duty last night. Though she had no wish to go any closer, Amelia found she had no choice, her feet were making their way without her say so. She had to see for herself - maybe she could still help. As she crept forward, a sudden sharp sound made her start and look down. There was broken glass on the floor here too. Which was odd, since the high windows were all intact.

"Amelia?"

A hand landed on her shoulder and Amelia nearly leapt out of her skin, crying out and wrenching herself away from the figure behind her.

"Amelia, it's alright, it's me!" Mr Pearson held out his hands, trying to calm her, and Amelia, gasping for breath, overwhelmed by the onslaught of fear and relief, collapsed into his arms.

"I thought..."

"What? Oh! No." Mr Pearson shook his head. "Though they'll probably fire me for all this happening on my watch. I only closed my eyes for a minute, you know!"

"Who is he?" asked Amelia, turning back to look at the dead man on the floor.

"No idea," said Mr Pearson. "My guess is, he was one of the thieves and his mates turned on him. Serve him right."

"Thieves?"

Mr Pearson said nothing, but looked past Amelia, who followed his gaze. More broken glass lay on the floor, centring on the display case beside which she spent so much of her time. The glass was broken, the Priest with Turquoise Eyes was gone.

Chapter 2 - The Collector

The intercom on the desk of Norton Whemple buzzed brashly and the American tycoon (as he liked to describe himself) stabbed the talk button with a stubby finger.

"What?"

"There's a man here to see you Mr Whemple," replied his secretary (he wanted to say 'Janine', but he got through a lot of secretaries). "He doesn't have an appointment but he says he's a friend."

"Send him up."

"Yes, sir."

Whemple sat back in his chair, unconsciously knotting his hands across the ample acreage of his stomach. For all his faults, he did have a sense of self-awareness and would have been willing to admit that he was not a 'nice' man. His annual salary, not including bonuses, was many times the national average and yet his annual tax bill was many times lower, thanks to creative accounting and a bank in the Caymans. He had made nearly half his workforce redundant last year by relocating their core functions to a third world nation where people worked for peanuts, almost literally. He had been connected to the mysterious disappearance of his former business partner, who had vanished from his luxury yacht just as negotiations for the dissolution of their partnership had become acrimonious. He had met his current wife while cheating on his second wife, yet he also had a mistress and a girlfriend and was cheating on both of them, simply because he could. As far as Norton Whemple was concerned, money could not only buy you happiness, but it enabled you to buy other people's and then sell it back to them at a tidy profit. There were other transgressions yet to be proved and too numerous to mention.

But despite all this, the fact that Mr Jago would shortly be entering his office made Norton Whemple uneasy. He reached for the bourbon and poured himself a large measure. There was something about the man that made Whemple's skin crawl, whenever they spoke he could hear the sound of knife being run along a whetstone. Still, Jago was useful.

A few moments later there was a slow knock at the door that made Whemple nearly drop his glass. Was it possible for a knock to sound threatening?

"Come in!" Whemple barked, hoping that volume would make him seem like the one in charge - which by rights he was.

The door opened and Jago slid in. It was a feature of Jago (he had no other name, at least not professionally) that he slid everywhere, seeming to insinuate his way through the world, edge first, like a blade. Everything about Jago had that quality; his face seemed all edges, as if it had been shaped with a angle-grinder. You could have cut yourself on the bridge of his nose or the line of his jaw. There was only one irregularity in his face but that too spoke of a blade; a scar carved a path through his features, starting just below his left eye and terminating at his chin. Someone had tried to kill him - they were unlikely to have been the only one. Curiously, if you just glanced at his face then all you saw was ugliness, but the more you looked the more you realised that he was actually a very handsome man. Or would have been. His face seemed to lack some element that would allow it to be good-looking. Perhaps a soul.

"Mr Whemple." The voice too was honed to a sharpness.

"Take a seat," said Whemple, and Jago slid into a chair. He moved with a casual power, rangy muscles twisting about his limbs like ropes.

"What can I do for you?"

"I need you to go to Egypt."

Jago nodded.

"There is an item there that I want you to get for me."

"Something that belongs to someone else?" suggested Jago, his words easing into the conversation like a stiletto through a man's ribs.

Whemple considered the question. "Well, I don't know about that. It's there for the taking so who's to say it's not mine as much as anyone else's?"

"Finders keepers?"

"Not exactly," Whemple hedged. "I didn't find it."

"And the person who did might feel it belongs to them."

"They might."

"You would like me to educate them?"

Whemple fiddled with the gold plated pen on his desk, which had been a gift from a US Senator (it would be tactless to say more). "I want you to bring me back this item. With as little 'unpleasantness'

16

as possible."

Jago inclined his head. The unsaid words 'by whatever means necessary' hovered across the table between them. Whemple had employed Jago for similar jobs many times before, and there was an understanding between them that things were to be done discretely. Which, in this context, meant leaving no witnesses.

"The usual fee?" inquired Whemple. "Plus expenses, naturally."

Jago smiled, or at least his mouth curved thinly across his face like a scimitar. "Times are hard, Mr Whemple. Living costs are up. Rental costs are a crime."

"Shall we say an extra five thousand?"

"Well that's very fair of you, Mr Whemple."

He never pushed for more, never haggled, nor even named a price. He simply commented on inflation, on the falling markets or the rising cost of living, and allowed Whemple to increase his offer by an amount that suited both. Likewise Whemple never tried to pay less than the man was worth, partly because that was bad business when it was a man whom he wished to employ again, but also because he did not know what would happen. Probably nothing. But he would always be wondering, always watching his back. It was easier to pay.

"All the details are in here." Whemple passed an envelope across the desk. The details inside were sparse, leaving room for Jago to take whatever action he saw fit, and handwritten by Whemple himself, leaving no digital trail. Jago would burn them after reading as a matter of course.

Jago took the envelope and teased the corner against his thin lips thoughtfully. "Something for your collection, Mr Whemple?" he wondered.

Norton Whemple did not answer. In this room he tried to say as little as possible that might be considered incriminating. If it was not bugged now then one day it would be. One day the Feds would come for him and it would be bad enough that he had had conversations with men like Jago, the best he could do was make sure that the content of those conversations was non-specific.

"Thank you for your time."

The thin, unsettling smile spread again across Jago's hatchet face. "Always a pleasure, Mr Whemple."

17

He got to his feet with cat-like speed and slid out the way he had come.

Whemple collapsed back in his chair and poured himself another drink. He sometimes wondered if it was worth working with men like Jago just for the sake of a hobby. But of course his collection was more than that. Like the hobbies and pastimes of all men who consider themselves 'tycoons', it was a way of keeping score. The items in his collection were eclectic and varied, but above all they were unique. There was not one that would not have enjoyed pride of place in a museum. There was not one that should not, legally, have been in a museum. But getting away with it was part of the game. Value was important, but if you had the money then anyone could turn up to an auction and lay down a few million for a Picasso or a Degas. Where was the sport in that? You might just as well head for the bathroom with a ruler. No, to really win at the game of collecting then you had to be obtaining items that were hard to get hold of, not simply because of rarity or cost, but because they were not yours to take.

Historical artefacts were Norton Whemple's preference. He had begun with a Roman statue from Pompeii, for which Interpol were still searching. He had items from Ancient Greece, from Mycenae, and from various early South American civilisations. He had accidentally started a national incident when he acquired a Native American Totem pole, and an international one when a priceless item of Chinese jade found its way into his hands. Over the years he had set up a network of informants, working in archaeological digs around the world, sourcing items that might make the grade to join his peerless collection.

But his greatest passion was for Ancient Egypt. Unlike all the other civilisations, periods and peoples represented in his collection, he actually had a genuine interest in Ancient Egypt. He had even read books on the subject - which for a man who had given up halfway through *Green Eggs and Ham* was saying something. His collection of Egyptian items was an enviable one, but it lacked one thing that he dearly wanted, one thing without which no Ancient Egyptian collection could be said to be complete. Now, suddenly and unexpectedly, the opportunity to remedy that deficiency had come up, and with the help of Jago he would soon have a new centrepiece for his collection. No matter what it cost.

Whemple had never really thought about what his collection cost. In monetary terms the question did not interest him, and beyond that.... You did not employ men like Jago unless you were willing to have someone (someone other than you) pay the ultimate price, but he still did not like to think about it. When the subject occurred to him then he simply looked at his collection and decided it was all worth it. The people who had died in order that he might enjoy these items were going to die anyway in a few mere decades, while the items themselves would endure through the centuries - so which was more important? Besides, it was unlikely that there was an item in his collection which did not have a legacy written in blood. That was the nature of history; people were forever killing each other. He might be adding to the sum total of blood on these trinkets, but his contribution was pretty minimal by comparison.

Leaning back in his chair, Whemple idly day-dreamed of how he might best display this latest addition, when Jago provided it. This one, if his information was accurate, was more than usually steeped in blood.

Chapter 3 - The Interpreter

Cambridge Police were swift to descend on the Fitzwilliam Museum, cordoning off the Egyptology section and questioning Mr Pearson and Amelia long into the morning.

"Do you know who the man is?" Amelia kept asking, but the police were unwilling or unable to say. Amelia found herself feeling a strange attachment, or even responsibility for the mystery man whose body she had found, and yet also a niggling resentment. His death had ruined her plans for the day. The theft was an inconvenience too, but the sarcophagus remained and so her work could theoretically continue, but try telling that to a bunch of homicide detectives.

Strange the way your mind behaved in circumstances like this.

When the police let her go in the early afternoon, Amelia wended the familiar path home, stopping to pick up a cheese and tomato roll from the nice little shop on the corner that she often used. On reflection she also bought a packet of crisps, a chocolate bar and one of those fruit smoothies you could probably make yourself for a fraction of the price but who has the time? She entered the flat and put her bag of notes and books on the floor by the chair in which she habitually worked. The little lunch she had bought, she placed on the kitchen table, then opened the fridge to check for milk. None. She had meant to pick up a bottle on her way home. Amelia closed the fridge and burst into tears.

It was a brisk bout, not the sort of thing she often did, but these were exceptional circumstances. When she was done, she went into the bathroom and splashed cold water on her face. It was out of her system, no need to worry further.

But she still found herself unsettled. Amelia was not a person who struggled with how to fill her days; there was always work to do and if she needed a break from it then there were books to read or movies to watch, and a pleasant walk along the Cam was always an option. None of these appealed right now. Something studious was out of the question with her mind in its current upheaval, but something mindless seemed somehow disrespectful, as if she would be letting down the dead man by continuing her life in such a shallow way. It was a great relief when the phone rang.

"I just heard - are you okay?"

Every time she heard Izzy's voice, Amelia felt a sly pang at her heart, an involuntary flashback to the first time she had heard it, and the news that voice had brought. It was nice, if a little odd, that she had become such good friends with her ex-partner's ex-lover (one of), but the circumstances behind their friendship were always there, like the background radiation of their relationship. At her low points she found herself imagining that voice whispering or even screaming Frank's name in high passion. It was hard to say the name 'Frank' with passion, it didn't lend itself in the way that names like Antonio or Kurt might have, but if anyone could then it was probably Izzy.

"I'm fine. Just a bit shaken."

"I'm coming round."

"There's really no need."

"Then you come here."

"I..."

"I'm not taking no for an answer, Amelia. You don't have to be the strong one all the time. You shouldn't be alone."

Amelia had never really thought of herself as the strong one, she just had a habit of getting on with things. She wanted to ask why she shouldn't be alone. It wasn't as if she had known the unfortunate man, and museum thefts happened, especially in university towns (if it hadn't been for the dead man then this would have immediately been put down as a student prank). And yet, now it had been offered, she found a crushing need for company, the need to talk about anything other than the morning's events.

"Where are you?"

It was not a day for being indoors and Amelia found that, anyway, she did not want to be in Izzy's room in the Halls of Residence. In that intimate setting she would have felt the need to pour her heart out, and she did not want that. Better to go out for a drink, and on a summer's day in Cambridge then the only way to drink was on the banks of the Cam, watching the rowers and punters go by.

"Do they know who he was?" asked Izzy.

"I'd really rather not talk about it."

Izzy nodded. "For sure. Was anything missing other than the mummy?"

"Izzy."

"Oh, you mean not talk about any of it? I thought you just

meant the dead guy."

"Izzy!"

"What? He is, isn't he?"

Amelia shook her head and sipped at her Pimms (also compulsory on a day like this). There were huge advantages to a friend like Izzy, one who so seldom knew the right thing to say and who enjoyed only a passing association with social etiquette, and yet who was also the wisest of counsellors. People tended to misjudge her because of the way she looked and her way of speaking, but Izzy was on course for a First and was considered one of the best and brightest of her year. She knew her subject and had a remarkable mind, albeit one that was prone to stray.

Amelia leaned back and stared up at the cloudless sky. She was not a sun-worshipper, her skin refused to tan and she seldom gave it a chance, preferring her natural paleness. But on a day like today she was willing to tolerate the sun, and if it burned away a few brain cells - which was the only explanation she could come up with for some of the sun-bathers - she was inclined to let it.

"Here." Izzy passed her friend a pair of sunglasses.

"Thanks." Amelia put them on. "So, what's new with you?" She consciously took charge of the conversation.

"Not much," Izzy shrugged. "Work is unbelievable. I don't know how they expect us to fit it all in." She finished her drink and poured another from the jug between them, as Amelia observed with a sardonic but non-judgmental eye, hidden by the sunglasses.

"Seeing anyone?" Amelia always asked. She wasn't sure what answer would make her happy. Did she want Izzy to be alone and miserable? Or did she want to believe that the affair with Frank had been meaningless and that he had been easily replaced?

"Not much," Izzy repeated. "Claire set me up with a guy and we went on a date last night. I don't get people who study geography. I mean, how much study does it really need? Everywhere is pretty much where it is, right? Places aren't moving about - or at least not fast. What's the point?"

"You've got me." Amelia had never had much time for geography either.

"I'm sticking to Arts in the future. I had a date with a Performing Arts 2nd year. He was cool. Kind of up himself - Performing Arts 2nd years tend to be. Weird that. Oh, and I met a guy in the bar the other night. We're going out next week. He works in that gallery - you know the one."

Amelia nodded slowly. "Not much?"

"Not *that* much," said Izzy defensively.

"Seems like you can fill your evenings."

Izzy smiled ruefully. "But is that really all you want?"

They both drank. The truth was - and Amelia did not like to admit it - that Izzy had actually liked Frank the same way she had liked Frank, and for many of the same reasons. She probably wouldn't have become friends with Izzy were this not the case, on the other hand it did irk.

"How's work?"

Amelia considered the question. "Do you think it's possible I'm going to make an archaeological breakthrough that will reinvent how we see a whole period of Egyptian history?"

Izzy nodded. "Sure. Why not?"

"I just don't seem the type."

"I think you can do pretty much anything you set your mind to."

"I guess."

Why did she find it so hard to accept that this might be real? That it might be her who made this breakthrough? In so many ways Amelia was doing exactly what she wanted with her life and yet she could not help seeing herself as one of the also-rans - someone who could have made it and didn't. Perhaps it was because, however much she loved what she did, there always seemed to be something missing, something that made her a failure. She had followed her dreams but she had seldom followed her instincts. She had taken the path to her goals as prescribed by the school system and the university system and the acknowledged hierarchy of Egyptology. It all seemed a bit flat. It was a pretty mean thing to say when you considered that so many people never got to do something they loved for a living, but there it was. It was a hard mindset to get out of.

"Want to get dinner?"

Izzy smiled. "I fancy Thai."

There was a little place on Green Street that was always quiet, and the pair stayed late, eating, drinking and chatting, until Amelia had almost forgotten why she had ever been feeling morose. They parted on King's Parade and went their separate ways.

It was as Amelia turned off the main road and into the network of side streets that took her home that she began to get the uncomfortable sense of being followed. It was the sort of thing you read about in books and always wondered if it was actually possible or just a convenient invention of authors who wanted to establish a little tension. Amelia had always assumed the latter, but now, though she could hear nothing, she fancied she could feel eyes pricking at the back of neck, and found herself wheeling about to look deep into the shadows. She saw as little as she heard and yet the sensation continued. With a shake of her head she consciously dismissed the notion as no more than the after-effect of that morning's events. It was perfectly natural for her to be imagining things. She continued to think this way until she was almost at her door, when she heard a definite sound from behind her, the sound of a breath.

She started around to see where the sound had come from and a hand snaked out of the darkness, sealing her mouth with a vice-like grip, silencing her scream. The hand was replaced moments later by a strip of tape, then a bag was pulled roughly over her head, plunging her into blackness. Throughout it all, she was held immobile by hands with a grip like steel, which now wrenched her arms behind her back and tied them there, painfully stretched. Her ankles were taped too and, within seconds of her first being aware that something was wrong, she was thrown over a man's shoulder and carried away.

In such situations a person dies a hundred deaths from anticipation first. Fear coursed through Amelia unlike anything she had ever known. She felt that she might pass out and then wished she would - anything was better than suffering through this. Though she remained unwillingly conscious, she was too strung out to analyse the path to her kidnappers were taking, or listen to any of the tell-tale sounds around her that might have revealed her location. The next thing she was aware of was being dumped into a chair, the bag being removed from her head and the tape being ripped from her mouth, making her cry out in pain. She blinked in the light that was being very deliberately shone into her eyes, stopping her from seeing the room. She was aware of at least three people standing around her, all keeping to the shadows.

"You are Amelia Evans?" a strongly accented voice asked.

"What do you want with me?" It was a horrible cliché but she wanted to know.

"You are Amelia Evans?"

"Please don't hurt me!"

"You are Amelia Evans?"

"Yes. But please don't hurt me!" Why would anyone kidnap her? This made no sense.

"You will translate."

"What?"

The speaker grabbed Amelia's face, pinching her cheeks between thumb and fingers, tight enough to draw blood as the inside of her cheeks were forced into her teeth. He stared straight into her face and Amelia found herself focussing on the greying roots of his badly dyed hair.

"You will pay attention. You will speak only when spoken to. You will do as you are told. Now, translate what he says."

He indicated a figure in the corner of the room, whom Amelia had not previously noticed. She could make out only an outline, as the man (she assumed male based on size) was wearing a hooded cloak that hid every feature. He was sitting unnaturally still, and from his direction came a sound like a blunt saw being dragged back and forth across piano wire. It took Amelia a moment to realise that the sound was the man's breathing.

Dyed Hair let go of Amelia's face then crossed to the hooded man. He bowed respectfully, pointed at Amelia, and made a talkie-talkie gesture with his hand as if operating an invisible puppet. It was so incongruous in the circumstances that Amelia almost burst out laughing.

The hooded man shifted slightly in his seat to look at Amelia, his face still hidden, his movements jerky and strained.

"Listen!" advised Dyed Hair.

The noise that issued from within the hood was like nothing Amelia had ever heard; a rasping, grating conglomeration of syllables that sounded more as if they were being made by rubbing two rocks together than by a human tongue and vocal cords.

"What does he say?" Dyed Hair asked.

Amelia's mouth went dry. She had no idea. She was fluent in several ancient languages, and some of those sounds she had recognised as having some relation to various dialects of Ancient

25

Egyptian, but nothing that could be called words and certainly no meaning.

"I... I'm sorry..." What would they do when they discovered she was worthless?

"You will translate!" Dyed Hair barked in her face.

"I don't know what he's saying!" Amelia nearly shrieked back.

"Liar! You understand the language of the Lost Dynasty!"

This couldn't be happening. That language hadn't been spoken for millennia. There was no one who could speak it, and certainly not Amelia. Reading was one thing, the spoken word was another entirely.

"I... I can't. I'm sorry."

"You are lying! They've got to you!"

"I swear! You have to believe..."

She was cut off by a sharp tapping sound that echoed hollowly around the room, cutting into the claustrophobia like a death watch beetle. Amelia's eyes, along with those of everyone in the room, were drawn to the arm rest of the chair in which the hooded figure sat, to see one finger rapping the wood, making a sound against it that no finger should.

Dyed Hair shut up instantly and stepped back as the hooded figure swivelled awkwardly in his chair, moving like a badly animated special effect. He turned to the wall and raised his hand, index finger extended. Amelia grit her teeth as the finger cut into the plaster on the wall, scraping against the buried brickwork with a noise like fingernails being drawn down a blackboard. With slow precision the finger moved, incising a character into the plaster of the wall.

"Yes!" Amelia started in excitement as she realised what the hooded figure was doing. "Yes, I can read!"

The hooded figure coughed out another incomprehensible mouthful at her, and this one needed no translation; shut up.

Amelia did as she was told, the fingers of her still tied hands knotted together, white-knuckled, as she watched the finger move. It was a horrifying and yet compelling spectacle, seeing that single digit scratch across the stone, accompanied by the hideous screech of bone on brick. Now she looked, Amelia could see the finger was black - not as in 'of African origin', but jet black. It looked like a dead twig, the joints standing bulbous along its bony length.

Finally the hand dropped and Dyed Hair nudged Amelia roughly. "What does he say?"

Not all the words were familiar, which was inevitable when you had only ancient inscriptions for guidance, but Amelia had studied as many examples of cryptoglyphics as she could, and was relatively confident as she began to translate. With her life apparently on the line, all spectres of self-doubt about her work had gone out the window.

"'She is found'," she read. "'We must go to her with all speed. Her place...' no, sorry, 'her *location*, is in The Arcana'."

The other men in the room exchanged a few words between themselves in what Amelia recognised as Egyptian (modern). With a natural flair for languages she had of course learnt a smattering to aid her on the visits she had made to that country that so dominated her dreams, but it had never held the same interest for her as the ancient dialects. Besides which, the men were making every effort not to be heard. She noticed for the first time that, while they were not all dressed identically, there did seem to be a unifying theme in their clothes, as if a designer had made a conscious decision to tie it altogether with a colour motif. Did cults take fashion advice? The idea made her want to laugh in a slightly hysterical way.

What would they do with her now?

Had she served her purpose? In which case she would be either set free or... or not. The former seemed horribly unlikely. In fact, her best chance seemed to be that they had *not* finished with her. And given that one of their party was unable to communicate with the others, that seemed possible. What a terrible thing to have to hope for.

Dyed Hair, who seemed to be the leader of the group, addressed the hooded man. "The Brotherhood will travel with you and aid you in any way we can." It was presumably incomprehensible to the hooded man, but Dyed Hair seemed to feel better for saying it. He now turned to Amelia. "We go."

That, Amelia felt, was non-specific. Did 'we' include her?

Suddenly the door slammed open and another man (whom Amelia immediately christened 'Noddy', because he had big ears) entered, talking quickly in Egyptian, panic in his voice. Whatever he said (and he had spoken too fast for Amelia's limited skills) it set the other men into frenzied activity. Two of them hurried to help the hooded man to his feet, another rushed to a chest by the wall and produced - Amelia's eyes widened in horror - guns.

Without warning the bag was pulled back over her head as the voices continued. Then a cry. The sound of breaking woodwork and a slam. More voices. Running feet. A door opening and closing. Amelia shrieked as the first gunshot went off, far too close for comfort. On instinct she kicked back and her chair overbalanced, sending her rolling to the floor as the fire-fight continued above her. Even with the bag over her head she squeezed her eyes shut, her fists tight balls of tension, her stomach a knot. She realised that she was still screaming.

And then - silence.

Amelia could not be sure how long she lay there, all screamed out, listening to the ringing in her ears that the gunfire had left. The feel of a hand on her shoulder made her start and shrink away, but this hand was far gentler than the last, and was accompanied by a voice that sounded like dark honey.

"Don't worry, Miss Evans, I'm not going to hurt you."

The bag was removed from her head once more and Amelia looked into the handsome face of a man of about her age.

"My name is Boris. You're safe."

Amelia tried to take this in, and tried not to look around her - Noddy had not made it through the fight. She attempted to think about something else, like the fact that - without wanting to play racial stereotypes - the man in front of her did not look like a 'Boris'. He looked, predictably, Egyptian. It was hard not to wonder; what the hell next?

Another man, this one blonde and in his twenties, hurried in. "They got away."

Boris nodded. "They had an escape plan. Should have guessed."

"We had to move fast," the blonde said, "because of..." He not very subtly indicated Amelia.

"Even so." Boris seemed upset with himself. "Try the usual spots, though I doubt we'll find anything. Watch the ports." He turned back to Amelia. "Would you like to go home?"

Half an hour later Amelia sat in her chair in her flat, holding a cup of her tea in her favourite mug which bore the legend 'Archaeologists Do It Slowly Over a Period of Years'. It was good to focus on the normal things, like the sudden appearance of Valerie, the Fitzwilliam Museum cat, who now joined her on the chair, shredding the arm rest with her claws. Valerie was one of those cats who adopt a number of people and show up at random times expecting to be fed, whether the person is a cat lover or not. But today, even Amelia was pleased to see her, as another little piece of normality to which she could cling. Still, it was hard to dispel the abnormal that had forced its way into her world when one aspect of that abnormality remained, seated on her sofa.

"You have a very nice flat," said Boris, pleasantly. He looked out of place in the academic domesticity of his surroundings. Though he was soberly dressed and 'normal' looking (if slim, handsome and elegant was normal), there was also a jungle cat quality about Boris. He looked *ready*, without being ready for anything specific. Like a coiled spring. It was akin to having a panther seated on the dented, rumpled sofa that Amelia had bought from a Salvation Army shop during her second year at university and had dragged around with her ever since. With quick fingers, Boris flicked through a few pages of the book that sat on the little table beside him - a John Le Carré borrowed from Cambridge Library - and clicked his tongue with interest. It was hard to avoid the impression that he was absorbing everything he saw and forming an impression of Amelia based upon it. The messy stacks of biro-scrawled notebooks, the notice-board pinned with stubs of theatre tickets, the open packet of Jaffa cakes, the underwear drying on the radiator, the ill-matched furniture, the thinning carpet by the window where Amelia paced when she was trying to think, the shelves of Egyptology texts, and the significant gaps in those shelves where Frank's books had used to sit - all seemed to contribute to the picture Boris was forming of the flat's inhabitant, Amelia Evans. "Very nice," he added politely.

"You're not police, are you?" Amelia was done being reactive. Today had pushed her about, knocked her down and kicked the shit out of her, but no more. She would be the one in charge from here on in.

"How did you guess?"

"You haven't asked me a single question yet. Police always have a million questions."

"Yes," Boris mused, "you've been having quite a day, haven't

29

you?"

"You know about what happened at the Fitz? You know who the dead man was?" The need to know still burnt at Amelia.

Boris met her gaze, apparently summing her up. "He was a colleague of mine."

"Have you told the police?"

"That would be awkward."

"Because he wasn't supposed to be there?"

"Among other reasons."

Amelia paused a moment, wondering if she really wanted to know what she desperately wanted to ask. "What was his name?"

"Claude."

It didn't help. Giving him a name didn't add anything or make the image any less looming in her mind. It didn't make her feel any better for finding him - as if by finding him she had been responsible somehow for his death.

"Sorry for your loss." Such an empty statement.

Boris acknowledged it politely without any obvious sign of emotion.

"Who are you?" Amelia continued.

"I told you, you can call me Boris."

"Is that your name?"

"It will do."

Amelia boiled over. "What do you want? Who were those men? Why did they want me? Who the hell is speaking cryptoglyphs in the twenty first century? And..."

Boris held up a hand. "I think I can answer most of your questions if you would indulge me."

"What?" Amelia was not sure what the man meant but his mellifluous voice had an oddly soothing affect. She felt a need to fight it. "How do I know I can trust you?"

Boris shrugged. "Of all the people you've met today I would hope I have made the best first impression."

"That's not an answer."

Boris nodded. "True. May I?" He helped himself to more tea from the pot which Amelia had made when they had got in, more out of habit than necessity. The pot had Paddington Bear on it and had been a birthday present from Frank. She had no idea why she had kept it, possibly because the break up had not been Paddington's fault so why should he suffer?

Boris sipped his tea. "That's excellent." He settled back on the sofa. "I'm not sure what I could tell you that would make you trust me. I'm not police or CID or CIA or anything like that. I represent a company called Universal Egyptology. We exist for crises just like this one."

"What crisis?"

"Ah," Boris held up a finger. "This, I think, is where we came in. Let me tell you a story."

Chapter 4 - The Queen of The Lost Dynasty

The first thing that hit Arthur as he got off the plane was the heat. As a child he had gone to the South of France on holiday with his family and, much as he had enjoyed himself, he had always found the heat a little hard to take. Arthur was one of those unfortunate people who wilt in the heat, and the heat in Egypt was in a whole other class. It was like a physical thing that hit him in the face. Walking from the air-conditioned plane out into the open air was like running into a solid wall of heat. At first he wasn't even sure he could breathe. He had fortuitously taken the precaution of putting on his sun-block in advance (Arthur did things 'in advance' wherever possible), but it just felt as if he had greased himself up to be fried. This whole trip was starting to seem less and less like a good idea, which was a hell of a thing to be thinking when he'd only just got off the plane.

Arthur took a deep breath and pulled himself together. He had to remember why he was here; for his career and, more importantly, for Helen. If he could not suffer a little heat for the woman he loved then what kind of man was he? Possibly the kind of man that she had implied he was, which was what had led to this whole expedition.

Having collected his bags - he had packed as sparingly as possible and yet still seemed massively overloaded - Arthur headed out of the airport, glancing hopefully about and wondering how he might recognise Miss Moran. This was not Cairo Airport, which was the country's main hub for tourists, businessmen and the like, he was 'down south', but there were still taxi drivers, family members and business associates there to meet his fellow passengers. Among them, one person stood out; a woman, perched on the bonnet of a jeep that looked to have been assembled from spare parts and then driven here via a war zone. As the woman saw him she sprang nimbly from the bonnet and strode across to Arthur. She wore a loose, hard-wearing shirt, khaki shorts and boots that seemed to have been designed to stamp out forest fires. Her eyes were shockingly blue, her hair had been bleached almost white by the sun, and her skin looked to have gone through sunburnt and come out the other side.

"Banning?" she asked, brusquely.

"Miss Moran?"

"Maggie. You building a house out here?"

"I..." Arthur was thrown.

"The bags."

"I tried to pack light."

"You failed. Come on."

Maggie picked up two of Arthur's bags, with a strength that Arthur would not have credited to her slight build, and headed back to the jeep.

"You're Professor Andoheb's research assistant?" asked Arthur, struggling to keep up.

"Site manager," replied Maggie, dumping Arthur's bags in the back of the jeep. "See if you can fit them all in. But if they're slowing us down, I'm chucking them out as we go."

She shot a smile at him that creased her cheeks. She was probably in her early to mid-thirties, but long years under a desert sun had made her look older than that, though she radiated a very definite aura of not giving a shit. It occurred to Arthur, as he struggled to load his bags, that beneath the tangled hair and sun-crisped skin, Maggie was a very beautiful woman. And one who would probably break his arm if he voiced that opinion.

"Get in and stop looking scared."

Arthur did as he was told (at least the first half of it), Maggie jammed the jeep into gear and they took off at a bone-rattling speed, the engine making a noise like the coming apocalypse.

"I've never been out in the field before," said Arthur. He felt some need to explain his tentativeness.

"Shocking," replied Maggie, with easy sarcasm.

"How long have you been out here?"

"On this dig or in Egypt or in the field generally?"

"Whichever. I was just making conversation really."

Maggie shrugged. "I move about a bit. Quite a bit. Off and on I've been in Egypt ten years. Prof and I go way back. He gives me a shout when he's on a dig. We work pretty well together. He respects you. Which is why I'm carting your bags back to camp rather than setting fire to them by the side of the road."

"I appreciate that," said Arthur, fervently. "Can I ask what all this is about?"

"You can ask, I guess. Prof'll give you the details. Long story short? We were out in the fringes digging where there's not supposed

33

to be shit. Turns out there's shit there."

"Really?" Arthur nodded sagely, as if this fully answered his question. "You're probably wondering why I came out here when I have no idea what you're digging."

"Nope."

"Professor Andoheb asked me," Arthur went on - talking made him less nervous. "I wouldn't have come out here for anyone else. He was my tutor at university - we bonded over a mutual love of Sherlock Holmes. He really inspired me"

Maggie shook her head firmly. "That was what? Five years ago?"

"Something like that."

"And he never asked you on a dig before?"

"Well yes, but..."

"And you said this is your first time in the field. Nobody else asked you?"

"Again, yes, but..."

"Are you rubbish at what you do?"

"I'm not an 'expert' *per se* but..."

"You don't strike me as a field archaeologist. You got a librarian's tan. Bookworm. Research. That type. Nothing wrong with that. All well and good. But when your sort ends up in the field, there's a reason."

Arthur sighed. "That's a long story."

Maggie nodded. "Feel free to keep it to yourself."

Arthur would have happily admitted that Maggie's assessment of him was perfectly correct. In fact he would have been proud to do so. He was a born researcher, never happier than with his nose buried in a book and more than satisfied to spend his life recording and analysing the finds of more intrepid archaeologists. It might not be glamorous, but the profession owed a great deal to men like him and it was a career path he truly loved.

His girlfriend felt differently.

"I'm not saying you should climb a mountain, or kayak across the Atlantic," Helen had said in exasperation, "but either of those would do you good. Don't you ever want to be more than a bookworm?"

Arthur felt he knew the right answer to this question, but it was not *his* answer.

34

"There must be a part of you that wants excitement, adventure, the thrill of seeing new places and doing new things!" Helen enthused.

"You'd think," said Arthur, tentatively, "but I'm really not sure there is."

"Don't you want to be Indiana Jones?"

Like all archaeologists, Arthur loved the Indiana Jones films, but felt that they had done his profession something of a disservice. Still, he was willing to compromise.

"In the event of Nazis attempting to steal important historical artefacts, I will spring into action," he promised, hoping to lighten the mood.

"It's a big world and you can't see beyond your own reading glasses!"

Arthur wanted to point out that if you couldn't see *beyond* your glasses then there was little point in wearing them, but felt, rightly, that now was not the time.

"I love you Arthur," said Helen, her tone softening. "But sometimes you are the most infuriating man. I'm just not sure I want to be with someone who has so little drive!"

That struck Arthur as unfair; he had a great deal of drive. He was a research archaeologist, and his drive to get to the top of his profession was real and single-minded. It was such focussed drive that it admitted little deviation into other areas. Which was, perhaps, what frustrated Helen.

"Someone with so little sense of adventure!"

That was a fairer. Arthur had very little sense of adventure and he had never seen it as a problem until now. Helen's words struck fear into his heart. He loved Helen very much and the idea of losing her was more than he could stand. If he had no natural sense of adventure then he was willing to fake it to placate the woman with whom he hoped to spend the rest of his life.

It had seemed like providence therefore when, the following day, a message arrived from his old tutor: 'Extraordinary find Western Desert. Come at once, if convenient. If inconvenient, come all the same. Andoheb.'

The last two lines were a direct quote from The Adventure of the Creeping Man, a Sherlock Holmes reference that was bound to fire Arthur's blood with the desire for adventure, and which explained why Andoheb had written an email like a telegram. There was a pleasing urgency to the request, and Arthur did not even stop to think before replying to say that he would be there without delay. Once he had had time to think, he began to regret it. He had allowed himself to be swayed by Sherlock Holmes and tantalising hints of 'extraordinary' archaeological finds. He had no business out in the field. There was too much in the way of sand and too little in the way of adequate bathroom facilities. But that regret had been quickly reversed when he told Helen. Her face lit up with girlish delight.

"Will there be danger?"

"I don't know." Would there be? He hadn't thought of that. But it was an archaeological dig so the possibility seemed a remote one. Despite the Sherlock Holmes reference, Andoheb had given no suggestion that there was anything actually adventurous about the dig.

"I think there will be," said Helen, hopefully.

"Jolly good," murmured Arthur.

"You're out in the desert, there are bound to be bandits, jackals, maybe even lions. There might be a long-lost tomb with traps in it - arrows firing from the walls, pit-falls opening up beneath you. There's sure to be armed treasure hunters as well, who will stop at nothing to get what they want. They might kidnap you. Threaten you. Torture you for hours until you you're screaming for - Oh God, Arthur!"

Grabbing Arthur by the lapels, Helen dragged him down on top of her on the sofa.

"I want you to know," said Helen earnestly, half an hour later when they were putting their clothes back on, "if you come back with one eye or a hideous scar across your cheek, I shall still love you."

"Oh." said Arthur. "Good."

"Maybe more."

"Right."

"Not too hideous," Helen qualified. "I mean there are limits, you know. Do be careful."

"Oh, I will."

"But not too careful."

"No."

"Try to strike a balance."

"Danger?" Maggie frowned. "What do you mean?"

"Has anyone lost an eye?" suggested Arthur.

"Not so far. We get treasure hunters. Tomb robbers. Just every now and then. Bastards. That's why Prof kept the details short sending for you. But sleep with a gun under your pillow and you'll probably be fine."

It was not an answer calculated to inspire any great confidence in Arthur, but right now he was less concerned about treasure hunters or tomb robbers and more about Maggie's driving, which, now they had got out of town, had escalated from dangerous to suicidal.

"Could you slow down a bit?"

Maggie shook her head. "It's a long drive. We want to be back in good time."

"And one piece, right? Maybe keep your eyes on the road?"

"There isn't a road," Maggie pointed out. "Anyway, who can see anything in this dust?"

"If you drove slower there wouldn't be so much dust." The jeep's speed was throwing up great clouds of desert dust all around them.

"But then we'd be late back," pointed out Maggie. "Best to cane it. Just keep pointed in the right direction." She nodded at a compass on the dash. "Not like there's anything out here to hit. The camels hear us coming."

That, Arthur could well believe. The deaf would have heard Maggie coming.

Three terrifying hours later, the gently undulating skyline of the desert was broken by a jagged shadow, rearing up out of it. As they grew closer, Arthur saw it was a vast rocky outcrop, erupting from the sand like a miniature mountain range plonked in the middle of the featureless dunes. An isolated island, several miles across, of towering spires, sheer cliffs and narrow gullies - the only landmark for miles around.

"Is that where we're going?"

"The locals call it the Sarranekh."

Some small while later, the jeep ploughed through a pair of rocky pinnacles and came to a jarring halt, engine grinding ominously. Maggie jumped out. As the dust clouds cleared, Arthur was able to see that the pinnacles formed a natural gate to a circle of rock, like an amphitheatre eroded by time. It was a natural place for the little camp set up by the archaeologists; a scattering of tents erected in the shade and shelter afforded by these broken outskirts of the Sarranekh. A few people were about, working at one thing or another, which did not stop Maggie from barking sharp instructions in a language Arthur did not understand but assumed to be Egyptian. Although he had lectured in England, Professor Andoheb was Egyptian himself and preferred his digging crews to be local, with Maggie the single exception. He invited archaeology students from Cairo Museum and other institutions to join him and learn on the job, surrounding himself with people whom he trusted and who, presumably, were used to being yelled at by Maggie. He also preferred his teams to be all male (Maggie, again, an honourable exception), which Arthur generously wrote-off as a generational issue.

"I'm away a few hours and everyone slacks off," muttered Maggie.

"I imagine the Pharaohs had similar problems," said Arthur, and immediately wished he hadn't.

Maggie levelled a diamond-edged stare at him. "Problem?"

"No," Arthur gulped.

"It's imperialism, isn't it?"

"What?"

"The English overseer and the native workers?" Maggie raised her eyebrows. "I know how it looks. I just don't give a shit. I'm good at what I do and nothing else comes into it."

Arthur nodded. He imagined that Maggie had had to deal with some sort of prejudice all her career, and he imagined that she had dealt with it extremely well.

"Arthur!"

Arthur turned to see the lumbering figure of his old tutor, hurrying towards him with hands outstretched and a beaming smile on his face. There was nothing small about Professor Andoheb, he was over six feet tall with a torso like a barrel, a face like the moon, and the general appearance of a good-natured bear. His personality and emotions were similarly big. His lectures had been everyone's favourite because they were enthusiastic, energetic performances that invariably left the Professor sweating and sore-throated. Arthur remembered when the Professor had related the story of Cleopatra's death and cried like a baby at his own telling.

"So good to see you!"

Arthur gasped as the Professor threw his long arms around the younger man and squeezed the breath out of him.

"Welcome to Egypt!"

"Thanks. Hot, isn't it?"

Andoheb let loose a peal of laughter that echoed amongst the rocks. "Same old Arthur. I can't believe we managed to drag you out here."

"Well it sounded exciting."

Andoheb grabbed Arthur's arm like King Kong picking up Fay Wray. "Exciting isn't the word, Arthur! You don't know the half of it. Has Maggie told you anything?"

"Not much."

"Excellent. Maggie!"

Maggie looked up from a conversation she was having with one of the conservators in the 'Finds' tent - she seemed fluent in the local language.

"My tent!"

In the Professor's tent, Maggie flopped back in a folding chair and put her feet up on the table, while Andoheb dumped an armload of maps down for Arthur to look at.

"The most extraordinary luck, my friend! And the sort of thing that makes all archaeologists hang their heads in embarrassment. A tomb was found here many years ago, back in the days of Carter when every inch of Egypt was turned over. A nondescript type of burial - thoroughly gutted by tomb robbers in antiquity. Everyone moved on, and *no one noticed* that there was another tomb underneath!"

"Underneath?" Arthur stared at the maps in fascination, suddenly he could see the appeal of being out here in the field, of being there to see something for the first time.

"Cleverly disguised by the natural shape of the rocks," Andoheb went on. "The tomb on top was a deliberate blind, no doubt put there to fool tomb robbers. And it worked."

"The tomb underneath is intact?" If that were the case then this could be the biggest discovery in Egyptology since Tutankhamen.

"As far as we can tell," nodded Andoheb, with relish.

"How did you find it?" asked Arthur.

"I was out here looking for something else," Andoheb shrugged. "The mass grave of an ancient battle. But I came across measurements that had been made of the area and something obviously didn't add up. The depth of the already discovered tomb didn't account for the space. Not dissimilar," he added, a twinkle in his eyes, "to the Adventure of the Norwood Builder."

Arthur beamed. "Or the treasure room in the Sign of Four."

"Exactly!" Andoheb clapped his hands in delight. Maggie, clearly not a Sherlock Holmes fan, rolled her eyes.

Arthur shook his head in wonder. "What made you think to take the measurements?"

"Oh yeah, tell him that," said Maggie, apparently amused by something.

"I didn't make them," admitted Andoheb with a sigh. "The area was being surveyed by Google Earth. Hence the embarrassment I mentioned."

Arthur shrugged. "You found it - that's what matters."

Andoheb clapped Arthur on the back hard enough to bounce his lungs against his ribs. "My thoughts exactly. Come with me."

They left the tent and headed up into the rocks, Maggie leading the way, climbing with practised ease and little obvious effort. Andoheb followed with the speed and enthusiasm of a far younger and smaller man, while Arthur brought up the rear, sweating like a horse, breathing like a steam engine and suddenly very aware that he never climbed anything steeper than a library stepladder.

"There!" Andoheb announced as they reached the top of a ridge looking down into a gully that wound a path through the rocks.

Arthur looked down. The original robbed-out tomb was clearly visible, but beneath it, hidden by a natural rock formation was a recently excavated path leading to a huge stone door. The seal on the door remained intact.

"You haven't been in yet?"

Andoheb shook his head. "Not yet. I wanted you here for that."

Arthur swelled with pride, but could not help being a little confused. "Why?"

He had been a good student, but not exceptional. He knew his subject, but there were men who had spent a lifetime studying, as opposed to his four years. He had no field experience and had

40

previously shown an almost pathological aversion to gaining any.

Andoheb smiled. "Two reasons. Firstly; I trust you, and secrecy remains our top priority. Secondly; you are a walking encyclopaedia."

"I am?"

"There's no internet access out here," Andoheb explained. "And we have to conserve our generator power for essentials. We can't be frittering them away on charging laptops. I don't know what we might find in there and bringing all the reference books needed to cover every possible eventuality would be impossible. But I don't need reference books if I have Arthur Banning."

There was something in that. Arthur might not have been an expert, but he had a great memory and, more importantly, a very organised one. At a young age, Arthur had decided to treat his mind like a library; facts were neatly catalogued, he knew where everything was, and talking louder than a whisper was frowned upon. That decision had paid off dividends when he moved into research - he had no need to reach for a book when the classification checkpoints for telling first dynasty pottery from second were itemised neatly in his head. He had, he would be first to admit, little in the way of instinct, he was incapable of making an educated guess let alone a wild assumption, but when it came to facts, you couldn't beat Arthur Banning.

Back at the camp, fires were lit and dinner preparation began as night fell. Maggie shared a joke with a group of the diggers, fitting in easily and automatically. Arthur now noticed that she switched between languages or dialects depending on who she was speaking to. Settling back in his chair, Arthur tried to take in where he was and what he was doing. It was still archaeology - the work he had done all his life - but this was another world. For the first time, he found himself quite grateful to Helen for forcing him into this. An undiscovered, undisturbed tomb. It was probably not the sort of excitement that she had had in mind, but for an archaeologist, it didn't get any better than this.

"Do you have any idea whose tomb it might be?" he asked Professor Andoheb, who sat beside him.

Andoheb's eyes were trained on the fire. "I have... an inkling."

"Tell me."

"You have heard of Queen Amunet?"

Arthur nodded. "I've heard stories. I thought she was a legend."

"So much about the Lost Dynasty is uncertain. Who's to say if she is legend or forgotten history?"

"You think this is her tomb?"

"I think it could be," said Andoheb, his eyes sparkling in the firelight. "Or perhaps I just hope it is."

The stories about Queen Amunet varied wildly, giving little picture of what sort of monarch she might actually have been. Tellingly there were none that originated verifiably from her own time - all the stories there were had been written by people who came later, blending history with drama, and even those stories had been retold many times and altered in the telling, so fact and fiction had become inextricable. Was she a saviour of the people who had beaten down a violent uprising? Or a terrible tyrant who had quashed a popular rebellion? Was she a witch, who, along with her High Priest, had used black magic to keep the people in her thrall? Or was it the Priest himself who had ruled and she was no more than a puppet? Perhaps she had simply ruled during turbulent times, when monarchs get blamed for everything from the weather upwards.

There were stories too about her coming back from the dead, which was a rarity in ancient Egyptian legend - the afterlife was supposed to be where you wanted to be, why come back? In Amunet's case it was to save Egypt.

They were great stories, but the more dramatic they became, the less likely it seemed that the Queen herself had ever existed. More likely she was a composite of various rulers of the Lost Dynasty - some good, some bad - and her Priest was a bogeyman, used to scare little Egyptian children into eating their greens.

Dinner was a convivial affair, and despite the language barrier, Arthur managed to pick up a few names of the people he would be working alongside in the coming weeks. As the fires died, the camp said their goodnights and headed for their tents.

The temperature dropped overnight, which was a huge relief to Arthur, who was not sure he could have slept in that heat. Still, he lay awake a long while, staring up at the canvas of the tent above him. He was in Egypt. It was a country whose history he had spent a great deal of his life studying and yet one that he had never planned on visiting. Now he was here it was scary, but it was also exhilarating.

He drifted off to sleep, to dream dreams of happy anticipation.

Arthur started awake with a gasp and spent the next fifteen seconds in a panicked game of 'where the hell am I?'. Once he had remembered, he tried to recall what it was that had woken him. He had heard something, of that he was sure, but he could not say what. He sat up in his bed. It was still the dead of night and the blackness was absolutely total - he could not even tell if his eyes were open or closed. He held his breath and listened. The desert produced many odd sounds by night as the wind stole across it and whistled through the rocky outcrops of the Sarranekh, but Arthur heard nothing that should have woken him. There was nothing, and yet he could not shake that sense of something not right.

Trying to put his ill feelings to one side he lay back down, determined to get back to sleep. Then, just as he was about to close his eyes, a flash of light passed across the wall of his tent. Arthur sat bolt upright, his heart in his mouth. There it was again. And from outside he heard the faint sound of sand crushed beneath footsteps - someone creeping past. The torch flashed once more.

It was one of the diggers. Obviously. Someone who couldn't sleep or needed to use the camp's limited facilities and did not wish to attempt it without a torch. Why were they creeping? So as not to wake anyone else. Very considerate. There was no reason to assume anything untoward. No reason at all. Which did nothing to stop the voice of Helen in his head, talking about bandits and jackals, kidnapping and torture.

The torch flashed again, near to the door of Arthur's tent, left partly unzipped to allow the cool night air in. Arthur's eyes widened to horrified saucers as, by the dim light of the intruder's torch he saw a face peer in through the open flap - deep-set, heavy lidded eyes, a cruel mouth, and a deep scar lacerating one cheek.

For a moment, Arthur was silent, fear numbing his vocal cords. Then the torch beam found his frozen face and he let loose a yell that could have wakened the dead.

The face vanished instantly, and from outside Arthur could now hear the sounds of others coming out of their tents to find out what he was screaming about. Flushed with sudden adrenalin, he leapt from his camp bed, pausing only to pull on his slippers, and ran out.

"What the hell was that?!" Inevitably it was Maggie taking charge, holding a gun roughly the same size as her head.

"There was someone in my tent."

For a moment Maggie stared at him intently by the light of her torch, deciding whether or not to believe him. The next moment she yelled something in Egyptian and the excavation party rushed into action, gathering torches and weapons, while she herself made for the rocks and the tomb beyond.

With no instructions of his own, Arthur remained frozen and bemused for a moment, then took off after Maggie, still too thrilled to be scared or worried that he seemed to be the only one unarmed. Maggie moved like a mountain goat, leaping barefoot from rock to rock, barely using the torch to find her way. Arthur struggled behind her but managed, more or less, to keep up, adrenalin still fuelling him.

At the top of the rise Maggie stopped and swept her torch about, hunting with her eyes.

"See anything?" breathed Arthur.

"Shh!"

There were others following behind them, but for now it was just Arthur and Maggie, alone on the rocky outcrop with the desert wind whistling eerily about them.

"Come out, come out," Arthur heard Maggie mutter to herself.

Arthur was very aware of his heart beating fast within his chest. He peered into the darkness, straining to see.

"They could be anywhere," growled Maggie.

"Who?"

"Thieves."

"Why come to the camp rather than go straight to the tomb?"

"Don't know. Maybe to see if we've taken anything out of the tomb yet. Why go to the trouble of busting in a door when they can let us do the hard work, then cut our throats as we sleep."

She set off again, Arthur still following, his heart now in his mouth. As the initial adrenalin rush cooled, anxiety found its way back into him. Maggie prowled through the rocks, moving fast like a hunting dog. The only light was from her torch and Arthur found himself constantly glancing about. There were so many places to hide down here, so many alcoves in the rock, so many shadows to fade into. Attack could come from anywhere at any time and he would never see it coming.

"Maybe we should wait until the sun comes up," he suggested.

"Shh!"

Consciously or unconsciously, Arthur found his eyes drifting over towards the stone door of the tomb. Even after the excavation, the door was still largely hidden from view, but somehow it was picked out by the moonlight. Perhaps the tomb's designers - the best and brightest architects that Ancient Egypt had to offer - had built it specifically with this in mind. There was an arch cleverness in going to such trouble to disguise the location of a tomb and then letting the moon itself pay tribute to the hidden occupant. That was the sort of thing that appealed to the Ancient Egyptian mind. Though he could appreciate this, Arthur currently found the door more disturbing than impressive or historically fascinating. Perhaps it was his imagination, but he felt as if he was being watched from that doorway. It *had* to be his imagination - the door was practically the only place that was well lit, the only place from which he could be sure he was not being watched. And yet it was the place that sent shivers down his spine.

He was relieved when Maggie finally gave up and they headed back through the rocks, up to the rise. As they reached the top, a pair of armed diggers approached from the camp and Maggie barked a command. The pair hurried towards the tomb door.

"From now on we'll have a guard on that door at all times. Come on." She led Arthur back down the slope towards the tents. As they walked, Maggie looked down at Arthur's feet. "Are you wearing slippers?"

"Yes," Arthur nodded. "Are you wearing a Wham! T-shirt?"

"Problem?"

"No."

"They're nice slippers."

"Thank you."

It was noon the following day. The camp was empty and the entire team had assembled around the tomb door. Arthur watched as Professor Andoheb selected a pick axe and walked solemnly towards the entrance. Things had changed since the days of Howard Carter and the Egyptology boom of the nineteen twenties, archaeologists were not quite so gung-ho about bashing their way into every tomb they could find, picking up everything they could carry, and getting out. That said, when you came down to it, the only way in was a damn great stone door and, regardless of how fastidious an archaeologist you were, the only way through was to take a pick axe to it. Still, if you were going to smash in the door to someone's eternal resting place, you could at least do it with a little solemnity.

Professor Andoheb lined up the pick with the seal, then took it back over his head, paused for moment, and swung. The sound of the seal cracking resounded and re-echoed around the rocks.

Maggie issued instructions then she, along with three other diggers, took pick axes and began to break the door in. It was hot work in the midday sun, even with the shade offered by the rocks. Arthur felt exhausted just watching them. After ten minutes of hard work, Maggie was red in the face and sweating heavily, but the door was breached. A breath of cold dead air swept out, which should have been refreshing, but was just unnerving.

"After you," said Maggie, passing a torch to the Professor.

Andoheb grinned like a schoolboy, snatched the torch and led the way. "Come on, Arthur. The game is afoot!"

Emboldened by the Sherlock Holmes reference, Arthur took a torch of his own and followed the Professor and Maggie.

It took a little while for their eyes to adjust to the sharp contrast between the darkness of the tomb and the bright shafts of their torches, but as they began to see more clearly, their eyes widened at what they saw.

"Remarkable," murmured Andoheb.

"Amazing," breathed Arthur.

"******!" said Maggie.

It was not just the decoration on the walls of the narrow corridor in which they stood that impressed them, it was the state of preservation. The paintings depicting scenes of ancient Egyptian life and death (a lot of death) looked as bright and fresh as if they had been painted yesterday.

"We need to record all this as quickly as possible," Andoheb said, staring in awe. "The change in atmosphere might damage them."

"I'll get the air conditioning equipment up here," said Maggie. Running a generator to preserve, as best they could, the conditions in the tomb would eat into their limited fuel supply, but it would be

46

worth it to save this for posterity.

They walked on, watched by silent figures in paintings that no one had seen for over four thousand years. As they rounded a corner, Andoheb, gasped sharply in fright and started back. Then, with a hollow half-laugh, relaxed.

"Guards," he said simply, indicating with his torch.

Even forewarned, Arthur's stomach lurched as the torch beam lit up the face of a life-size wooden statue with a ferocious expression, looking out from an alcove carved into the wall. It seemed to be staring at him personally, its ivory eyes shining in the harsh light.

"What's all this say?" asked Maggie, her torch picking out the hieroglyphics on the wall. "Would be nice to know who's down here."

Andoheb stared at the writing, a curious smile playing about his lips. "I don't know. Can't read a word."

Maggie frowned. "What kind of Egyptologist can't read hieroglyphics?"

Andoheb said nothing but led the way on. Arthur thought he was moving faster now, childlike enthusiasm overcoming his better scientific instincts. Of course, Arthur understood why the unreadable hieroglyphics had so excited him - they were cryptoglyphs of the Lost Dynasty. The case for this being the tomb of Queen Amunet was getting stronger.

The tunnel now descended sharply, still lined with paintings and pockmarked with occasional statues. As they went deeper, these guards, set there to protect the tomb's occupant from thieves and marauders, became first more ugly, and then less human.

"Supernatural protectors," muttered the Professor, admiring the sharp beak and jagged fangs of a particularly gruesome example. He was, Arthur knew, thinking again of the Witch Queen - such a monarch would surely have inhuman guards to safeguard her eternity.

Finally, the three arrived at a door, the first they had encountered in their long descent. The royal seal was still intact on it. Maggie glanced at Andoheb.

"Come too far to turn back now," the Professor nodded.

Maggie drew a hammer and chisel from her pack. The sharp sound of rock being chipped away echoed up and down the tunnel so it sounded as if it was coming from all around them.

The seal fell, revealing a hole. Andoheb bent to peer through, shining his torch into the hole and the chamber beyond.

"What do you see?" asked Arthur.

Andoheb drew in a breath. It may be a cliché, but there is only one thing that an Egyptologist can say in this situation. "Beautiful things."

Chapter 5 - The Universal Library

"Wait," Amelia held up a hand to stop Boris's narrative. "This happened last night?"

"It's now arguably more accurate to say that it happened two nights ago." said Boris, glancing at his watch and inadvertently making Valerie mew irritably as he stopped stroking her for a split-second - she was a needy cat.

"But it happened the same night that the Priest went missing from the Fitz?"

Boris inclined his head. "That is correct, yes. In fact, a little time zone calculation will tell you that my colleague was killed in the museum just after Professor Andoheb entered the tomb of Queen Amunet."

"The tomb is definitely hers?" Academic curiosity briefly overcame Amelia's other questions.

"I think we can infer that from the events that followed," said Boris.

How much of what she was being told she accepted, Amelia was yet to decide, but at the first mention of Queen Amunet and a possible connection to the Priest, a name had rung like a bell in her head. Ramose. The High Priest of Queen Amunet was everyone's favourite possible identity for the Priest with Turquoise Eyes, based on the period, the richness of the tomb, and the fact that tomb robbers had apparently been too frightened to open the sarcophagus. It all pointed to Ramose, but there was a lot of wishful thinking involved as well - Ramose was one of the most colourful characters in Egyptian history. 'Colourful' in this case being a euphemism for bloodthirsty, terrifying and monstrous.

"Does your company work with Professor Andoheb?" Amelia tried to focus on the present.

"No."

"Then how did you know about the excavation? You said it was secret."

A small smile played around Boris's mouth. "It's the sort of thing we keep tabs on."

"Why was your colleague in the museum that night?"

"Because we knew what point the excavation had reached," explained Boris. "And we anticipated... something." He took a sip of tea and winced - it had gone cold while he was talking. "Although what actually occurred we did not see coming. Poor Claude would have been taken quite unawares. We expected the Mummy to be stolen."

Amelia frowned. "It *was* stolen."

Boris looked at her with a curious expression on his face. "Who said it was?"

"Well it's not there," pointed out Amelia.

"You found the broken window. Where was the glass?"

"Outside."

"Broken from the inside."

"But the door was unlocked so..."

"That is how Claude entered. Where was the glass from the mummy's display case?"

"All around the case," said Amelia, knowing that what she was saying was true, however much her mind fought to refute the conclusion to which it pointed. The broken glass had been scattered in every direction around the epicentre of the case itself.

"If someone had smashed the glass from the outside, surely the glass would have fallen in," Boris continued, as if it was the most logical thing in the world. "Glass all around the case suggests something breaking out."

It was rapidly dawning on Amelia that, just because this man had saved her from kidnappers, did not mean he wasn't crazy himself. She shifted imperceptibly in her seat and allowed her eyes to flick momentarily towards her little kitchen in search of the nearest carving knife.

"You think the mummy broke out? That he..." she sought for the right words, "went for a little walk?"

Boris nodded calmly. "Seems the logical supposition."

"Playing fast and loose with the word 'logical' there."

"You know the legends that surround the High Priest of Queen Amunet."

"'*Legends*'," stressed Amelia.

"Legends start somewhere. The ones about High Priest Ramose do not paint a pleasant picture. And all of them refer to his loyalty 'to death and beyond'."

"Ancient Egyptians had a powerful belief in the afterlife," Amelia inadvertently slipped into a lecturing tone of voice. "They

50

pretty much based their whole civilisation around it. Pledging loyalty beyond death isn't so unusual."

"True," said Boris. "Might I...?" He indicated his empty cup.

"Of course, where are my manners?" Amelia stood; there was something deeply surreal in the man talking about the living dead wanting a refill.

"It's alright, I can get it myself." He busied himself in the kitchen as he spoke. "Yes, Egypt is all about life after death, but Queen Amunet is the one who said she'd be coming back. Which is unusual. So how far do we think the Priest's loyalty might extend?"

Amelia tried to get her head around what she was hearing. Should she be playing along? Humouring this man? "So, you think that the mummy in the Fitz 'sensed' the archaeologists entering the Queen's tomb, woke up, and is now heading back to Egypt?"

"That's simplifying it somewhat, but in essence; yes."

The kettle whistled - Amelia had always preferred to have a kettle that sat on the hob as the whistle reminded her of her Grandma - and Boris poured the boiling water into the pot. Despite the situation, Amelia was quietly pleased that he used the teapot, not simply dropping a teabag into a cup (or God forbid a mug) like an animal. Tea etiquette carried a certain weight for Amelia.

"I think he would run into some problems."

Boris nodded, with an expression like that of a man whose dog has learnt a complicated trick. "That is a very good point."

"I mean he couldn't just buy a plane ticket."

"Certainly not."

"A mummy on a Boeing 747 would excite interest."

"Even if he understood the concept of air travel, which we have to assume he would not."

"So..." Despite herself, Amelia was fascinated to know where this might be going. "You think he had help?"

There was that 'good girl' expression again. "People who have waited in anticipation of this day."

"Like your lot," pointed out Amelia.

"But with very different intentions."

"People who have waited thousands of years?"

"We can assume a family 'business', passed from father to son," Boris conceded. "Or, more likely, they are one branch of a larger organisation. There are some strange people out there."

51

"You don't have to tell me," Amelia muttered.

"It's likely that there would have been disruptions through the centuries," Boris went on. "But as long as there is someone who remembers, then these traditions continue, even if they no longer remember why. Even if some salient points have been forgotten or misconstrued along the way."

"Salient points?"

Boris levelled his dark eyes at her. "Language, for instance. Sugar?"

Amelia felt a chill shiver its way down her spine. How had she not seen where this was leading? He thought that this ancient sect were the ones who had kidnapped her, and that the man in the hood was a millennia-old Mummy who only spoke a dead language. She idly wondered if she could dial 999 on her phone without Boris noticing.

But then again - assuming this was all nonsense - who *had* kidnapped her? Who had been beneath that hood? Who could write cryptoglyphic sentences with such perfect fluency? Boris was clearly certifiable but he was currently presenting the only answer that made sense - albeit to a certain value of the word 'sense'.

"No," said Amelia. "To the sugar. No, thank you."

"They call themselves the Brotherhood of Egypt," said Boris, passing the cup to Amelia.

"Not the Brotherhood of Amunet?"

"Oh no." Boris shook his head. "According to the legends, Amunet will return to save Egypt. They believe they are acting in the national good. We have reason to believe that they know about the excavation. We also have reason to believe that they have been watching the Fitzwilliam Museum for some time. They would have to be - a mummy strolling through Cambridge would excite almost as much interest as one on a plane."

"Might be written off as a student thing," suggested Amelia. You saw some strange things on the streets of Cambridge and ninety percent of them were 'student things'.

"Initially perhaps," Boris admitted. "Because the Brotherhood were watching from the outside, we put Claude on the inside ready to catch them in the act if they tried to break in. Which, of course, did not happen."

Amelia sipped her tea. She felt something move against her leg

52

and looked down to see Valerie rubbing her body along her shin. It was a measure of how distracted she was that Amelia actually leant down to scratch the cat behind the ears rather than irritably pushing it away.

"After it killed Claude," Boris went on, "we can assume the mummy went out through the window, where it was met by the Brotherhood - they presumably had some way of identifying themselves to avoid Claude's fate. It took us the better part of the day to track down where they were hiding and we arrived as you observed. Just in time."

"Earlier would have been better," said Amelia, hastily adding, "Not that I'm ungrateful." She yawned. She was no longer sure that all this was actually happening, or that she was hearing what she was hearing, the unreality of the story blending with her own tiredness.

"You should get some sleep." Boris put down his cup, apparently satisfied that Amelia was as convinced as she was ever likely to be. "Thank you for the tea."

"Thank you," said Amelia. "For everything."

Boris waved this off. "Just doing my job."

"Okay." She was not sure she understood what that job was. Who were Universal Egyptology? And why did such an organisation consider saving kidnapped women to be all in a day's work?

"There was one other thing I wanted to ask you," said Boris, as they walked to the door.

"Oh yes?"

"Are you busy at the present?"

"Why? Are you asking me on a date? Because I've had a long day."

"No." Boris turned to face her, that compelling and inviting smile on his face once more. "I thought perhaps you might like to see this through."

The fact that there was any part of her that was excited by this idea surprised Amelia. She was by trade and nature an academic, and yet the invitation sent a pleasant frisson shivering through her body and a fast-moving montage of images through her mind of what it might entail. But it only lasted a second - a bright flash of thrill that was immediately extinguished. There was work to be done, a language to be deciphered, and she was far too busy at the moment. Plus, the whole thing was crazy and this man a certified loon.

53

"No. But thank you."

Boris pulled a rueful face. "That is a pity. We have many skilled linguists on our staff of course, but none who can read cryptoglyphs. Something which is bound to come up again. Do you know of anyone?"

Amelia shrugged. "The only other man who was making real headway in deciphering them was Professor Joseph Muller. He worked here, at the university, but he disappeared in the late 70s and hasn't been seen since. There was a scandal."

"Scandal?"

"He was a brilliant Egyptologist - my work is largely based on his notes - and a great lecturer. But he embraced the 60s in a big way - free love, free drugs. He never really let go of it. Things got out of hand. The university 'let him go' when he turned up to a lecture naked and suggested everyone else join him. I've no idea what happened to him, though I guess if you ask around someone might know. I think he's probably dead now."

"Unfortunate," mused Boris.

"Certainly for him."

Boris stood in thought a while. "If I cannot convince you to help us track down the Priest, perhaps you might help us in another way."

"Really not my..."

"We have a number of documents written in cryptoglyphs which may be relevant and which have never been translated."

Amelia could not stop her eyes from lighting up, this was like waving a bottle of vodka at an alcoholic. But she determined to remain firm. "No, thank..."

"In fact they've only even been looked at by a handful of people. They are amongst the rarest Ancient Egyptian texts in the world."

If Amelia had had a tail it would have been wagging, but again she tried to suppress her enthusiasm. "Even so..."

"They're part of the Universal Library, the largest collection of rare historical documents in the world, containing texts from practically every ancient civilisation you care to name. Very few people even know that it exists."

Amelia opened her mouth to speak but no sound came out, and the look on her face betrayed her.

"It would only be for the day," said Boris, his voice gently wheedling.

"Which of these do you think it is?" asked Izzy, filled to overflowing with enthusiasm. "This one? No, that one. Gotta be that one! With the gargoyles and the wiggly bits of architecture round the roof."

Her mistake, Amelia thought to herself, had been mentioning the library to Izzy in the first place. For one thing the Universal Library was supposed to be a secret - although that was of little real concern as Amelia trusted Izzy completely. But she had done what so many did when they talked to Izzy; she had forgotten that her friend was an accomplished classicist with a vested interest in old books. After Boris had left that night, Amelia had felt an overwhelming urge to tell someone at least some portion of what had happened to her. Amelia was not overburdened with friends to begin with, and when you added in the limiting factors of a friend she could trust, who would be awake at this hour of the night (early morning really), that left only Izzy. During the ensuing phone call, Amelia had made the mistake of mentioning a secret library filled with rare books, and realised too late that she was talking to a serious student and not a Valley girl. As soon as she heard about it, Izzy was insisting that she come along.

"I'm not sure I'm allowed..." Amelia began.

"Please Amelia! Please, please, please, pleeeeeeeze!" It was stuff like that that made it so easy to forget what Izzy was.

Amelia knew that if she wanted, she could forbid it, but in truth she rather liked the idea of having someone else along. This whole thing was getting out of hand and, while it seemed unlikely that it was all an incredibly elaborate ruse to trick her into something, she would feel more confident and comfortable with a friend by her side.

"Okay," said Amelia, and yanked the phone away from her ear as a high pitched squeal of excitement from the other end of the line threatened to burst her eardrum.

So it happened that the pair found themselves in London, emerging from South Kensington Underground, not far from The Natural History Museum, an area replete with handsome buildings whose stately facades might easily disguise a secret library.

"He said to meet him here," said Amelia, as they stopped on a corner and tried to keep out of the way of the constant pedestrian traffic of London. (You are not supposed to stop walking in London, if you stop then you are automatically in the way of someone who must be more important than you because *they* have somewhere else to go.)

"What does he look like?" asked Izzy. Amelia could not help noticing that while she herself just seemed to be in people's way, the foot traffic, or at least the male portion of it, simply flowed around Izzy, slowing slightly to take her in as they passed. It was not as if she was wearing anything particularly enticing - jeans and a sensible blouse - it was just Izzy.

"He's tall, quite slim, dark hair and eyes. I'd be stunned if he wasn't wearing a tailored suit." Boris had struck her as a man who seldom appeared out of a tailored suit. "I think he's Egyptian - originally anyway, he doesn't have any accent."

"Is he good-looking?"

Amelia gave her friend a look.

"I'm just asking. I'm just trying to spot him."

"He's very handsome, yes," acknowledged Amelia.

"'Very'?"

Amelia ignored her friend's tone, turned to continue looking for Boris, and started as she found him directly behind her, appearing as if from nowhere wearing an impeccably tailored suit.

"Miss Evans, so nice to see you again." Boris's dark eyes flicked to Izzy. Most men's eyes did this, but Boris's were more suspicious than interested. "You brought a friend."

"This is Isobel."

Boris nodded slowly. "Perhaps I should have specified that I am not giving tours."

Amelia met his gaze steadily. "Perhaps I should have specified that I am not in the habit of meeting strange men I hardly know without exercising a degree of caution."

"Burn," said Izzy, backing up her friend.

Boris smiled indulgently. "That is perfectly reasonable. My apologies Miss Grosvenor, you are most welcome."

Izzy beamed, while Amelia wondered how Boris had known her surname. However he had known it, she suspected that he had deliberately dropped the name to remind Amelia who was in charge.

"This way please."

Boris led the two women, not into one of the stately buildings but into a waiting car.

"Why did we meet here if we're going somewhere else?" asked Amelia.

Boris gave her a look: don't ask questions to which you already know the answers. "I wonder if you would be so good as to put on these blindfolds."

Izzy eyed the thing suspiciously. "Last time a man asked me to do that, it...," she mused on the memory for a second. "Actually it was pretty cool, but that wasn't in the back of a car."

"If we say no to blindfolds?" asked Amelia.

Boris shrugged. "Then I don't get to look out the window."

He nodded to the driver. A partition rose between the front and back seats, sealing them in, and the windows faded from transparent into opaque, plunging the back of the car into darkness. There was a click as Boris turned on the light. "I can only apologise if these precautions seem extreme, but the Universal Library had been a closely guarded secret now for centuries. And while we're delighted that you've agreed to help us, we're not prepared yet to give away its location to newcomers."

"Who are Universal Egyptology?" asked Izzy. "And why do they need a library like this? And what's it got to do with the dead man in the Fitz? And the missing mummy? And Amelia getting kidnapped? I like your suit."

"All in good time," said Boris. "And thank you; Savile Row."

"Boris is an expert at not answering questions," confided Amelia.

As well as the windows being blacked out, Amelia now noticed that the sounds of London - one of the world's loudest cities - had vanished, suggesting that the car was soundproofed as well. They were travelling in a sensory deprivation tank on wheels. They could be going round and round in circles for all she and Izzy could tell.

About twenty minutes after they had got in, the car finally came to a halt.

"We're here," said Boris.

The partition descended, the windows became clear once more and a loud clunk announced that the doors had been unlocked. The trio got out into a nondescript underground car park which was nowhere near as impressive a sight as that for which Amelia had been quietly hoping.

"This is a relatively recent addition," said Boris, perhaps seeing the disappointment in the faces of the two women. "We like to keep up with the times. This way please."

The lift to which he led them was decked out in brass and velvet like a Victorian antique, but it set off downwards with barely more than a hiss, dropping, as smooth as silk and coming to a halt with a polite 'bing'.

Boris gave Amelia and Izzy a final look, then opened the doors and led them through.

This was more what Amelia had had in mind. Row after row of dark oak shelves stretched into the distance, sealed beneath a vaulted ceiling from which hung electric chandeliers that gave off a discrete orange glow - nothing too obtrusive. The shelves were heavy with books, each one looking like the sort of thing for which a collector might spend his whole life searching. The shelving was punctuated by long tables with reading slopes built into them and adjustable lamps sprouting from their centre. Leather club chairs sat squatly in nooks and at the end of aisles, each with a reading stand beside it that could be swung into place in front of the chair and adjusted to suit the individual reader. Each stand had its own light built in. The smell of old leather and paper hung in the air, heavy enough that you could taste the antiquity. Figures moved between the shelves; men and women, neatly and soberly dressed, moving with quiet intent. Those handling the books wore white cotton gloves and each carried a slim, wooden page turner like an emblem of office. Above all else there was the silence. It cloaked the room so only the sound of rustling pages and the occasional shriek of a scratching pen cut through it.

"I've died and gone to the library," Izzy breathed. Amelia felt the same way.

Boris pointed and they walked on, their feet making not a sound on the hushening carpet. People glanced at them as they passed but they were apparently of little interest compared to the books. Amelia looked at Izzy. Her eyes were wide and shining, her mouth open in happy amazement, her head jerking this way and that, trying to look all ways at once; everything of interest. Amelia wondered if she herself looked any better, this place was a book-lovers paradise - she could quite happily have moved in here.

In one of the stone columns that supported the roof was set a narrow but heavy-looking door. Boris opened it to reveal a cast iron spiral staircase, burrowing still further down. Their footsteps rang loudly as they descended, echoing off the stone interior of the column. At the bottom they came to a far more plain door which Boris opened, leading the way into a sterile, low-ceilinged room. The layout was similar to the vast hall above, but here metallic shelving was filled by sealed drawers, lockers and cases, stretching on, row after antiseptic row into the distance. In the background they could hear the soft hum of an air-conditioning unit maintaining optimum temperature.

"The Vault," explained Boris. "This is where the most fragile of our collection is stored."

They walked through the endless stacks, each identical row labelled with a sequence of numbers and letters, which apparently meant something to Boris but might as well have been Martian for all Amelia could comprehend. They turned down one of the avenues and Boris stopped in front of a drawer. Carefully, almost reverently, he pulled the drawer out, revealing a papyrus in astoundingly good condition.

"It is over four thousand years old," he said. "We have several documents in cryptoglyphs but this is considered the most significant. None of our scholars has ever been able to read it, or indeed any of them."

"And you think Amelia can?" asked Izzy.

Amelia levelled a hard stare at her friend - there had been altogether too much incredulity in her voice. True she was making the same mistake about Amelia that Amelia had made about her earlier - it was easy to forget that a friend may also be intelligent or even expert in her field - but the mistake is easier to forgive in ourselves than in others.

"In fairness," said Boris, "our scholars do have other more pressing matters. We decipher such things on a need-to-know basis depending on what crises are currently occurring in the world. Up to now, being able to read cryptoglyphics has not been a priority. Now it is, we're quite happy to get someone to help and then that knowledge will be passed on through future centuries of Universal personnel."

"In fairness," Amelia added, in acid tones, "it is also bloody hard to read and some of us have devoted a career to it."

"That too," acknowledged Boris.

"I'll take a look at it then, shall I?"

"If you wouldn't mind."

Amelia turned her attention to the papyrus. She suddenly felt rather put on the spot. She had put herself forward as an expert in cryptoglyphics - the *only* expert - even though she had only found the essential key a matter of days ago and was nowhere near deciphering the alphabet as a whole. What she had learnt she could extrapolate to other characters, but there remained a real chance that she would not be able to read more than one word in five.

"What does it say?" asked Izzy, naturally impatient.

The layout was unconventional, the painted characters swirling about a central point like a whirlpool rather than laid out in nice tidy rows. It was hard to know even where to begin, so Amelia started with words she knew (or hoped she knew). 'Tomb' - that had been one of the first she had deciphered. 'Cat' - always a feature in Egyptian inscriptions. 'Queen' - another she had learnt from the sarcophagus of the Priest with Turquoise Eyes. She read on, starting to get an idea of how this was supposed to be read.

"I think it's the location of a tomb." It was fast occurring to her that the strange layout might have some occult significance, perhaps it was an incantation of some sort. This was a document intended for the eyes of a few initiates, not the common man. One particular character was bothering her. It seemed important, perhaps even the title of the incantation. Unfortunately the character was located in a spot where time had done some damage to the papyrus, so it was only partially visible. She squinted at it, joining the lines and filling in the blanks in her head.

A cold chill stole over her.

"What is it?" asked Boris, his quick eyes picking up the change in her expression.

"Arcana," said Amelia. "This papyrus is called The Arcana."

The lights in the Vault went out.

Chapter 6 - In the Dark

As they were plunged into darkness, Amelia felt Izzy grab her arm, squeezing tighter than a tourniquet.

"Remain calm." Boris's smooth voice came out of the inky blackness beside her. "There is a back-up generator for emergencies such as this one, which will I am sure... Ah, there it goes."

On the floor, along the bases of the shelves, lines of cool fluorescent lights lit up. They were dim, but they were light, and their presence was oddly calming.

"What's happening?!" asked Izzy, panicked and still clinging to Amelia's arm like grim death.

"Hard to say at this point," said Boris. Though his voice remained level, Amelia could hear the anxiety, and any hope that he might be about to announce that this sort of thing happened all the time evaporated. He did *not* know what was happening, and he feared the same as Amelia. The figure in the hood, the one who Boris thought was the Mummy of the Priest with Turquoise Eyes, or even the High Priest of Queen Amunet, had said 'Her location is in The Arcana'. Here was a document called The Arcana, which seemed to give the location of a tomb; the tomb of a Queen. It was hard to avoid the horrid possibility that the hooded man - the Mummy, Ramose, call him what you want - needed this papyrus to find 'her', and had now come to get it.

"Surely you've got guards," said Amelia, more desperately than she would have liked.

"The fewer people who know about this place the better," replied Boris, unhelpfully. "Our agents know how to look after themselves of course, and there will be a few in the building, but actual guards... We prefer to rely on the fact that no one knows where we are."

Was that an accusation? It might have been. No one knew where this place was and yet someone had apparently found it. Was he thinking that Amelia might have brought along someone other than Izzy? Someone who might have trailed the car? She hadn't of course, but in the circumstances she would not have blamed him for suspecting that.

"I think it might be best," said Boris, "if we were to leave now."

"I'll second that," said Izzy fervently.

But as they were about to head for the exit, the character of the light in the Vault changed again. A stream of red lights cascaded along the row of white ones at the base of the shelves, making the light in the room flicker with a horror movie ambience. Boris stared, his face set.

"The silent alarm," he said, grimly.

"Meaning?"

"There are intruders in the building. Come on."

This time it was a sound that stopped them in their tracks; the metallic clang of feet on the staircase, then noises of people entering the room, followed by voices. Now there were sounds of movement, but softer - they knew that someone was down here. They were splitting up and spreading out to cover the room. A shiver of terror snaked a cold path up Amelia's spine as she heard a sudden, harsh voice, louder than the other more cautious ones, speaking the ugly, incomprehensible syllables of the Lost Dynasty. In that instant, there was no room in her mind for this being merely the 'hooded man' - it was the Mummy.

Izzy's grip tightened like a vice on Amelia's deadening arm, and Amelia glanced back at her friend. It was strange to see Izzy scared, she normally took everything in her stride. Only on the night they had first met, when she had shown up crying, had Amelia seen her friend out of control. Now, as she had then, Amelia found it easier to be strong for Izzy's sake. Had she been alone, then holding herself together would not have been an option, but with Izzy there as something to focus on, she could keep herself in one piece and her mind in one place.

She tugged at Boris's sleeve as he peered out between the rows of shelves. He turned back and made a quick series of complicated gestures.

'What?' mouthed Amelia - the gestures could have been sign language or interpretive dance for all she knew.

Boris rolled his eyes and mouthed, 'Stay here'.

Amelia replied with a thumbs up - which, she told herself, had the sort of simplicity one appreciated in gestural language.

Boris stole off through the shelves, quick and silent, that panther-like quality which Amelia had noted in him suddenly coming good. Without realising they were doing it, Amelia and Izzy shrank down to crouch on the floor, hugging as close as they could to the shelves. Amelia could hear Izzy's quick, panicked breathing, and feel her friend's heart pounding against her. Or perhaps both were her own. She looked down at her hand, red and white light flickering across it; she was trembling. From elsewhere in the room, other sounds were now reaching her. She held her breath and listened. Her assumption had been that the intruders had split up to search for them, but now, listening to that clattering and clunking, she began to wonder if the search was for The Arcana. What she was hearing was locks being broken, drawers being opened and centuries' old documents being thrown to one side. Had Amelia not already labelled the Brotherhood of Egypt as 'the bad guys' then this behaviour would have confirmed it. Every fibre of her screamed out against such reckless mistreatment of historic literature. Part of her wanted to leap up and yell at the men to put everything back where had they found it, carefully. Another part of her wanted to point them in the direction of The Arcana, as that would presumably halt their wanton destruction and since they were going to find the thing in the end anyway. Was there any harm in them getting it? It didn't belong to them of course, but in the circumstances she would still have liked to know why it was so important to them. Was stopping them worth risking her life over?

It was as these thoughts were passing through her head, handily distracting her from contemplation of her situation, that Amelia heard a noise from just around the corner and her blood froze. Someone was coming towards them. Suddenly her breathing seemed even louder, like a steam train setting out, while her heartbeat sounded like Fred Astaire on a hardwood floor. The footsteps drew closer and she became aware that the owner of them had an unusual gait, a shuffling, dragging, half-step that was slow but relentless. She could also hear the unseen person breathing in slow, long rasps, each breath like a death rattle passing over dry, papery vocal cords. It was a sound she had heard before.

Trying to control the panic that was pouring into her so that it seemed to be seeping from every pore, Amelia began to edge backwards. At first she encountered resistance from Izzy, who was behind her, but her friend soon caught on and, as quietly as they could, moving in tandem on hands and knees like some strange eight-legged beast, they retreated down the row. They had not quite reached the halfway point when the figure - the hooded man, the Mummy - came into view. Every muscle in Amelia's body went tight. All her instincts screamed at her to run, but all she could do was stare. It was tall - taller than it had appeared when she had glimpsed its shadow in the little room in Cambridge - and lean to the point of emaciation, its fingers bony claws. It walked, not so much hunched, but with its whole body bent like bow. It was still draped in a hooded cloak, hiding much of it including its head, but through the folds, illuminated by the flashes of white light, Amelia could see dirty linen strips of bandage about its exposed legs and arms. It was impossible. Boris could not be right. It had to be a man dressed up as a mummy. But however much her logical mind argued for this conclusion, her gut fought against it. No man moved like this - a stringless puppet that ought to fall at the first breath of wind and yet conveyed a tremendous power and strength. No man carried with him the aura that shrouded the Mummy - it was hard to describe through the usual sensations; a feeling of immense age and the scent of death. It carried with it the cold emptiness of the tomb, seeming to prickle Amelia's skin even at this distance.

Slowly, with a dry crackle that could have been its bandages, its bones or its parched skin and shrivelled sinews, the Mummy turned its head, and the light from the floor caught the face beneath the hood. All doubt left Amelia. The face was a patchwork of bandages and age-blackened skin; its nose eroded by time into a pair of black holes; its mouth a ragged cave of rotted teeth and dry gums. The overhang of the hood hid where the Mummy's eyes should have been, but in that shadow, Amelia glimpsed a gleam of turquoise.

The Mummy's mouth opened to emit a noise like a wind blowing across a dry desert. It clutched the shelves with a scrawny hand, and began to walk towards Amelia and Izzy, its pace quickening as it did so.

Perhaps if she had been there alone, Amelia would never had moved. Perhaps if she had not already had one run-in with the Brotherhood, then she would never have moved. Perhaps if Frank had not cheated on her, then she would never have moved. Or perhaps it was some combination of factors, but whatever the case, Amelia Evans was done taking shit from people.

"Come on!" Shouting might not have been the smartest thing to do, since it advertised her presence to the rest of the Brotherhood, but in the event it made no difference. As Amelia sprang to her feet, dragging Izzy down the aisle with her, away from the approaching apparition, the Mummy let out a blood curdling howl. Now Amelia could hear the Brotherhood hurrying towards them through the vast vault. She didn't care. Away from the Mummy was what mattered, everything else she would deal with.

She rounded a corner at speed and bumped into someone.

"Sorry," she said, automatically, before realising that this was one of the men apparently trying to kill her. She raised a hand to strike, but the man grabbed her, forcing her back against the shelves. Next second he was doubled over, nursing a part of his anatomy to which only nice things are meant happen. Izzy had been too scared to do much up to this point, but a man forcing his attentions on a woman landed right in her area of expertise. When men would not take 'no' for an answer, then Izzy knew exactly where to aim.

"Good kick," murmured Amelia, a little dazed.

"A knee is more efficient, but you get more power from a kick," replied Izzy, the voice of experience.

"Worth remembering."

"Shall we?"

"Yeah."

They took off again, ducking and dodging between the stacks, describing a path so random that surely no one would think to follow it. They had no path in mind and no idea where the exit was, but that was a problem for another moment. The size of the Vault had not previously been clear to Amelia. Because of its lofty roof and grand design, the library had looked as massive as it was, but the Vault had a low roof and self-effacing appearance which made it seem small, when in fact it stretched for what seemed like miles. You could get really lost in here - which was currently a mixed blessing.

"I think we lost them," panted Izzy, as they came to a halt, far from where they had set off. "You think they'll keep after us?"

Amelia shook her head as she doubled over to catch her breath. "I think they're too busy looking for that papyrus."

This too was a mixed blessing. Why hadn't she had the foresight to stick it in her pocket? That would probably have destroyed it, but wasn't that better than letting it fall into the hands of a rogue mummy and its cohorts? No. It was no good, Amelia's mind would not countenance even the idea that the destruction of an important historical document might be a good thing. Besides, they still had no idea of the Mummy's purpose. Perhaps if they all sat down and talked about it they could work something out. Where was it written that mummies had to be evil? She wondered if Boris might know more than he was saying. She also wondered where Boris was and if he was okay.

"What now?" asked Izzy, immediately turning to the older woman and expecting a plan.

Amelia held up a hand, asking for another minute to get her breath back. Though she was slim, it was more through diet and metabolic predisposition than exercise; she did not run as a rule. As she stared at the floor, something caught her eye. She straightened and looked back at the last crossroads in the shelves. That was interesting.

"What is it?" asked Izzy, hopefully.

"The red lights." At the base of the shelves, the little red circles streamed along the white bands of light like buoys in a fast-flowing river.

"What about them?"

"They go different ways depending on where we are."

Izzy frowned. "So?"

"I think they lead to the way out."

"Just because they go in different directions?"

"Because in the case of an emergency that's something you'd need to know and this would be an easy way of showing it."

Every avenue of the Vault looked the same. You'd have to work here for years to be able to find your way around, and even then in time of panic it would be easy to take a wrong turn. A map was all very well, but if the building was on fire who would have time for that? This made sense.

"Come on." Amelia took charge. "And keep your ears open."

They crept on in the direction in which the lights led but were brought up short almost immediately by sounds elsewhere in the Vault; cries, thuds, the sounds of a struggle and, finally, a gunshot.

The two women looked at each other and hurried on. There was nothing they could do one way or the other.

They heard nothing more as they continued, but the silence was as unnerving as the sounds had been. The fear now was that there were still people out there, and they just couldn't hear them

66

coming. Amelia felt her nerves had been shredded to a ragged edge, she was no longer sure if she was perceiving anything correctly. Were the noises she had heard before a figment of her stressed imagination? Or perhaps it was this silence that was all in her head? All she could do was follow the lights through the appalling quiet, until Izzy grabbed her arm and put a finger to her lips.

They both listened. Amelia shivered and felt Izzy do the same as they heard the footsteps approaching. Hastily, now more careless of the noise they made, they hurried on. The footsteps quickened too. They ducked down alternative avenues, no longer following the lights, just anxious to get away. But the feet followed. At one point it seemed they were gone and Amelia allowed herself a moment of relief, but they returned a minute later from a different direction, now closer and closing fast. The women began to run. The feet matched them, seeming to always know a quicker route. Now they ran blindly, bumping into shelves as they went, skidding round corners, no thought of direction, only of speed.

But to no avail. Amelia cried out as a hand grabbed her.

"It's alright! It's me!"

"Boris!" Amelia gasped in surprise and relief - emotions which quickly turned to fury. "Why the hell didn't you say it was you?!"

"I didn't know it was *you*!" Boris pointed out. "You could have been them."

"We're not them," Izzy argued. "They're them. We're us."

"Good point."

Only now did Amelia register that blood was running down Boris's face. "You're hurt."

Boris dismissed the idea casually. "Just grazed. Lucky really. It was enough to knock me over so they thought they'd killed me and left me for dead."

"Are they gone?" asked Amelia. She knew she ought to hope that the intruders were still here, that there was still some chance of catching them, but could not.

"We'll do a proper sweep later," said Boris. "But they seem to have gone. They got what they came for."

"The Arcana."

Boris nodded. "They now know the whereabouts of the Queen's tomb."

There was a pause before Izzy spoke. "So what?"

67

Though prosaically put, Amelia thought it was a fair question. What was the worst that could happen?

"Truthfully," said Boris, "we don't know what the Priest wants. We know some of the legends - they can't all be true but none of them are good. The only absolute is that he wants to restore Queen Amunet to life."

"Like him?" Izzy pulled a face.

But Boris shook his head emphatically. "Oh no. He wants her to be more than a mummy. A mummy is little more than an animated corpse. He is planning to restore her completely to life."

"That's impossible."

Boris raised a quizzical eyebrow. "Bold words for someone who was just chased by a mummy."

"Not all legends about the Queen are bad," said Amelia. She found the old romances of a love that survives beyond death rising in her mind. Was it possible that the Priest just wanted to be reunited with his lost sweetheart?
Who knew she had such romantic dreams left in her?

"The dead belong dead," said Boris firmly. "Whatever their intentions we really can't have them wandering about. Universal lost an agent in Cambridge, there's another three injured upstairs, one on the critical list. I think we can interpret the Mummy's intentions by his actions and those of the Brotherhood."

Which was hard to argue with.

"So now he's on his way to Egypt?" asked Izzy.

"Now that he has The Arcana," nodded Boris.

"How?" asked Amelia.

"Most likely by boat," said Boris. "As you pointed out, he can hardly buy a plane ticket, and security restrictions are pretty strong these days. So..."

"No." Amelia shook her head, she had been thinking. "I mean, what use is The Arcana? It's in cryptoglyphs."

"The Mummy can read crypto..." Boris tailed off as the same realisation hit him.

"But his followers can't understand what he tells them," Amelia finished.

"And we've got their only translator," mused Boris.

Despite not being wild about the word 'got', Amelia nodded. "They're bound to figure something out, but it should give us one hell of a head-start. Especially if they're taking a boat. We can be ready for them when they arrive."

Boris looked at her, arching a questioning eyebrow. "We?"

She had said it without thinking, but as soon as Boris asked the question, Amelia knew that she was in this for the long haul. It was a million miles out of her experience, it was dangerous and insane, but there was no way she was missing it.

"We," she said, plainly.

"And that includes me," said Izzy firmly. Boris and Amelia both opened their mouths to disagree but Izzy gave them no chance. "No desiccated Ancient Egyptian gets to pull something like that on me and get away with it."

Boris smiled. "Very well. 'We' it is." He shook his head. "I wish we knew how they found this place though. I don't like the idea of them being one step ahead."

Chapter 7 - Two Journeys

In the secluded doorway that he called his own when night fell, Old Joe (he was not quite sure when he had stopped being simply 'Joe') curled up. It was just off Market Square and was not such a bad place to sleep at this time of year. When winter rolled around then a place in a local shelter was definitely preferable, but in summer and even through a mild autumn, this was a good spot, sheltered from the wind, wide enough for him to stretch out full length, and deep enough to store his personal items - while not materialist, there were a few possessions that meant a great deal to Old Joe, and which he had carried with him for years.

From the corner of his eye, as he started to drift off to sleep, he saw the little group approaching. The majority of them seemed relatively average but the tall one in the centre was the sort of thing you did not see on the streets of Cambridge every night. Or at least, the sort of thing that most people did not see on the streets of Cambridge every night. Joe saw stuff like that all the time, and so remained unphazed - he had seen stranger on many occasions. The world as Joe saw it was not necessarily a better place to live, but it was certainly a more interesting one.

The group reached him and came to a halt. It would seem that he had visitors. If he'd known he would have tidied up the doorway.

"Something I can do for you gentlemen?" asked Joe, with an olde worlde courtesy that he found sadly lacking in many of his contemporaries.

When the answer came it did so in a manner that would have baffled anyone other than Joe. It was not a manner of speech in which any had ever spoken to him before, but fortunately he spoke to people in that manner quite regularly, keeping up his familiarity with the language and earning an undeserved reputation for talking gibberish. Had he stopped to think about it, then Old Joe might well have wondered at how extraordinarily lucky this group was to have found him, quite probably the only man alive in the world today capable of conducting such a conversation. But Joe was not in the habit of stopping to think about things. Thinking had lost its appeal some decades since, and he was not altogether sure that he missed it.

"Would you come with us?" one of the group asked, speaking in unremarkable English.

"Is there food?" asked Joe - it had been a somewhat lean day.

"If you would like."

"Can I bring my things?" It did not do to leave your property lying about - there were thieves and, worse still, street cleaners.

"Of course."

The rooms to which the group led Joe, taking a route off the beaten path and clinging to the shadows, were spartan at best. They did not look as if they'd been lived in for more than a few days and had the air of somewhere that might be vacated at any minute. Packed bags were by the door, the floors were dusty and had no carpet, and the shelves were bare save for a few dead flies. Still, the food was good and relatively little seemed to be required of Joe in return. He occupied himself in observing the people who had brought him here. The tall man seemed to the leader, certainly the others showed considerable deference to him, and yet they did not seem able to understand him, which surely presented some hierarchical difficulties. Fortunately, Joe was able to translate, easing the flow of communication. They all seemed very grateful, and made him feel quite welcome.

Outside of the tall man, who remained nameless, the group's senior member was a man called Youssef, and it was he who did the lion's share of the talking, in English and Arabic Egyptian. Much of that talking was to a cat. Again, to many this might have seemed unusual, but Old Joe was more accommodating. People thought that he was odd all the time - it did not do to judge. For all Joe knew the cat was an excellent conversationalist, although he himself had always found them to be snooty and stand-offish.

The cat looked familiar to Joe - he fancied he had seen it around the town. It did not talk back to Youssef, nor did it speak to anybody else, and yet it seemed somehow to make itself understood. That was interesting. Despite the passage of years and a certain waning of sanity, Joe still retained an academic interest, particularly in language and communication, and he pigeon-holed the observation for future study.

"Tomorrow?" Youssef asked. "By private plane?"

The cat apparently confirmed this.

"Go with them," Youssef said, speaking directly to the cat. "Find the right moment."

The cat replied with a haughty expression, common to all cats, which could have been understanding or disdain.

"The women might have been useful but that cannot be helped; the man must not reach Egypt."

"Egypt?" Joe spoke up as the word recalled one of the more reliable memories in an eclectic selection that mixed and matched between fantasy and reality. "Wonderful country. Went there in my youth. Although I daresay it's changed now."

Youssef turned to look at Joe, and smiled. "Would you like to find out?"

Old Joe could not help noticing that the cat was looking at him as well.

There were a lot of things that Amelia did not like about plane travel, and it was a relief to find that one of them, the appalling wait at check-in, would not be necessary, as Universal Egyptology had their own plane. All that remained was her dislike of being a thousand feet up in the air in a metal box waiting for the laws of physics to notice that none of this was possible. Because of her career, trips to Egypt had been unavoidable, and in fact highly desirable, and flying was the only efficient way to do it, so Amelia had bitten the bullet on many occasions. But, given the choice, her favoured mode of transport would have been a slow train, chuffing romantically through country after country. She and Frank had planned to take the Orient Express one day. One day.

"That's it?" Izzy stared incredulously as they crossed the tarmac towards the plane."I'm sorry, would you rather we take *your* plane?" suggested Boris, sarcastically.

"I'm just saying," Izzy went on, "I'd have thought an organisation that can afford a library like the one we saw... I'd have thought they'd have a nicer plane."

"We put the money where it matters," said Boris. "It's a perfectly good plane. What is your objection?"

Izzy shrugged. "No specific objection. I was just hoping for a few more frills."

"Ah. You had in mind something more lavish. With a bar and a screening room perhaps?"

"Honestly? Yeah."

Boris smiled and shook his head. "Sorry to disappoint you. Miss Evans? You seem quiet."

"All good," said Amelia, her voice coming out in a high pitch squeak that she had not intended.

"She doesn't like flying," Izzy confided.

"Izzy!"

"What? You don't. He was going to find out anyway, when you start popping sedatives like M&Ms."

Boris put a comforting hand on Amelia's shoulder. "It's a very good plane. The journey will be an easy one."

Amelia nodded. She had been on lots of plane journeys and they had all gone fine. Why was it then that she could not get the image of them hurtling to the ground in flames out of her head? Perhaps because that was the sort of image that arrested the attention.

When Joe awoke, they were already beside the sea. That was not a useful location given that Britain is surrounded by sea, but he had no more specific information than that. Somewhere on the south coast presumably, since they were heading south.

Wherever it was, it was certainly not a major port, and what they were travelling on was certainly not a commercial vessel. It would be a cramped journey. Speaking of which... Joe looked about him. Where was the tall man?

As Joe wondered, a long wooden box was carried onto the little ship.

"What you got in there?" wondered the man who was either selling or leasing his boat.

Youssef replied with a look.

"None of my business really." The ship's owner demurred. He was used to renting his boats out to all kinds and it did not do to go asking questions. If someone was using your property for illegal purposes then knowing about it in advance just created more problems.

"How long does it take to get to Egypt?" wondered Joe, more out of curiosity than anything else.

"A week and a half. Maybe two weeks."

Joe nodded. It was always nice to learn new things.

"Not as quick as by plane," Youssef added, half to himself. He watched as the long box was stowed below decks, his eyes fiercely intent.

"Well, no," Joe acknowledged. "But sea travel is so much nicer, wouldn't you say?"

It was hard to say what Youssef was thinking when he looked back at Joe. His face was set hard, but then suddenly cracked into a smile. "I like you Joe. I think you will make this journey go all the more quickly."

"How long does it take to get to Egypt?" asked Izzy, peering out of the window to the ground, far below.

"Six to seven hours," answered Amelia, mechanically. "Longer with refuellings."

"Do you think you'll be able to pry your fingers out of the arm rest at any point during that?"

Amelia glared at her friend. Take off was always the worst. Apart from landing, that was really the worst. And turbulence was really, really the worst. The rest of the flight was just bad. Still, Boris had not been lying when he had said that this was a good plane. It might have looked less impressive than a commercial flight, but it was the smoothest and least terrifying take-off through which Amelia had ever closed her eyes and prayed she wouldn't be killed. The smoothness had not stopped her from clinging to her seat like grim death and now, an hour in, she had still not let go.

"She does have a point," said Boris. "Keeping your muscles contracted like that for such a length of time is very bad for them. You should really relax. Try taking a pill."

"Taken one. Taken five."

"And you're still tense?"

"This is where an in-flight movie would have been useful," Izzy pointed out. "We could watch *Despicable Me*. No one can be tense watching *Despicable Me*."

"I'll mention it to my superiors when we get back."

"I'm not sure you will."

It was hard to say if Izzy was flirting with Boris or just chattering the way that Izzy did. One of the things Amelia had learned since hanging out with Izzy was that men defined flirting based on the appearance of the woman they were talking to. Virtually any conversation with a beautiful woman was categorised 'flirting', while there was almost nothing a less attractive woman could say that could not elicit the excuse 'we were just talking'. Two different worlds. Either way, the current bickering between her travel companions gave her something to focus on besides the view out of the window. Another of the frills that Universal Egyptology had disposed of was blinds to cover the windows, and hard as she tried not to look, Amelia still found her gaze drifting. There was something profoundly unsettling about seeing clouds from above, it wasn't natural.

She closed her eyes and tried to ignore all the little sounds that seemed to be coming from the plane itself - the rattles, the clunks, the scratching and grating, the grinding and squeaking. At one point the plane seemed to make a noise like a cat's meow.

As far as he remembered, Old Joe had always enjoyed travelling by boat. He had taken a cruise liner once, sometime around the mid-sixties he fancied, and although that was an era during which his memories were not to be trusted, he was pretty sure he had enjoyed it. He was enjoying himself now, three hours out of port, riding the waves, feeling the salt spray on his face. It was the best shower he'd had in years.

Not all of his fellow passengers were enjoying it so much, some were looking decidedly green around the gills. They mostly seemed to talk to each other in Egyptian, Joe noticed, another language he was wont to slip in and out of as a matter of course. Languages got tangled up and interwoven in his mind unless he concentrated.

The tall man had now reappeared - though Joe had not seen him come onboard. He mostly remained below decks with Youssef, and Joe was often ushered down to translate the conversations between them. They seemed stilted conversations to Joe, as if, even talking through him, there remained a barrier, though perhaps not one of language.

Youssef looked at his watch. "It's time."

Joe translated and the tall man inclined his head in understanding - while Joe remained in the dark.

"Leave me," the tall man replied in his cracked voice.

Again Joe translated. Youssef stood, bowed and left. Joe followed, then, as an after-thought and because he did not wish to be impolite, he turned back to bow.

When you came right down to it, there was something odd

about the tall man. Not his appearance - Joe had long since ceased to find anything odd about anyone's appearance - but his manner. He had a face that was hard to read; it struggled to form expressions and by the time it achieved one the moment had likely past. But as he bowed, Joe could swear that he read something like confusion on the tall man's face, as if he was trying to remember something.

It probably wasn't important. As he left the cabin, Joe glanced at the clock on the wall, and idly wondered what it might be 'time' for.

The shriek from the cockpit was so sudden and so violent that it rendered all three passengers dumbstruck and immobile for a moment. Boris recovered first, springing athletically from his seat and rushing for the door, with Izzy just a beat behind. Amelia, nerves already in tatters from the horrors of flight, took longer, struggling to undo the seatbelt that she had refused to unfasten just because the pilot had turned off some light (how the hell did that make it safer?!).

"It's locked!" Boris put his shoulder to the door as the screams continued beyond it.

Amelia had just managed to make it out of her seat when the hinges gave to reveal the horrid tableau within. The screaming had stopped now. The pilot (she thought his name was Mike - they had been introduced) was beyond screaming, and perhaps for the best. Blood streaked every surface, it was spattered over the control panels and slicked across the windscreen. Mike himself was slumped over the controls, his shirt soaked in his own blood. His face, thankfully, was mostly hidden, but that part that was visible had been shredded, the flesh hanging loosely from his bones.

Boris took a cautious step forward, motioning Izzy back behind him. As he did so, a bloody ball of teeth and fur shot out of the cockpit, making for the luggage area, leaving gory paw prints in its wake.

The plane lurched, the weight of Mike's corpse on the stick turning its nose downwards. Boris rushed into the cockpit, unceremoniously pushing Mike's body from the seat and grabbing the controls.

Though her worst nightmare was happening around her, Amelia could not stop staring towards the luggage. "That was... that

76

was Valerie."

She would know the museum cat anywhere, it had spent enough evenings on her sofa, watching her work with its unblinking green eyes. It had been the first living thing to know that she had cracked the cryptoglyphs. She had confided secrets to that cat - it seeming less crazy than talking to herself. She had cried in front of it.

"Leave it," Boris instructed coldly.

"But... But how...?" Amelia could hear her own voice rising with hysteria.

"We have more immediate issues," said Boris, firmly. "I suggest you get yourself into the cockpit now and see if the two of you can close the door to keep that little bastard out! Izzy, get that out of here."

Izzy had been staring, white-faced, at Mike's body. "I can't."

"If you know how to fly a plane then now would be the time to mention it, but if not then I'm afraid you have to move that."

"*That*?" Izzy glared. "He..."

"Is dead," said Boris. "It's not a person, it's a thing. And it's in the way. Amelia, help her."

It was an effort but, with something to do, Amelia managed to shake off the terror of the situation and the horror of what Valerie had done. She grabbed the collar of Mike's shirt, trying not to think about how wet it was, and hauled him out of the cockpit.

"Keep a look out for the cat," she said to Izzy, who still couldn't bring herself to touch the body.

As she dropped poor Mike to the floor, Amelia got a glimpse of what was left of his face. How had Valerie done that? Though she was no cat lover, and had always assumed that this was the sort of thing that cats probably dreamed of doing, she would never have imagined... She knew this cat! Perhaps Valerie had been somehow trapped in her luggage and had come out angry and terrified and... Even as she thought it, Amelia knew that she was grasping at straws. There was so much more going on here than an angry cat.

And there it was.

Amelia felt its gaze on her before she saw the animal itself. Any lingering hope she might have had that this was a normal cat having a bad day evaporated as she looked into those glassy, pitiless eyes. It was not just looking at her, it was targeting her.

77

Cat and human moved at the same instant; Amelia running for the cockpit, Valerie springing from the luggage towards her. Izzy was at the door and slammed it hard behind Amelia as soon as she was through, then held it in place on its busted hinges. Amelia stood with hands on hips, catching her breath. From outside, a long, low meow crept through the door. Amelia had never heard anything more threatening.

"Can you keep the door closed?" asked Boris.

"Yeah." She was not sure how, but they would. She could hear the sound of clawed feet pacing on the other side.

While Izzy held the door in place, Amelia searched for ways of jamming it shut.

"Were you and Mike... Did you know him well?" asked Izzy.

"Yes," Boris replied, his tone cutting any further inquiry on the subject short.

The pilot's locker yielded a heavy tool kit, a box of bottled water and first aid kit, which together were enough to hold the door closed. Amelia sat down on the tool box with her back to the door, adding her weight to the improvised barricade - no way Valerie was getting in now. But with the immediate danger of the cat removed, she was finding it much harder to ignore her greater fear.

"Are we still going down?"

"I think at this point, down is probably the right direction," replied Boris.

"Wouldn't it be a softer landing over the sea?"

"Perhaps. But we would have needed to refuel soon, so stopping to find the sea is not an option. Stopping, however, is an inevitability."

"We have to land?" Amelia blanched.

"We're *going* to land," replied Boris. "The question is what sort of job we make of it."

Amelia swallowed uncomfortably. "Do you know how to fly?"

"I've been taking lessons."

"How far did you get?"

Boris looked at her and managed to smile. "Does it matter?"

The plane plummeted towards the ground.

Chapter 8 - Ghosts of The Western Desert

The dancing light of the fire threw Ahmad's face into horror film relief as he leaned conspiratorially towards it. The rest of the excavation team, seated about him, unconsciously followed suit, edging closer. He shook his hair - black but shot with a peppering of grey - and waggled his fingers, relishing his time in the limelight, then began to speak.

"In a time long gone and long forgotten," Maggie whispered a simultaneous translation to Arthur, "there was a battle here. Not a great one. Certainly not a long one. But a savage one. And, more importantly, an unfair one in which the wrong the side won. And so the souls of the dead could find no rest in whatever afterlife they believed in, and were doomed to roam these rocks until the end of time. It is an old story, and one that Osman knew when he set out that day," Ahmad deftly introduced his lead character with the skill of a master storyteller.

Though he could only understand the story through Maggie, Arthur could not take his eyes from Ahmad, and still listened to the words he could not understand as they rolled off the digger's tongue in rich, bass tones that communicated a world of meaning beyond the words themselves. Ahmad gestured as he spoke; he shot sly, knowing looks into the faces of his audience; he grinned with hidden meaning; sometimes he would leap to his feet, his whole body becoming part of the terrifying and ultimately tragic story of Osman. As they sat around the camp fires at the end of a day's work, the team took it in turns to tell stories - mostly ghost stories - but there was no doubt that Ahmad was the master.

"He looked back to see where the footsteps were coming from," Ahmad continued, "but saw nothing. Perhaps it was just the echoes of his own feet tricking him. So Osman set off again, and tried to ignore the sound that padded persistently at his back. He tried to ignore it when another set of feet was added. And then another and another. But he kept on telling himself; *the echoes of the Sarranekh can play tricks on you*. Still, he hastened his pace and remembered the warning of the old man at the oasis, 'Stick to the path and all will be well'. Then suddenly!" Ahmad thrust his face forward towards the fire, making his audience jump. "Out in the rocks, he heard a new sound. A pitiable crying, wailing and calling for help. He closed his ears to it and walked on, with the procession of other feet still behind him. And now the wailing seemed to resolve into a word, 'Osman!'. It called for him. *Screamed* for him. He put his hands over his ears to try to block it out. Then the voice was joined by another, 'Osman!'. And another, and more, until the voices to his sides equalled in number the feet at his back. Osman's pace quickened further as the shadows began to lengthen. His head twitched this way and that. Had that shadow moved? He broke into a run. He could not hear the footsteps any more for the screaming around him, but he saw the shadows move - they swept along with him in a dark tide, the shadows of sharp peaks of rock turning into claws that reached for him. They surged past him and rose up; an ever-shifting mass of darkness out of which cried the screams of a thousand dead!" Ahmad paused to let the image register. "It was too much for Osman. With a cry of terror he fled off into the rocks, leaving the path behind him." Ahmad settled back as if the story was over, though everybody knew there would be one sentence left which required their participation.

Arthur was the first to crack. "What happened to him?" He asked, Maggie translating.

Ahmad shrugged. "He was never seen again. But they say - those who walk the path through the Sarranekh regularly - they say that when you walk that path now, you hear another set of feet at your back, and another voice screaming from the shadows."

The party around the campfire relaxed back as the story ended, Ahmad taking the well-earned plaudits. Arthur was glad to see that he was not the only one whose gaze had unwillingly shifted to the peaks and spires of rock that towered over them, and the deep, echoing gullies that ran between. Almost every story that was told around the fires of an evening centred on the ghosts of some long-forgotten battle that still haunted this area, preying on passing travellers, jealous of the life that they had so unfairly lost. One look at the Sarranekh and it was all too easy to believe. And yet, for all that he was extremely susceptible to such tales, Arthur looked forward to the evening's storytelling. It was convivial, it made him feel like part of the group. It was the sort of thing that archaeological teams had been doing in these deserts for decades and beyond. Take away the vehicles in the background and remove the gentle hum of the air-conditioning unit in the Finds tent, and they could be a

Victorian expedition. Take away a little more and they could be a party of tomb builders in the time of the Pharaohs. Oral storytelling around a campfire went back to the dawn of man.

Taken overall, desert living did not suit Arthur. He did not like to admit it, but when it came to sleeping rough, a tent in North Wales would have been too rough for him. He felt strongly that he was doing his girlfriend, Helen, proud in the way he tolerated this life, but after three weeks of it he would probably have felt that he had suffered enough, had it not been for other compensations.

Though he had come out here to have an adventure at Helen's insistence, Arthur was sticking it out because of what they had found. Even the most insular and sedentary of Egyptological bookworms would have been hard pushed not to find some enthusiasm for a dig like this. It was not just the wealth of the tomb that kept him there, it was everything about it. So little was known about the Lost Dynasty - the books on the subject were yet to be written, and Arthur had every intention of writing one, for here was a treasure trove of information. Even if the cryptoglyphs remained unreadable (and he had heard of a researcher in Cambridge who was said to be making progress), the knowledge that could be gleaned from the plethora of objects they had found, stowed safely for Queen Amunet's afterlife, would upturn the archaeological world. It was early days in the 21st century to be making 'find of the century' claims, but Arthur was comfortable making them.

They were all calling the tomb's occupant that now. It had not been confirmed of course - could not be without a translator - but so much pointed to that conclusion, that it seemed almost certain they had indeed found the tomb of the legendary Queen Amunet. They had located the most sought-after tomb in all Egypt and they had found it intact. Arthur had a hunch that it was not the sort of adventure that Helen had had in mind when she had sent him out here, but it was one that suited him, and one for which he was prepared to put up with the hardships of desert living. Every time he found himself in the lushly decorated burial chamber, photographing the wall paintings or delicately dusting carved wood statues, Arthur had to pinch himself to make sure he wasn't dreaming.

And yet, at the same time, he would find his eyes drifting to the heavy stone sarcophagus that dominated the centre of the room, and he shivered.

The lid of that sarcophagus had been lifted on the first afternoon - respect for the dead was all very well but no one had the patience to wait. A good archaeologist is a combination of scientist and eight year old child. Lying within was the ornate wooden coffin of the Queen. It was painted with her features - or a stylised version of them - overlaid with gold leaf, inset with precious stones and metals, and painted in the gaudy Egyptian style. Most notably, and most unusually, painted around the Queen's neck was a gold chain with a jewel hanging from it. Enormous care had been taken by the artist in representing that jewel, and rays extended from it, as if a magenta-coloured sun hung around the Queen's neck.

This coffin would be the last thing that they moved, and so it sat in silent state as they went about their work, slowly dismantling and emptying the chamber. Every now and then, Arthur got the feeling that it was watching him.

That was ridiculous of course, and it was not a fear that he would have voiced to Andoheb or Maggie. Still, when he was in the chamber alone, he would often go over to look into the carved wooden face and meet the gaze of the two unblinking ivory eyes with their jet pupils, just to convince himself that there was nothing to fear. But deep down he knew that it was not those inanimate eyes he felt - that face was just an effigy. Beneath that, inside the coffin, lay a body, and it was her eyes he felt, pricking at the back of his neck. Sometimes he could swear that he heard her whispering his name.

But when the day was done and the workers returned to the camp in the evening, all such thoughts were swiftly dispelled. Andoheb was still the entertaining, effervescent character he had known at university, the local diggers, university students and support staff were good company (even if his conversations with them were limited by the language barrier), and Maggie was less intimidating once you got to know her. Those evenings around the campfire made life here more than merely interesting, they made it fun, and if Arthur had not quite forgotten the strange events of his first night, he had now begun to wonder if he had imagined the face of the scarred man in his tent.

There were other reasons beyond the good company and scary stories that Arthur found the evening to be the most pleasant time of the day. Firstly, it was cooler, which was a tremendous relief. It was also the time that he could really get stuck into his cataloguing work. For all that he had embraced the excitement and adventure of field archaeology, Arthur remained a researcher at heart, and the pleasure of writing up notes, measurements and comparative morphology of the finds was one he saved for the long, cool evenings. After the stories were done, Arthur retreated to the seclusion of his tent and, with his laptop glowing before him, he worked long into the night, transcribing his own tightly written notes, Andoheb's curvaceous scrawl, and Maggie's curt, broken observations. His tidy mind instinctively and automatically organised the disparate notes into a cohesive whole, chronological in layout, cross-referenced through subject and location in the tomb. From time to time he felt the absence of his own books or, better yet, a library to call on, but for the most part Andoheb had been correct; Arthur carried most of this information with him. Without reference to photographs he was able to compare the canopic jars from the tomb with those of other dynasties - noting points of similarity and difference. He recognised the greater use of certain symbolic devices in this tomb to any other he had read about. He was able to put the details in the context of the whole.

It was such engaging work, and it gave him such pleasure to do it, that Arthur found himself labouring late in the night, long after the rest of the camp had gone to sleep, the screen of his laptop his only light, the tapping keys the only sound.

Tonight, after Ahmad's chilling tale, was such a night. Arthur was not sure how long he had been working when his screen began to dim. The battery of his laptop was considered one of the camp's electrical essentials and was recharged daily via the generator, but when he worked, Arthur had only the battery's lifespan. He checked the indicator at the bottom right; half an hour's power remaining. That was disappointing as he had barely started on the glorious scarab brooch that had been brought up out of the tomb earlier that day. He glanced at his watch; two in the morning. That was considerably later than he had thought. Perhaps it was just as well that he got himself to bed.

Checking and double-checking that everything had been saved, Arthur began to undress, leaving the laptop on to light the tent. But as he stopped typing, a sound caught his attention and he paused to listen.

Footsteps in sand are a distinct noise and one to which he had become used, but after Ahmad's story they immediately made him shiver. Which was foolish - it was just a story. But these footsteps were different to the familiar sound. The steps were sloughing and unclear and the rhythm was off, like someone still learning to walk. And yet they did sound like steps, and forceful ones at that. Someone out for a walk? The steps - if that was what they were - were accompanied by another noise, a rhythmic rasping that sounded like someone with a serious sinus problem snoring. But if they were walking, they could hardly be snoring. Was someone sleepwalking? Did you snore whilst sleepwalking?

The laptop switched into power save mode, plunging the tent into darkness and making Arthur start. He fumbled for the torch he kept hanging by his bed and then froze. The noise was now beside him, just the thin canvas sheet of his tent wall between him and it. It sounded less like snoring now, more like the death rattle of someone moments from oblivion. For a moment Arthur remained where he was, unnerved and unsure what to do next. Then he thought back to that first night - the tomb was guarded now, as was the 'Finds' tent, but that did not mean they were safe. How would it be if the camp was under attack - perhaps by an asthmatic tomb robber with a bad leg - and he failed to raise the alarm? He hurried across his tent, unzipped the flap and shone his torchlight out into the darkness.

Nothing.

Arthur held his breath. The sound seemed to have vanished. Unzipping the flap completely, Arthur went out. His hand shook as he pointed the torch this way and that, peering up and down the avenues between the tents. It had not seemed as if the noise was moving fast and yet the source of it appeared to have vanished completely, swallowed up into the desert itself. He shivered and turned to go back into his tent - the dead quiet confirmed that they were at least not under attack. It was most likely just another of the weird sounds that haunt the Sarranekh, or an elderly and injured jackal that had scampered off when it heard him. But as he turned, something in the torchlight caught his eye. There were tracks in the sand. They did not look like the tracks of a man and yet were certainly not the tracks of an animal. Whoever or whatever had passed had carved deep grooves into the sand with its feet, dragging them like an old man, and yet the depth of the step suggested a tremendous power.

Little sleep came to Arthur that night, and so the following night, he went to bed early after only a few hours of studious typing. He paused as he pulled the sheets around him, listening for any disquieting sound, but heard none.

Despite his tiredness though, he did not get a full night's rest. Even with hard, physical work exhausting him, the strange locale, strange nocturnal noises, and sharp temperature shifts between day and night often kept him from a good night's sleep, and tonight he woke in the early hours. The sun was just rising, the early morning light reflecting off the fine sand to throw an unearthly, almost glazed, light upon one defenceless panel of his tent. Arthur rolled over, determined to get back to sleep. But as he lay there he heard a noise that turned his blood to ice in his veins. There were the uneven steps again, there again was the laboured, rasping breathing. Trying desperately to control his own panicked breaths, Arthur looked up in the direction from which the noise came and saw a shadow pass fleetingly through the patch of light on his wall. It was that of a figure, he was sure.

This time he did not hesitate, he sprang from his camp bed and looked out through the door. It was bright enough already that he had no need of the torch tonight, but again he saw nothing. But there in the sand were the tracks, the same as before.

Arthur only took a moment to come to a decision. Wondering if he should be waking Maggie at this point, he dressed as quickly as he could and went out, following the tracks. They were leading, he realised, up into the Sarranekh, in the direction of the tomb. Once he hit the rocks the tracks stopped, but Arthur continued on. As he crested the rise, a pair of rifles were instantly levelled at him.

"It's me!" He held up his hands and the two guards on the tomb (Karim and Nasr) lowered their guns. "Just taking a walk." Arthur explained, accompanying his words with the gestural sub-language he had taken to using with the Egyptian contingent of the dig. "Couldn't sleep."

The guards nodded their understanding. Or at least nodded - it was hard to be sure.

"You see anyone else tonight?" Arthur ventured.

Karim and Nasr frowned; perhaps in incomprehension, perhaps because if they had seen anyone then obviously the whole camp would know about it.

"Stupid question," Arthur admitted.

The guards nodded. Again, it was hard to be certain why.

Later that day, Arthur went to the 'Finds' tent. Everything they had removed from the tomb so far, no matter how small or seemingly insignificant, had been measured, photographed, recorded and catalogued with its own number. He went through the catalogue, looking for some discrepancy that might suggest theft. Nothing.

"You alright?" asked Maggie, looking in on him.

"Yeah," Arthur, waved a hand absently.

"There is actual work to be done, you know?"

Arthur nodded. "You didn't... You didn't hear anything last night?"

Maggie shrugged. "Nothing special. You hearing bogey men?"

"Must be."

Maggie stood there a moment longer, not quite accepting Arthur's easy dismissal. "If there's something you need to tell me, Arthur." However brusque she could be, Maggie took her job seriously.

But Arthur shook his head. "My imagination."

Two days later word reached them of an approaching sandstorm and everyone was pressed into service making the camp safe. All the tents were moved closer into the shelter of the rock walls, protecting them as much as possible. The precious finds were secured; tents made fast; everything tied down, weighed down or nailed to something big and heavy.

"The guards will have to spend the night inside the tomb," said Maggie. Although it would take a madman with a death wish to go out during a sandstorm, she was not leaving the site unprotected.

"How bad a storm is it?" asked Arthur.

"About as bad as they get."

"How bad do they get?"

"Can't see a foot in front of you. If you're not wearing goggles you can't even open your eyes. If you do you'll lose them. Try to breathe and you'll breathe in sand. Try to cough it up and you'll choke on sand. Which is probably preferable to having it slowly flay you alive."

Arthur listened aghast. "Have you been in one?"

"Yep. Nearly died," commented Maggie in her matter-of-fact

way. "Made an arse of securing my tent. One of the flaps came loose. By the time I got it back down, I'd had the skin stripped off my face. Had to spend the next three hours holding the tent in place." She touched her cheek. "Still got some scars. You can't see them for sunburn now."

"Always a silver lining."

Maggie grinned. "You want to worry about how you look, don't live in the desert."

Arthur idly wondered how Maggie might have looked if she had lived a more normal life back home. It was a hard imagining, and in the end he found it difficult to believe that she would have been any better looking with moisturised skin, make-up and coiffed hair. The desert suited Maggie, it brought out the best in her.

"You gonna stand gawping all day or get that tent secured?" Maggie asked. "I'm not coming to save you if you do it wrong."

The storm hit just after sundown and Maggie had not been exaggerating. Arthur huddled in his bed, staring at the walls of his tent as they billowed in and out. The noise was incredible. Deafening. A roaring and a rushing and a screaming, as if his head was inside a blender filled with gravel. After hearing Maggie's stories, he eyed the tent door as if it was an enemy, waiting for it fly open and let that abrasive mayhem into his tent. There would be no sleep for him tonight.

The storm howled on. The sun began to rise and still there was no let up.

Then, Arthur saw it. There, passing slowly along his wall. The shadow of the figure. How was that possible? How could anybody be outside in that? The shock of it, and the curiosity, stunned all Maggie's warnings from his head. He had to know. No matter how dangerous and stupid it was, he had to know. With inevitable steps, that he barely felt he was controlling, Arthur crossed the room to the tent door. His fingers trembled as he reached for the zip.

The hideous noise from without suddenly increased as he opened the zip a fraction, letting in a sharp, high-pressured hiss of wind and sand. Fumbling his goggles onto his face, Arthur peered out. But the gap was too narrow, he had to open the zip further if he wanted to see, and he *had* to see. The sand whipped at his face as he pulled open the zip, and he spat sand onto the floor. But, if only for an instant, he saw outside, and there, in the eye of the storm, the wind and sand lashing about it, was the figure of a man, tall and dark, swathed in a cloak. He was battling against the storm to move but other than that seemed unaffected by it, was not trying to find shelter, was not struggling to breathe, did not seem to be having his skin flayed from his bones. Or if he was, it did not bother him. Arthur did not - could not - look for long, but somehow the figure sensed him. It turned its head. The dark confines of the hood masked its face, but that face was looking directly at Arthur. Then, as soon as it had looked, it turned back, moving on, vanishing into the sandstorm, heading in the direction of the tomb.

Arthur managed to close the zip. He pulled off the goggles and threw them across the tent before collapsing to his knees, retching and coughing, choking up sand. His eyes watered with effort and with pain as the grit scored his throat.

It had been a stupid thing to do. But he was not sorry he had done it. The apparition of his first night - the scarred man - perhaps that had been his own wild imagination, but *this* he had seen. Though he could not say what 'this' had been.

Despite his certainty, come the morning, and with the storm finally died out, Arthur held back from telling Maggie or anyone else about his experience. It all sounded crazy, and besides, there was work to do. Everything had been properly secured and it all looked to have survived the storm, but sand covered everything. Moving the camp to the base of the cliffs came with the advantage of protection but the disadvantage that the sand piled up against them. All the tents had to be dug out, sand had to be shaken from everything. Half the desert seemed to have emptied itself on top of them.

"I'm going to relieve the guards," said Maggie, as work was beginning. "They've been in that tomb long enough."

"Mind if I come?"

"There's work to be done."

"I'll do it," Arthur answered, standing up to the site manager.

Maggie shrugged. "Come on then. If you're coming."

They trudged up through the rocks, now liberally covered with sand, making the route more treacherous as their feet skidded beneath them, or at least Arthur's did.

"No problems last night?" Maggie was clearly picking up on Arthur's mood this morning.

Arthur shook his head. "You? Good night?"

"Pretty good. I don't like to spend sandstorms alone."

It had not escaped Arthur's notice that Maggie occasionally slept in tents other than her own. Whose did not seem to matter too much to her. She was not a woman who formed emotional attachments, but living out in the wilderness a person could get lonely and she dealt with it how she dealt with everything - she tackled the problem head on. It was not a subject on which Arthur wanted to quiz her, but if he had then he was relatively sure she would be plain and upfront about it. It was just sex. The students, workers and so on were here, at most, for a month at a time - who cared?

The entrance to the tomb was sheltered by a rock alcove so, although sand was on the ground outside the tomb, it had been relatively safe from the wind. This meant that the sand outside the tomb was undisturbed. As they approached, Arthur felt his stomach contract.

"What the hell's done that?" Few things got past Maggie. She stooped to examine the tracks in the sand that had arrested Arthur's attention. The difference was that he had seen them before.

"I think there's something I need to tell you."

"Don't tell me you were up here last night?"

Arthur shook his head. "But I think I saw the person who was."

As he related the story, Maggie listened more attentively than she had to anything he had said since arriving here. At the end, she nodded slowly.

"Don't tell anyone else."

"Why not?"

"Because I said so," Maggie retorted, then softened. "Look, I'm not one to label cultures superstitious, but I don't go in for political correctness either. There's a few stories about this place that have got some of the team nervous. I was with Tarek last night and he was close to blaming Queen Amunet for the storm. Ruined the mood," she added. "I don't need people crying ghost when tomb robbers turn up."

"You think it was a tomb robber?"

"Has to be," said Maggie. She said it with conviction, but there was a hint in her voice that she was convincing herself as much as Arthur.

"I don't see how it could be," Arthur began tentatively. "I

89

mean, in that storm..."

"These aren't locals with a rope and a shovel," Maggie interrupted. "Tomb robbers these days are mercenaries. Funded by wealthy collectors. Think they're above the law just cos they've a few billion to chuck about. These people are well-equipped. It's tomb robbers. Has to be. Now, not a word."

Arthur nodded. He respected Maggie, and respected her knowledge, and even if he hadn't he would have done as he was told. But not even she could convince him that what he had seen last night had been a tomb robber.

The following night Arthur was once again roused from his sleep, but this time by something more solid. He jerked awake to find Maggie on top of him with her hand firmly over his mouth. Truth be told, and however devoted he was to Helen, Arthur had had dreams like this. There was just something about Maggie. But a dream was one thing, reality was something else.

Maggie put a finger to her lips before taking her hand away from his mouth. She then leaned down over him and Arthur felt her breath against his ear.

"Dress quickly and come with me." She spoke so quietly that her voice was barely more than an inference.

She got up off the bed, leaving Arthur to shamefacedly reassess his view of the situation. He pulled on his clothes while Maggie alternated looking out of the tent flaps with urgently gesturing for him to hurry. Then, as Arthur stood to join her, she pushed a gun into his hand. Her eyes met his in a significant 'I'm trusting you' look.

Arthur had never fired a gun in his life and had no desire to do so now. He understood the principle; you pointed the end with the hole in it at the thing you no longer wanted to be there and squeezed. But actually doing it... He really hoped he would not have to find out.

Moving stealthily, Maggie led the way out of the tent and through the camp. They were heading up into the Sarranekh, but apparently not for the tomb. The route they were taking was a longer one which would bring them out on the western side of the gully in which the Queen's final resting place was situated. From this side it was a sheer drop down, but it gave a good view of the tomb's entrance. As they approached the top of the cliff, Maggie stopped and gestured Arthur down to his hands and knees as she did the same. She then pressed her finger to her lips with extreme force, emphasising the point. Arthur nodded, his heart thudding somewhere just behind his tonsils.

They crawled forward and peeped over the top of the rocks. The tomb's door was picked out by the early morning light, another clever quirk of Ancient Egyptian design. Since the sandstorm, Maggie had moved the guards permanently inside, ostensibly because the nights could be cold, though Arthur suspected she was trying to lull any would-be robbers into a false sense of security. But there was someone outside the tomb. A figure was pacing up and down relentlessly - up and down, up and down. It was tall and thin, it wore a hooded cloak, and it walked with an uneven, broken gait. Arthur stared, wide-eyed until Maggie pulled him back down out of view.

"Is that what you saw?" Again, her words were little more than breaths, with Arthur reading her lips as much as listening.

He nodded fervently, then mouthed. 'Who is it?'

Maggie shook her head - she did not know.

"Why don't they go in?"

Again the head shake. If this was a tomb robber, or even the advance party of a team of robbers, why would he behave like this? Pacing outside the tomb like a dog at a gate, waiting for the return of its master.

The two again peered out at the figure who had now begun to slow in his perambulations. He stopped to look at the sun as it crept higher, then took a long look at the darkness of the tomb's entrance. Then, with a certainty that made Arthur's blood run cold, he looked directly at where Maggie and Arthur were hidden. They could not be visible, but the figure seemed to know he was being watched none the less. Though the hood still hid the face within, for an instant, barely more than a heartbeat, the morning light caught something beneath the hood, and Arthur was sure he saw a flash of turquoise.

Finally breaking the stare, the figure stalked away in that strong but clumsy step, heading back toward the camp.

"Come on!" hissed Maggie.

"Why's it going back to camp?"

"Don't know. Gonna find out."

They skittered down the rocks in haste, even Maggie's surefootedness failing her occasionally. As they went, various fears rose and fell in Arthur's mind; what if they returned to find everyone dead? But if the figure had wanted to kill them, it could have done that any night. Which was not as comforting a thought as it might have been.

They hurried into the camp, minutes later, to find all quiet.

"Where'd it go?"

A quick search showed the camp to be empty and they headed back up towards the tomb. But this too proved fruitless.

Maggie kicked a rock angrily. "Where the hell did it go?"

"I guess it got back faster than us."

"Then where?!" Maggie snapped. "There's nothing but rocks and desert!"

Arthur left her to herself a while, pacing, muttering and kicking at things. Only when her frustration had dissipated a bit did he dare to speak. "Maggie, what the hell was that?"

"Tomb robber," Maggie replied, firmly. "He knew we were watching him. Must have doubled back and gone that way." She pointed up beyond the tomb, roughly north into the Sarranekh. "That means he was in camp tonight for a reason. Maybe checking to see how far we've got with bringing stuff out the tomb. Then he comes up here to..." She paused.

"To what?" urged Arthur, almost accusing.

"I don't know."

"Why didn't he go in?"

"Maybe he knows we've got guards in there. Maybe's he's got a contact amongst our people. These collectors offer big money, you know. Everyone's got their price."

"If he knew there were guards, then why come up here at all?"

"We move the coffin today," said Maggie, not answering the question. "I'll tell the Prof what's going on."

"What about everyone else?"

"No. If there's a chance we've got a mole, best to keep quiet."

Arthur couldn't help smiling. "You trust me."

Maggie rolled her eyes. "You're a boy scout, Arthur. That may not have much to recommend it, but it does make you trustworthy. Boring. But trustworthy."

"Did you," Arthur was almost afraid to ask. "Did you see anything under the hood?"

Maggie's face did the answering for her. "I thought I saw something, yeah."

Arthur drew in breath. "There's a mummy of the Lost Dynasty in the Fitzwilliam Museum in Cambridge. Some people think it's Ramose, the High Priest of Queen Amunet."

"Oh yeah?" Maggie's voice was sceptical even before she'd heard anything specific to be sceptical about.

"It has turquoise eyes."

"Very pretty I'm sure."

"Do you know the stories about Amunet's Priest?"

Maggie shook her head. "You're as bad as Tarek."

Chapter 9 - The Lost Dynasty

The sharp tapping on the palace floor announced the arrival of Ramose, High Priest of Pharaoh Amunet, but it was said that by the time you could hear the priest coming, he could already hear you. Sitting, waiting for him now, Mahu was ready to believe that the priest could hear his thoughts. There was no one living in Egypt - which was as good as saying that there was no one living in the world - who did not fear Ramose. That said, if there was one person, then it was the man sitting next to Mahu.

The sound of the priest's snake-headed staff on the floor, getting closer, made Setka look up, but his expression suggested no more than mild interest. Mahu wished that he had Setka's equanimity, but of course it was different for Setka.

The doors were opened by a pair of slaves, who very properly averted their eyes as the High Priest entered. It was hard to judge how old Ramose was, partly because his waxy skin could have been any age between 18 and 80, but also because it was impossible to imagine that he had ever appeared any different to how he did now. Ramose could never have been young, certainly never a baby, and he would surely never grow old - he would not stand for it. He was as unchanging and eternal as the gods he worshipped. Or maybe that was just how successive High Priests liked it to appear. There were always men like Ramose at the apex of Egypt's religious pyramid - they all looked the same, they all moved the same, they all spoke the same granite hard message.

Seeing Ramose close up was different to watching the priest from a distance, performing rituals and so on. He dominated the room. His lean body was curved like a bow as he leant on his staff, yet he was still tall enough to tower over all those around him, bar Setka himself. His features were angular and dark, but punctuated by the bright turquoise-coloured eyes that had given him his nickname. Those eyes lighted on Setka now and sought to pin him down with a stare. Setka met it.

"Setka." The priest had a voice like polished stone - hard and unyielding but smooth as silk.

Setka bowed politely and Mahu followed suit - he was obviously not going to be acknowledged, but that was fine with him. Mahu was used to vanishing in most company - he was not important - but beside these two men he felt like a dwarf amongst giants. Both men were tall, but it was the size of their personalities that made Mahu seem to shrink. As their eyes locked, Mahu swore he could see the air between them shimmer with heat.

"You asked to see me?" There was perhaps a hint of surprise in the High Priest's voice - people did not generally ask to see Ramose, quite the reverse in fact.

"Your new orders for the palace..." Setka began.

"The Pharaoh's orders," Ramose corrected. Egypt did not have Queens, or female rulers of any kind, it had Pharaohs, and the fact that some of them might have been born women was quite inconsequential. Once they were Pharaoh, they were assumed to be male. They were divine anyway so gender made little difference.

"Of course," Setka acknowledged his error. "The scale of the project is..."

"Quite in keeping with the scale of the Pharaoh's majesty." Ramose seldom let people finish sentences. He could invariably tell what they were going to say, and what they were going to say was of no consequence to him and had no impact on what was going to happen.

"Undoubtedly." You did not get far with Ramose by contradicting him, and Setka was playing the game well - Mahu would have run off in terror by now. "But the amended timescale is..."

"What the Pharaoh desires," Ramose completed the sentence with finality. As well as having the hardness of rock, Ramose's words had the weight of rock as well, falling into place like bricks into a wall, creating an impenetrable barrier against further discourse.

"It's impossible in the time." A short blunt statement seemed to be the only way Setka would be allowed to complete a sentence.

"All things are possible to the gods." Ramose smiled like a cobra.

"Then the gods had better build it, because to men it is impossible."

Ramose met Setka's stare with that humourless snakish smile. People did not speak to him like that. But, as ever, Setka was different.

"The gods will help them find a way," he said.

95

"What form will that help take?" asked Setka. Even for him, he was pushing his luck.

"Motivation," answered Ramose. "The gods will provide."

Ramose was not priest of any one god, he was the religious leader of the country, encompassing all the gods and the priests of those gods. And because all men existed only to serve the gods, Ramose was their master too. Not officially of course, but as he spoke for the gods, interpreted their desires and passed them on to the people, it might appear to an outside observer that the commands came from him. Someone more cynical than Mahu, or someone less attached to his life, might have noted how often the wishes of the gods seemed to coincide with the desires of Ramose. But Ramose's desires reflected those of the Pharaoh, and the Pharaoh was a living god, so it all made sense.

"I fear the work will not be completed on time," said Setka. It would be too much to say that he now seemed afraid of Ramose, but he did seem apprehensive about what the Priest's response might be.

"Then the gods will be angry," said Ramose. "They may demand retribution unless they are appeased."

Since Ramose had become High Priest, the sacred crocodiles had been the usual method of appeasing the gods. If Ramose was the earthly proxy for the tongues of the gods, then the crocodiles performed the same function for their stomachs. It had not used to be this way. Much had changed when Ramose had been appointed High Priest by the Pharaoh Amunet. In quiet corners of the kingdom, where there was no chance of being overheard, people wondered in whispers whether the Pharaoh her/himself even ruled, or if Ramose had carried out a bloodless coup, leaving the Pharaoh as a figurehead, existing only to make Ramose's word law. It was known that Ramose was a master of magic who could bend others to his will by thought alone. Had he used this talent on the Pharaoh? But even if it was true, what could any of them do about it?

"The new capital is the desire of the Pharaoh," said Ramose, "which means that it is the desire of the gods. And that makes it the desire of every person in Egypt. The temple-palace will be the starting point from which the rest of the city will spring. The date chosen for its completion is an auspicious one and it will be finished on this day."

Setka said nothing. You could not argue with someone who

96

spoke about the future with the such certainty. To Ramose, the future was as immutable as the past.

"We are living at the dawn of a new age," Ramose continued. "You should be glad to be a part of it. I am sure your mother would have been."

For a moment, Mahu thought he saw a flicker of anger - or even distress - pass across Setka's face, but he did not let the emotion master him. The exact nature of Setka's ancestry was not something Mahu knew anything about, and was not something into which he was likely to pry too deeply. Noble blood flowed in Setka's veins, but only on his mother's side. That noble blood gave him a certain level of protection, it meant that he could talk to Ramose with more confidence than anyone else out in the workers' village. But since the blood came from his mother, it was not enough to give him noble status. He was barred from such professions as priest or court official. In some ways that was all to the good, as Setka had talent as an architect, and had carved out a position for himself that straddled the two worlds between which his parentage tugged him. But such a career left him at the whim of men like Ramose, and in the end Ramose was powerful enough that he could have Setka killed for any reason he pleased, or no reason at all. There would be some fuss at the spilling of noble blood, but Ramose had weathered worse. He had become all-powerful under the Pharaoh and the gods - and even their power over him was a matter conjecture.

Ramose did not wait for any response, he simply turned and exited the way he had come, his steps measured out by the taps of his staff on the floor. Setka watched him go.

"Can we go now?" asked Mahu.

Setka started a little, as if only just remembering that the other man was there.

"Yes. We won't get anything more out of him. Maybe this was always futile."

"What now?" asked Mahu, as he walked out beside the architect.

"Now we work. As fast as we can."

"Do you think we'll finish on time?"

There was a sadness on Setka's noble face as he replied. "Yes. I'm sure we will. I just hope we won't need the gods 'help' to do it."

They left the magnificent reception room with its towering

97

columns and looming statues of the Pharaoh. Like all great architecture, it gave the impression of having been here forever - it gave the impression that Queen Amunet had been Pharaoh forever - but in fact the room had been finished only two weeks ago, built by the men whom Setka and Mahu represented, the men of the workers' village. When they walked out through the main doors, they did so into a building site. The rest of the vast temple-palace complex was growing around them, the first part of a yet to be built capital city that would stretch out around it as far as the eye could see, dwarfing even the Sarranekh, beside which it was built. It would be the centre of the world for a yet to be conquered empire stretching as far as the mind could contemplate. Such were the ambitions of Pharaoh Amunet. Or of her High Priest.

"And I suppose you'll take the credit?" Djhutmose sneered at Setka, narrowing his eyes accusingly.

Setka sighed. "I understand how it might seem like that. You don't see me as one of you but... neither do they!"

"And you're keen to change that."

Djhutmose was absolutely 'one of us', born in the workers' village and risen to a position of some authority as Chief Overseer. Never the less, whenever Mahu looked at the man, he was reminded that our friends and neighbours have an equal right to be jerks.

"You're trying," Djhutmose continued, "to win your way into the court - back to where your blood says you ought to be. And you're trying to do it off the sweat and toil of my workers."

"I swear to you I'm not!" Setka pleaded. "I know it seems like I'm working everyone too hard, but this is the deadline the High Priest gave me."

"I was there," Mahu put in, almost surprised at the sound of his own voice interjecting.

"Who asked you?" snapped Djhutmose.

Mahu closed his mouth and retreated into his seat.

Setka went on. "I know this deadline is insane. I made it clear that it was insane, but all I got in return was threats. And I don't think High Priest Ramose will be slow to deliver on them."

"The High Priest would respond to logic and reason if he heard it," said Djhutmose. "But you're too busy fawning and kow-towing - not wanting to upset anyone in case it costs you your place in court. I

98

could have told him that this schedule was impossible but of course you insisted on doing it yourself. *You're* the one with the court connections after all so *you* have to be the one who deals with the nobility."

"I am also the architect," pointed out Setka.

"And what's that to do with it? The architect just draws a picture. You're hogging the credit, making sure that if anyone gets elevated because of the success of the project, it'll be you. You'll work my men to death to meet their impossible demands just to get what you want. You don't want to be an architect all your life and you've set your sights on something a bit higher. Well you're not the only one with aspirations, you know. It's my men who've to build it. I'm the one who's in charge of labour so I'm the one who should be talking to the High Priest about the deadline."

"That sounds logical."

The assembled men spun around. The voice had come from a shadowy corner of the room, a hard yet smooth voice that spoke with total confidence and utter authority. Mahu felt his stomach contract as he recognised the outline of the lean figure, wreathed in shadow, that stood in the corner.

"High Priest," said Setka, and for the first time since he had known him, Mahu heard fear in Setka's voice. "We did not hear you come in."

"I imagine not."

How had he come in? The door was on the other side of the room. There was no way that he could have got from the door to the corner without being noticed. Had he been here all along? Mahu ran back through the conversation in his brain, looking for any slight against Ramose that anyone (most particularly he himself) might have uttered.

Djhutmose had been as stunned as the others, but he recovered himself quickly and determined to make use of this rare opportunity, bustling forward to greet their unexpected and inexplicable visitor.

"My Lord High Priest, what an extraordinary honour it is to have you visit us here in our petty squalor."

"Keep your distance." Ramose remained shrouded in darkness, holding out his staff to keep back any who might approach him.

"Of course." Djhutmose took several steps back. "I wonder if I might..."

"Present your case for postponing the completion of the temple-palace?"

Djhutmose gulped for a few moments. "Not necessarily, High Priest. Not postponing so much as..."

"Returning to the original time-frame."

"Exactly!" Djhutmose leapt on this. "If I could explain to you the difficulties involved, then I am sure a man of your discerning intellect would..."

"See things from your point of view."

"Yes." Djhutmose smiled, and it occurred to Mahu that some people might actually be too stupid to be frightened.

"I have no time now." The voice now seemed to be made of the darkness itself. "Come to my quarters tomorrow evening. We will talk then. Perhaps you will leave seeing things from my point of view."

High Priest Ramose left through a door which turned out to have been behind him all along, though no one in the room could remember there ever being a door there before. But there must have been, Mahu told himself, mustn't there?

The suite of rooms in which the High Priest currently lived on the site would not be where he lived once the palace was complete. They were fine rooms, which would eventually be used to house visiting dignitaries, but something more austere in its grandeur was planned for Ramose, something with easy access both to the temple and the Pharaoh's living quarters, so the Priest had a foot in both the religious and secular worlds.

The following evening, Djhutmose set out for the temple-palace site, in the shadow of the Sarranekh. When he arrived, dressed in his finest, he was ushered by a pair of silent slaves through the recently built halls, flagged with polished stones. This was the life. This was what he was made for and who was to say it could not be his, just because he had been born in the workers' village? That life was alright for most of those who worked there - they didn't have the brains or ambition to know any better - but for someone like him? All he needed was an opportunity to make the right sort of friends, and here was just such an opportunity. This was how Setka tried to play it, but that man had no idea how to play the game. Djhutmose would do better.

Reaching a door, one of the slaves knocked. He waited, then

seemed to receive a response (which Djhutmose did not hear) for he opened the door and held it for the Overseer. Djhutmose entered. The walls of the room were painted with religious scenes, as befit a High Priest (they would be repainted when the room's purpose changed). Statues of deities stood by the walls and the furniture was richly made and covered with finely woven fabric. Seated about the room in attitudes of languid repose were nine cats, glossy and sleek. They watched Djhutmose as he entered, their green eyes focussed hard on him, taking in his every move; the nervous shaking of his hands, the shuffling of his feet, the movement of his throat as he swallowed.

One of the cats was sitting in the lap of Ramose himself, enjoying the way the High Priest tickled it behind the ears. As Djhutmose entered, Ramose brushed the animal from his lap and it stalked away haughtily with its tail in the air. You had to be very comfortable around the gods to treat a sacred animal with such familiarity.

"Djhutmose," said the High Priest in welcome, and Djhutmose wondered when he had told the priest his name.

"Lord High Priest."

"Please sit."

Djhutmose did as he was instructed.

"Now, I believe you were going to explain to me why you are behind schedule."

"I'm not saying it can't be done," Djhutmose began hastily. He was hardly going to climb the social ladder if he started out by saying that he couldn't accomplish what was asked of him. "It's just the workers."

"They are lazy?" Ramose raised an arched eyebrow with elegant precision.

"Not lazy exactly," Djhutmose continued, "but slow. I suppose. Used to working at a certain pace. And to finish on time requires a far quicker pace than that. Slow to adjust to your wishes. And my instructions," he added, wanting to make it clear that he was all in favour of the schedule. His position on this seemed to have changed without his realising it.

Ramose said nothing, but held out a cup and a slave instantly poured wine into it. He sipped thoughtfully before speaking.

"If my slave spills wine, is that my fault?"

"Of course not High Priest!" Djhutmose felt he was on safe ground here - *nothing* was High Priest Ramose's fault.

"Oh, you're quite wrong. The master is always at fault."

A queasy feeling started to creep into Djhutmose's stomach.

"If an experienced slave does something wrong then it is because I have spared the whip. So, when I get a new slave and he makes some small mistake - as they all do - I have him thrashed to within an inch of his life. That way he knows what I do over a small infraction, and fears what I might do over a greater one. Did I have you thrashed for a small error?" This last question was directed to the slave, who wordlessly shook his head. "Of course. I had your tongue cut out." Ramose redirected his attention to Djhutmose who was now shaking uncontrollably. "You would think this would make a man less loyal, but a strange thing about the human animal is that, no matter how horrific the torture inflicted, they still fear death. Even when they wish for its sweet release, they still fear it. Not even the certainty of the next world is comfort. I believe the gods made us like this to make life a little easier. For them, of course."

Realising that this conversation was fast getting away from him, Djhutmose forced his trembling mouth open to speak. He had little idea of what he could say, but he had to say something. "Lord..."

Ramose levelled his turquoise stare at Djhutmose, and the Overseer felt that he was staring into the bright and brilliant mouth of hell.

"I do not care if work is behind schedule because your workers are lazy or slow or overworked or dying on their feet. I only care that it is behind schedule. And that is your fault."

Djhutmose felt pinned to the spot, he could not move, aware only of the cold fear pouring into his body, freezing him to immobility.

"I have spent a lifetime motivating men to do things they thought they could not do. I accept no excuses. If you cannot motivate them, then I will." He sat back in his chair. "You may eat now."

Djhutmose looked about him for food and was about to ask what he could eat, when he realised that the words had not been directed at him. The cats were on their feet, their eyes seeming to glow with malicious intent as they circled him.

"The door is there if you wish," said Ramose. "Please don't wait for me to dismiss you."

The ability to move seemed to return to Djhutmose with a rush. He fell upwards to his feet, stumbling like a drunk, gulping and grunting like a hunted pig. On rubber legs, he dashed for the door. As soon as he moved, the cats moved too. Down the hall Djhutmose ran, unsure if this was the way he had come but no longer caring. All he cared about was getting away. Night had fallen while Ramose had been talking and the rooms were lit by torches, casting a flickering light that made every shadow leap up cat-like in Djhutmose's imagination. Behind his own ragged breathing he could hear them; the pattering of paws and sharp little claws on the floor, the threatening meows from far away which were then answered by others from much closer. Had that one come from up ahead?!

He skidded to a halt in an empty hall - he could make a stand here. They were just cats! Sacred or not, they were animals and he was a man. There was nothing to be frightened of.

To his left a torch went out, and a mew crept out of the darkness that it left behind. All around Djhutmose the torches started to blink out of existence, vanishing one by one, till there was just one left. It was not enough to illuminate the room, all it showed was the reflective green eyes of his pursuers as they closed in on him.

They brought Djhutmose's body to the workers' village the following morning, carrying it through the building site to ensure that it was seen by all as it passed. It was wrapped in a blood-stained linen sheet. The sheet was pulled back and the assembled men gasped. Some turned away, unable to look.

Mahu could not help but look, could not look away.

"Do you think they tortured him?" He did not want to know the answer but could not help asking.

"I don't know," said Setka grimly.

The eyes were gone - a favourite punishment. But they did not seem to have been put out, as was usual; the sockets were ragged, the flesh torn. In places his flesh seemed to have been scratched away, in others there were what looked like bite marks. It was hard to tell how much of this had happened while Djhutmose was still alive. Mahu prayed that none of it had.

Setka raised his head, listening. This close to the site, the sounds of work were always present, but now they were redoubled. Every man was working for his life.

Ramose's temple-palace would be finished on schedule.

Chapter 10 - The Mummy Rises

The excavation had been fast-approaching the point of moving the Queen herself anyway, so no one was that surprised by Maggie's sudden announcement that today was the day. Though the removal of items from the tomb had been carried out with the care and respect typical of the modern archaeologist, not since the first day and the opening of the tomb had matters proceeded with such solemnity. Queen Amunet had lain in peace in this room for millennia, civilisations had risen and fallen while she rested here. There had been something intrusive about their entrance, and there was something almost violating about removing her from that spot which had been designed as her final resting place (whatever the legends might say about her 'return'). The team filed into the burial chamber with a funereal dignity, almost as if this was a burial rather than an exhumation, and stood about the sarcophagus, looking down and contemplating the solemn and tricky task ahead.

Beneath the decorous coffin, the ropes that had been used to lower it into place forty centuries ago still survived. They were certainly not useable now, but they lifted the coffin just far enough to allow modern ropes to be wormed underneath, cushioned with folded canvas so as not to scrape the decoration. A wooden scaffold was hastily erected around the sarcophagus, its load-bearing capacity tested with the bulk of Professor Andoheb. Pulleys were attached to the scaffold and the ropes passed through. A stretcher from the First Aid tent (again tested on the good-natured professor) was placed to one side ready to slide beneath the coffin once it was clear of the sarcophagus - nobody wanted that precious cargo to be kept hanging in the air for any longer than was absolutely necessary.

All this preparatory work was done in near-total silence. Instructions were issued in low, tempered voices, as if even this might somehow be lacking the solemnity demanded of the task at hand. Andoheb was more quiet and introverted than Arthur had ever seen his old mentor, and Maggie's focus on her work seemed less professional and more deferential.

Finally, all was in place. Maggie and a handful of diggers took the ropes in their hands while Arthur and Enam stood ready with the stretcher and a plank of wood to support it. Andoheb took a final nervous look at everything, then nodded to Maggie, who gave an order in Egyptian - take up the slack.

The ropes tightened about the coffin, and Arthur heard Andoheb try to swallow through a dry mouth.

Another instruction: on my order... pull!

The coffin rose. Andoheb gulped breath.

Pull!

Another half foot.

Pull!

Arthur could hear his heart pounding in his ears.

Pull!

The blue and gold coffin rose up out of the sarcophagus, escaping the confining walls that had flanked it for the last four thousand years.

Pull!

The makeshift lights that had been strung up in the tomb to make work possible, now caught the coffin for the first time and made it gleam. It had looked beautiful before, now it looked rich. It emanated wealth, power and beauty, just as its occupant had in life.

"Enam," Maggie snapped, and the man beside Arthur slid the sturdy wooden plank across the top of the stone sarcophagus.

"Arthur!" Her voice was like a whip crack and Arthur hurried forward with the stretcher, sliding it along the plank, beneath the hanging coffin.

As ever, Arthur could not understand what Maggie said to the Egyptians, but her tone made the meaning clear: carefully.

The coffin lowered, millimetre by slowly eked out millimetre, edging towards safety and the moment when they could all breathe again. The coffin settled onto the plank - safe and secure.

The ropes were still beneath it, and pulling them out risked damaging the ornate decoration, so Maggie went around, cutting each one with a knife. The scaffolding was quickly dismantled to get it out of the way. This done, Ahmad, Nasr, Mahmoud and Maggie took the poles that ran though the stretcher, one at each corner of the sarcophagus.

Lift!

The coffin rose again, safely swathed in the yielding stretcher.

Forward!

With Andoheb peering anxiously beneath to ensure the coffin did not catch or graze anything, the four stretcher-bearers inched forward, holding their load high, until they cleared the stone sarcophagus.

Lower!

The poles were settled more comfortably onto the shoulders of the three men and one woman, the coffin slung between them. Andoheb darted this way and that, on tip-toe one moment, on his knees the next, checking, checking, checking for anything that might be wrong, wringing his hands in anxiety.

Forward. Slowly!

The procession began to move, led by a pair of diggers with torches; then the stretcher bearers; then Andoheb, still dancing nervously about; then the rest, with Arthur in their midst. The strange thought occurred to him that they were re-enacting a ritual last seen here when the tomb had been sealed, but in reverse. A procession not wholly unlike this one had surely entered this tomb four thousand years ago, carrying in the dead Queen. Now they were taking her out the same way.

Navigating the coffin through the tight passageway that led into the tomb without bumping it on the walls proved the most nerve-wracking part of the operation yet. Why had they made the tunnel twist like this, so the coffin could only be edged around it, one hair-raising inch at a time? Why had they made it so narrow when they knew very well they had to get a coffin down it?

"Do you think they had this much trouble when they brought her in?" asked Arthur, wondering at the short-sightedness of the designers.

"Remember people were generally smaller back then," Andoheb replied, his eyes never leaving the coffin. "They built for efficiency as well as beauty. When you're tunnelling through rock then you make a passageway as big as it has to be and not a millimetre more."

There was a clear-sighted logic in what he said, and Arthur was reminded what made Andoheb a great archaeologist: imagination. It was a facility that he himself lacked, only able to recite facts from books. Which was useful, but when the facts had not survived, you needed a man, like Andoheb, who could make a leap.

Finally, up ahead, there came into view the bright, sun-lit rectangle of the tomb door. They started to feel the sun's heat again and, unconsciously, the pace started to speed up.

"Steady!" Maggie had reverted to English - even she was affected by the tension of the moment - but her tone conveyed her meaning more than adequately.

"Have a sheet ready!" said Andoheb nervously. The bright colours of the coffin's decoration had not seen sunlight for a very long time, and would not retain their brilliance long if exposed.

Reflecting on the moment afterwards, Arthur found himself oddly underwhelmed. Every revelation of the coffin so far had been almost miraculous. It had felt historic. He had expected the passage out into daylight to feel similarly extraordinary. But in the hot light of day the coffin seemed diminished. Its colours seemed less bright, its workmanship almost crude. He had seen props in Hollywood films that held up better. The harsh reality of daylight robbed it of the power it had certainly possessed in the cold tomb. That was how it was meant to be seen - if it was meant to be seen at all. Out here it was just another artefact.

None of which stopped the champagne corks from popping back in the camp. The coffin was stowed in the finds tent, in a crate built specially to hold it, lined with cotton wool.

"You don't want to open it now?" asked Arthur, his voice almost pleading. "You don't want to see what's inside?"

Andoheb laughed. "I knew you'd catch the bug if you came out here! We don't know what we'll find inside. We don't know what state of preservation to expect or what manner of grave goods might be on the Queen's person. If woven material or papyrus is in there then we have limited resources for conserving it out here in the middle of the desert. It would be lost to science. Then there is the Queen herself. Everyone wants a well-preserved Mummy and if we open now, without the proper facilities, we could do untold harm. No. We leave her sealed up for now - that's where she's safest. The Finds tent is cooled, and with a bit of luck she won't even know she's been moved. A true archaeologist always does what's best for the archaeology." Then, with a twinkle in his eye, he added, "But he still wants to rip off that damn lid."

Arthur smiled. Maybe he was becoming a true archaeologist.

Maggie joined them, knocking back a glass of champagne in one gulp and pulling a face. "Warm."

"Move a bottle to the Finds tent," suggested Andoheb. "That's where all our air-conditioning equipment is now."

Maggie nodded. "I'm doubling the guard tonight."

"Good." Andoheb took a thoughtful sip of his champagne. "We'll take the Queen back to Abu Satur first thing in the morning, with a few of the most time-sensitive items. You're alright to stay here and finish up?"

Maggie nodded. There were still a few things in the tomb that needed to be brought out, a few things that needed recording. This had been a hurried dig - a race against discovery, against possible tomb robbers, against media intrusion, and even against other archaeologists (who can be ruthless in the right circumstances).

"You'll come with me, Arthur?" Andoheb asked.

Arthur nodded fervently. He had enjoyed his time out here more than he had expected, but the idea of staying in a hotel rather than a tent, somewhere with adequate bathroom facilities and a proper mattress, had an undeniable appeal. The excitement of the dig had held him here more than he would have thought possible, and had certainly made him re-appraise his thoughts on field work, but there were still aspects he would be glad to see the back of.

"Unless you need me here," he hastily added to Maggie, not wanting her to feel abandoned.

Maggie nearly spit out her champagne suppressing her laughter. "I think we'll manage, Arthur. But thanks for the offer."

The rest of the day was taken up in packing - making sure that everything was stowed safely and properly catalogued. Despite the busyness of the camp, Arthur was sure he saw, or perhaps sensed, more than mere urgency in Maggie. Andoheb's enthusiasm and the excitement of removing the Queen had temporarily erased any recollection of why they had stepped up their timescale, but Maggie had not forgotten. She was alert and edgy, and seemed, to Arthur at least, to be eyeing their comrades carefully. They had worked together a while now, and Arthur thought she would trust any of these men with her life - but that was not to say that she would trust them altogether. Someone here, she thought, was a mole for tomb robbers, and she was on the look-out for who. It did not surprise Arthur when, come the evening, Maggie skipped dinner in favour of a nap. She had placed herself on guard duty outside the Finds tent, along with Tarek and Nasr. They were men she felt she could trust, but perhaps she still wanted to keep an eye on them.

Night fell, and for one last time Arthur settled onto his camp bed. Once the Queen and the other finds were secure in Abu Satur - in maybe a week or so - Andoheb would return to the dig. But, though he had not said anything yet, Arthur was not planning to accompany him. The idea had been growing in him throughout the day. Though he was very glad to have had this eye-opening experience, as soon as the chance to leave had been mentioned it had not left his mind. Field work was something he might dip into again when interesting opportunities came up (or when Helen seemed a bit angsty), but it was not the career for him. Once they reached Abu Satur he would tender a difficult but grateful resignation, and head for home. With a bit of luck he could volunteer his services as nursemaid to some of the artefacts, so he might still be of use even after quitting. He knew that Andoheb hoped to have some of the items conserved in Britain, if he could convince the local authorities that this was a good idea. Andoheb was a man with a foot in two countries; his homeland and his adopted home. He was Egyptian to the core, and believed strongly that it was here that the Queen and her possessions ultimately belonged. But he was also no fool - like it or not, England was where the money was, and the Queen deserved the best. It would be a hard sell, but he hoped that the mummy at least could be conserved by people he knew from his days in the UK. Then she would come home to stay.

But wherever the Queen belonged, Arthur knew he belonged in England. He missed his home and his girlfriend, and was anxious to get back to the former so he could tell the latter that he had done as she had asked, proving himself the bold adventurer that she wanted him to be. He was looking forward to that reunion very much.

Perhaps it was because of this decision, and the quiet excitement it had raised in him, that Arthur could not sleep. He tossed and turned for a few hours, experimenting with the sheets, but the bed refused to be comfortable - or at least insisted on being even more uncomfortable than usual. It was oddly fitting that his last night here would be another sleepless one. The dream of a hotel bed floated before his eyes provocatively, teasing him with its clean sheets, flaunting its downy pillows, and flashing tantalising glimpses of its firm mattress.

With such enticing images before his eyes, sleep moved from

unlikely to impossible and Arthur decided not to waste any more time trying. He got up and dressed; a walk would clear his head and perhaps make sleep come a little more easily. Strolling out of the tent into the pleasant cool of night, he nodded a 'good evening' to Walid, another of those who had drawn the short straw for guard duty, on patrol about the camp. How comfortable he had become here; with the people and the place, his little tent, evenings about the campfire, Ahmad's ghost stories, Samir's cuisine. It had become almost a second home. A peal of laughter made him glance down the row of silent tents to see Maggie, seated outside the Finds tent, playing cards with Nasr and Tarek.

He would miss Maggie. Not least because he would not be able to say a proper goodbye to her, as he wasn't intending to reveal his plans until they reached Abu Satur. If he did tell her then she would only tell him to stay and to stop being so pathetic about it. Or possibly she would be completely indifferent, as if his presence here had been little more than an inconvenience anyway. Arthur paused to wonder *why* he would miss Maggie. Perhaps it was because of that straightforward attitude - so many people dissembled their true meaning; Maggie was never less than honest. She was unlike anyone else he had ever known, and whether that was a good thing or a bad thing, it was why he liked her.

Arthur walked on.

Leaving the encircling of rock in which the camp was situated, he turned left and followed the outer line of the rock wall east, away from the camp and with the desert to his right. It was a direction which he had not really explored during his stay. Come to think of it, he had explored almost nothing of their surroundings during his brief tenure. There had been work to be done of course, but he had also had a definite nervousness about wandering off on his own. You could hardly get lost if you stayed within sight of the Sarranekh, but who knew what you might encounter out here? Tonight however, the nerves seemed to have taken a night off. He was more relaxed now, out on his own in the wilds, than he had been at any point throughout his stay. He was aware that there was an oasis somewhere in this direction. In his mind he conjured up an image of palm trees and a crystal clear pool, where lions and giraffes temporarily suspend hostilities to drink shoulder to shoulder. In other words, a Hollywood oasis. It would be good to see what an actual oasis looked like before

111

he left.

It was after about half an hour's walk that Arthur came to the 'oasis', which was at first a rather disappointing prospect. The crystal clear water, illuminated by the high moon, was a muddy brown colour, silty and unappealing. The knowledge that he had been drinking this water (albeit filtered) for the last month did not make it look any better. There was vegetation, but it was pretty sparse and nothing as majestic as a palm tree was anywhere to be seen. Still, there was something about the sight of standing water that made him long for home even more than he already had been. It was funny the things you missed when you didn't have them. They say that people who move to Holland have a sudden craving for hills when they return to their native Yorkshire, to the extent that the idea physically excites them. Arthur could well understand it now. The sight of water, there on the ground as part of the landscape, was almost erotic. Sort of nature-porn. He sat down to stare and to dream of the lakes and rivers he would see when he got back home. Ponds too. And streams. Rills, rivulets, lochs, weirs, waterfalls, puddles. And rain! Just the thought gave him a thrilling tremor. He wondered idly how Helen might feel about a holiday to the Lake District. Or moving there permanently.

With his thoughts thus pleasantly occupied, he spent almost an hour sitting and staring at the muddy water. So caught up was he, that he did not notice the padding approach of feet until the jackal was there in front of him.

Arthur gulped on seeing it, and tried to remember if jackals ever killed people. If they did then Maggie would certainly have mentioned it. The jackal cocked its head to one side, looking at him in that way in which animals assess everything, mentally categorising them as something to eat, be eaten by, mate with, or ignore. After some consideration, it seemed to place Arthur in the last category (the only one he was one hundred percent comfortable with) and he ceased to figure in the jackal's life decisions. It stooped its head and drank.

Arthur watched. It wasn't a lion and a giraffe, but a jackal and himself seemed to fulfil at least one requirement of the Hollywood oasis brief. It was a certainly a moment, a moment that would stay with him for the rest of his life and that he would enjoy recounting to Helen. She would ask if it had attacked him. Did it bite? Did it draw blood? Did he fight back? Did he have a gun or was he forced to kill it with his bare hands? The jackal raised its head again, listening for any more threatening creatures than Arthur, then resumed drinking.

Perhaps he could make up a story about the vicious jackal to tell Helen and keep the truth as his own secret. The reality appealed to him far more, but to Helen it would be devoid of excitement. In some ways they were quite different people, but that was the spice of a relationship. Arthur glanced at his arm - two days ago he had tripped while running down through the rocks when he was late for lunch, and had cut himself. It was healing but would still be visible when he saw Helen, and who was to say that it wasn't a jackal bite? Helen would be too excited by the sight of his blood to care about the absence of tooth marks.

The jackal looked up once more and turned its gaze back to Arthur. This look was not the appraising one of before, but one of... Arthur was not a fanciful person but he wanted to say 'understanding'. As if the jackal recognised Arthur's worldly concerns and sympathised. Perhaps it wasn't keen on the desert either. A nerdy jackal who never fit in with the pack and found killing whatever it was that jackals killed a bit of a task. Perhaps he didn't see eye to eye with his mate on everything either.

All of which was crazy nonsense to be thinking. Was it even a boy jackal? Either way, Arthur was definitely better off making up a story for Helen.

The jackal turned - revealing that it was indeed a boy and probably didn't have any problems with the lady jackals - and padded off into the night. Arthur stood. It wasn't going to get any better than that, and it was now late. He didn't feel any more tired now than he had when he had set out, the beauty of the locale and the encounter with the jackal had served to enliven him more than coax him to sleep. But perhaps the walk back would take care of that. And if not, who cared? It had still been more than worth it. At no great pace, Arthur walked back the way he had come, following the line of the rock wall, heading west.

The protecting circle of rock meant that Arthur did not see that anything was wrong until he passed back through natural gates that led to the campsite. When he did so however, and saw the little white tents up ahead, bright in the moonlight, he immediately noticed the tatters of one blowing in the nocturnal wind. For an instant, fear took hold of Arthur, urging him to not to go on. But he mastered that fear and broke into a run.

"Maggie!" he yelled as he entered the camp, knowing in his heart that there was no one asleep to wake, and that he would get no answer. Some of the tents had been ripped asunder and boxes of supplies were overturned. The sand was an upheaval of footsteps, telling that something had happened here. Arthur ran from tent to tent but the place was deserted, not a soul to be found. The van, on which he had been scheduled to travel with Professor Andoheb, was still parked next to the Finds tent. It had already been loaded for the journey but now the back doors were open, and Arthur already knew what he would find when he looked inside. Various boxes and bags remained in the back, but the biggest crate, around which they had all been packed, was missing. Queen Amunet was gone. Everyone was gone. Arthur was alone.

With a sick feeling in his stomach, he looked over to where Maggie and the other guards had been. There had obviously been a struggle. And there was blood on the sand.

Moving without his instruction, Arthur's legs folded beneath him, dropping him to the ground, emotionally wasted. The desert in which he had finally felt at home seemed to have swallowed him whole. What in the hell did he do now?

The question was answered for him as a hand suddenly gripped his shoulder. Arthur lurched away with a yell, scrabbling desperately across the sand on his hand and knees, almost crying with fear. He twisted about to face his assailant. But the face that met him was that of Maggie. She stood unsteadily, looking down at him, her face stained with blood, her clothes wet with it.

"Arthur," she said, almost admonishingly. Then she dropped to the sand.

Chapter 11 - Maggie's Story

The bulk of them had come from the rocks. Maggie and her guards had been ready for that, and if that had been all then they might have repelled the attack. But, perhaps knowing how predictable such an approach would be, the tomb robbers hit the camp from east and west as well.

A cry from an outer tent was the first Maggie knew something was wrong. One of her sentinels had been jumped.

"Arm up." Her gun was in her hand in an instant, as she peered out into the darkness. Lights were going on around the camp as per her plan, but they were going off just as fast. They were everywhere, and Maggie realised that there were far more of them than she had expected. She cursed her own ill-preparedness. The collectors kept getting bolder - they'd pay anything for a prize like Queen Amunet; in money and blood. Bastards.

The shooting started seconds later and Maggie grit her teeth at the searing bite of a bullet catching her arm, knocking her back.

"Maggie?!" Nasr looked back at her, eyes full of fear.

"I'm fine! Shoot back!"

Just a flesh wound, and her left arm too, which meant she could return fire in short order. But there was too much confusion, too many people running this way and that. Few of the volunteers and hired hands had been in a fight before - they were diggers and archaeology students! When the shooting started people panicked, and Maggie and her guards could not risk firing at the indistinct figure running towards them in case it turned out to be one of their own. From all sides the attackers closed in.

A sound from behind her made Maggie spin around, fast enough that the blow to her head was glancing rather than devastating. Still, it was hard enough to knock her to her knees.

"Stay down." The voice was reptilian, low and hitting the sibilants. It spoke English with an American accent, and Maggie wasn't about to obey it.

"Screw you."

The second blow knocked her out cold.

How long she was out Maggie couldn't be sure, but it was still dark when she was urged back into consciousness and into the hot embrace of a screaming pain at the back her head.

"On your feet." The American voice again. He was nudging her with his foot to bring her round, the nudges rapidly becoming kicks. "Come on, you've got a walk ahead of you."

"Wouldn't it be easier to kill me and leave me here?" suggested Maggie. Her hands had been tied, which was going to make getting out of this a lot harder.

"Yes. But my orders are to kill only if necessary. Don't make it necessary."

Some people, Maggie reflected as she pushed her reluctant body first onto knees then feet, while her head throbbed relentlessly - some people are cut out by nature to be mercenaries. The voice was that of a man who would have done anything for money. People who are cruel for their own pleasure are of course not nice people, but the fact that they take pleasure in their cruelty gives it a curious honesty. Those who are cruel for money are a different breed - they presumably know better, but the money makes it okay. Just a job. Just following orders. She wasn't sure, but Maggie had a hunch that she could put a name to the American mercenary. It was tempting to mention it - maybe it would put him off-guard. Or maybe it would make killing her 'necessary'.

The excavation team had been grouped together ready to march out. The robbers hadn't come in vehicles, knowing that they would need the element of surprise. Chances were they had some sort of transport waiting for them on the north side of the Sarranekh. Once they were there then it was game over - locked in the back of a van there would be little Maggie could do. That gave her two to three hours to free herself and get away. What she would do then was less clear, but one step at a time.

"Keep an eye on that one." As if he was reading her mind, the American pointed at Maggie, letting her see his face clearly for the first time. It was a sharp, hatchet of a face. It might almost have been called good-looking had there not been a quality of nastiness to it - too much edge to be handsome. There was also the scar that cut an ugly path across it.

"Why 'd you look into Arthur's tent?" asked Maggie. There was no harm in testing the water a little. "You get off on watching people sleep?" That might be pushing her luck.

The scarred man looked at her a long beat before answering. "Someone new in the camp. Needed to see who he was. Speaking of

116

which; where is he?"

Maggie had not noticed Arthur's absence from the group and now cursed herself for drawing attention to it.

"Don't know."

There was something very casual about the way the American backhanded Maggie across the face - a habitual action.

Maggie looked back up, tasting the blood that dripped from her nose. "Still don't know."

This time he punched her in the gut and Maggie doubled up. The American looked down at her dispassionately. "I believe you."

It occurred to Maggie that her natural ability to rub people up the wrong way, something she had been doing most of her life, was not her best asset in this situation.

"Let's get moving."

As the group moved out, heading for the rocks, Maggie did a quick headcount. Tarek and Nasr looked the worst for wear, both bloody and bruised, but all the volunteers and hired and hands were there and still walking. Aside from Arthur, the only person missing was Professor Andoheb. Maggie searched about with increasingly frantic eyes and finally found him laid out on a stretcher, dragged by two of the tomb robbers. He was not moving. Beside him, two more men carried the crate containing the coffin of Queen Amunet between them.

"Mr. Jago?" Enam spoke up from within the group of prisoners. Maggie slumped a little - she had really wanted to be wrong about there being mole. "I don't think I should be here."

The scarred man looked at him for a moment. "No, I don't think you should."

The gunshot echoed through the Sarranekh and Enam fell, dead before he hit the ground.

"Can't abide traitors," muttered Jago.

Maggie didn't much like them either, but she could spare some sympathy for poor Enam. He'd been a digger all his life, and the money these people offered would have been more than he had made in twenty years of back-breaking work. No doubt they'd told him that no one would get hurt, and you couldn't blame a man for wanting more. Or at least not when it ended like this. He had confirmed Maggie's suspicions about the identity of the American. The name Jago was like an archaeological bogey man, a story that

Egyptologists told their diggers to keep then on the watch out for tomb robbers. Everyone had heard the story, and every dig that came to a mysterious and tragic end was attributed to the ubiquitous spectre of Jago. Maggie being Maggie, she had long wanted to come face to face with him, although preferably not like this.

Jago led the party up into the rocks, over the ridge and down through the gully, passing by the empty tomb. As they walked, Maggie let her feet become heavy, so she slipped back through the group, seemingly by accident. The chance would come. It had to. But she was rapidly realising that it would need to come sooner rather than later. Her sleeve was now wet with the blood flowing steadily from the wound in her arm, blood dripped from her nose, and she could feel a stickiness at the back of her neck which suggested that that crack to the head had also drawn blood. She was starting to feel woozy. Whatever move she was going to make, she needed to make it while she still had the strength to do so. She flexed her hands in their restraints - some sort of rope. That was the first mistake these people had made; a cable tie would have been far more efficient. The second was how they had seen Maggie. People tended to treat Maggie as bigger than she was, because she radiated an air of being a big, strong person, when in fact she was curiously petite. And with very slim wrists.

The path rose again, leading up out of the gully. It was an ancient route, probably used by robbers since the days of Queen Amunet, and today was no different. It was a route littered with side paths, alcoves and crevasses, in which bandits of bygone days had no doubt hidden, ready to ambush unwary travellers taking an ill-advised short-cut. No wonder there were so many ghost stories about the Sarranekh. As they climbed higher, one of Maggie's increasingly heavy feet caught a rock and she fell headlong to the ground, unable to put out her arms to protect herself as she fell.

"On your feet!" This voice was English. "I said get up!" The voice came closer as the man approached, eager that his boss should not be the only one who got to beat up a defenceless woman.

As soon as he was in reach, Maggie looped her feet through his legs and twisted, sending the man sprawling to the ground.

"Stop!" A gunshot that might have been a warning, but probably not, ricocheted off a rock by Maggie's head as she rolled gracefully onto her feet and took off into the darkness, ducking between the rocks, using her size and agility to weave a winding and awkward path. Her hands were almost free now, as she had been working them gradually through the rope as they walked.

"Get after her!"

"Leave her." Jago spoke. "She's not important. She's walking dead anyway. Let her bleed to death if that's what she wants."

Maggie crouched in the shadow of a rock hollow, listening. The man might be right, but Maggie liked to think that she was too stubborn to die so easily. (Actually Maggie liked to think that she was too stubborn to die at all.) Jago was underestimating her and overestimating her injuries. All she had to do now was go back to camp, where there were medical supplies, and patch herself up.

Of course, that wasn't what she was *going* to do. If she left them now then she would never know where they were heading and never be able to find them again. She was not sure what fate Jago and his cronies had in mind for Andoheb and the rest of the team, but she was damn sure she wasn't going to abandon them to it. Tearing off the right sleeve of her shirt she tied as tight a bandage as she could bear around the wound on her left arm. That would do for now. Gingerly she touched the back of her head and felt the hair matted with blood. There wasn't much she could do about that but it seemed to have stopped bleeding.

Into the darkness she set off, following the light and sound of the group, keeping off the main path, sticking to the shadows, moving as quietly as she could through the rocks. Since she had been a kid, Maggie had loved climbing. While other girls had built sandcastles on the beach, she had made a bee-line for the most treacherous cliff and terrified her parents by climbing up it. Looking back, it had been a profoundly stupid thing to do and she was lucky to be alive, but it stood her in good stead now.

The party continued on northwards through the cliffs, and Maggie became all the more convinced that they were to be met at the far side by cars, which would take them on to a plane. What would she do then? She couldn't stop them like this. Trying to ignore the throbbing in her head, Maggie paused to think. Once they arrived at their meeting place there was bound to be a pause while they had something to eat and sorted themselves out before moving on - they had no reason to hurry. She was as sure as she could be about the direction in which they were heading - allowing for the little

119

deviations in the path, they had been going north for the last hour. If she turned back now, if she pushed herself hard, she could get back to the camp, arm up and come back to make a fight of it. It wasn't a great plan, but right now she could not think of any other. Hastily, she turned around, heading back the way she had come.

It was then that she realised she was not the only one tracking the tomb robbers. At first she just saw one man, as the moonlight glinted off the barrel of his gun, and assumed it must be a rearguard of the robbers. But he was keeping off the main path like she was. And he was not alone. Now she saw others, creeping through the rocks, their faces intently set with stern purpose. All seemed to be Egyptian, all seemed to be armed. Given the circumstances, it might have seemed that these newcomers were on Maggie's side. They might be the Egyptian authorities come to arrest the tomb robbers. Perhaps Andoheb had managed to put in a call to the locals when the attack started. And yet there was something about them that made Maggie discount such a conclusion. Something about them that made her palms itch. They were coming in her direction.

Making herself as small as she could, Maggie curled up into a narrow split in the rocks. She could still see out, and could see this new group as they approached, moving stealthily. How had so many people managed to get behind them?

Towards the back of the group was a tall figure who seemed to be in charge. There was not much that frightened Maggie, but as she recognised the figure a sharp tremor of icy fear trespassed through her. There was no doubt that it was the same strange figure whom she and Arthur (and where the hell *was* Arthur?!) had seen outside the tomb only a few nights ago. There was no mistaking the angular form, shrouded in a cloak, or the disjointed gait. From within the hood, she caught a flash of turquoise.

The Priest with Turquoise Eyes. Never had Arthur's story seemed so plausible to Maggie as it did now, as the figure bore down on her. She was not a fanciful woman, but in the dark, in the rocks, with the solid, uneven footsteps growing nearer, it all felt horribly possible. The figure was bare metres away now, and Maggie winced as the air around her seemed suddenly stale, almost unbreathable. She saw the hang of the cloak, pass her hiding place, close enough that she could have reached out and touched it, and smelt the scent of ancient death it seemed to waft with it. She knew that smell - he smelt like the inside of a tomb.

Just as it seemed that he was about to pass, the figure stopped and Maggie held her breath. She could hear a rasping, rattling sound like a broken air conditioner, and realised that it was the figure breathing. How long it stood there, seeming to suck the life from the air around it with each laboured breath, Maggie could not have said. It felt a long time, but could not have been that long since she held her own breath throughout. Then it moved on. The hard footsteps grew fainter, and Maggie allowed herself the luxury of breathing again.

Who was this second group? More tomb robbers, about to rob the robbers who had robbed them? What would their attitude be to the captives who had been taken from the camp? There was no way she could answer these questions. She had to get back to camp, get a gun, maybe make a better job of staunching the flow of blood from her arm, and get back here as soon as possible.

Who could imagine what might happen in her absence?

"And now we've wasted quite enough time." Maggie stood up from the chair in which she had been seated throughout her story, while Arthur had cleaned and bandaged her wounds. Almost immediately she dropped back into the chair, her legs refusing to hold her. "God dammit!" Maggie smacked her thighs urgently, trying to massage life into them. "Work, damn it, work!"

"You need to rest," said Arthur. "Have something else to eat."

"I've eaten! I need to help them!"

"Well you can't help them like this!"

For the first time since Arthur had known her, Maggie looked desperate. She stared up at the rising sun. "I can't help them at all! Whatever was going to happen has happened already. Either they've been taken off by the first group of robbers or ambushed by the second - and I don't know what that might mean. And I've been sat here on my ass eating breakfast!" Being helpless was not something that came easily to Maggie.

"What now?" It was probably the last thing that Maggie needed to hear but Arthur sure as hell didn't have any answers. He wanted to be helpful - he was relatively sure that Maggie would have bled to death if he hadn't been there to wake her, to make her eat and drink, and to tend to her injuries - but he simply didn't know what to do. Nothing in his life thus far had prepared him for this.

"We have to go for help," said Maggie, resignedly.

But that would be easier said than done. A few minutes later, Maggie had something else to curse about.

"Bastard sons of bitches!"

The jeep and all the other vehicles had been vandalised.

"You really need to stay sitting," said Arthur.

"You know how to fix an engine?"

"No."

"Then shut up."

"The tank is drained," said Arthur, as firmly as he could. "Whether or not you can fix the engine isn't going to matter."

Maggie struggled to her feet, looking down at her own legs suspiciously. "Okay. That's a start."

"I really think you should sit down."

"And then what, Arthur?" Maggie asked. "We've food enough for a while I guess, but no one is coming looking for us. Our friends are in trouble. Maybe we can't help them but if we don't try then... I don't know what the hell use we are as people." She pointed. "The nearest town is that way. If we don't have a car then we walk. Get some food together and plenty of water."

"How long a walk is it?" asked Arthur, nervously.

"Five hours if we push hard. Maybe six or seven."

Arthur looked at Maggie as she tested her legs - pushing hard under a desert sun was not an option for her. Stubborn though she was, she would drop before the first hour was out.

"I'll do it."

Maggie looked at him. "What?"

"You can't walk that far and you know it. I'll go, and I'll bring back help."

He waited for Maggie to mock him, ridicule him, and pour scorn on even the idea that he could do something like this. But she looked at him seriously, maybe even with respect.

"You can do it?"

"I'll have to."

"Well alright then. You're a good man Arthur."

It might have been a nice moment, but was spoiled as Arthur saw Maggie's gaze drift from him out into the desert and her face stiffen. Arthur turned and saw what she was looking at. Out in the distance was a small dust cloud, approaching at speed. A car.

"Any chance it's someone friendly?"

"How many friendly people have called on us in the last twenty four hours? No one's due to come here. This dig's been kept secret from the nice people. It's only nasty ones who've taken the time to find out about it."

Arthur nodded.

Maggie loaded a hand gun (of some variety - Arthur was no expert). "Ever fire one of these before?"

"No."

"Ever killed anyone?"

Arthur felt that his answer probably went without saying. "No. You?"

Maggie tested the weight of the gun in her hand. "Not intentionally. Circumstances. Things happen. But that's another story."

"I really hope I get the chance to hear it."

"That's the spirit."

The car, a battered Land Cruiser that looked to have participated in a demolition derby before setting out, pulled up. Maggie, crouched behind a crate, levelled her gun. Arthur followed suit, without much hope that it would make a difference.

The driver's door opened and a short, dark-haired woman got out.

"Hello?!"

"You're in my sights! I can kill you from here!" Maggie barked back.

The dark-haired woman looked shocked. "I wish you wouldn't."

"Who are you?!" asked Maggie. "What do you want?"

"Have you seen a mummy come this way?"

Maggie frowned. "What do you mean, 'come this way'?"

Amelia Evans shrugged. "If you'd seen it, you'd know it."

Chapter 12 - Stranded

Amelia was not one hundred percent sure at what point she blacked out, but she was definitely still conscious when the plane hit the ground with a sickening crunch that sounded like a limb breaking. The force threw her forward and the wind was knocked out of her. Then there was confusion; a rush of images and sounds tumbling over each other as if her memories had been put on a spin cycle. It was somewhere in the midst of that she had blacked out.

When she awoke was not important. *That* she awoke was all that mattered. She peeled open bleary eyes and wondered why she seemed to be staring up at the floor, which was not the natural order of things.

"Buh..." She opened her mouth to speak but coherence had been shaken out of her.

With her mind still set on 'Red Alert! Panic Stations!', she tried to piece together some semblance of a damage report. She ached everywhere and there were a few areas of more urgent pain, but nothing you would call catastrophic. Her bottom lip appeared to be bleeding, there were tender spots on her head and rear, as well as multifarious bruises and scratches, but she seemed to have got through the plane crash largely unscathed. She was a lucky woman. Not as lucky as those whose flights are not plagued by killer felines, but still.

Only now did her brain remind her that she had not been alone. She sat up sharply, making her head spin and then ache afresh as she knocked it on the head-rest of a seat hanging above her. The plane was upside down.

"Izzy? Boris?"

"Miss Evans?"

Amelia peered through the wreckage to see Boris, pale-faced but forcing a wan smile.

"Should have put on the belt. So much going on, didn't think about it. One should always buckle up."

"Are you hurt?"

"I'm alive," said Boris. "Though I may be stuck. Miss Grosvenor is over there. Can you move?"

Amelia tried and found that she could, though her body complained pointedly that lying still would be a better use of her time.

"She hasn't regained consciousness," said Boris.

Amelia could hear the strain in his voice, but making sure Izzy was alright had to come first.

"Izzy?" The red-headed girl didn't move, her naturally pale skin looking paler. "Izzy!" Amelia tried gently shaking her. "Izzy, someone's taking your drink."

"S'mine..." Izzy's eyes shuffled open. Then she screamed.

Amelia took her younger friend in her arms and held her, whispering comforting nonsense until her breathing became calmer and her vice-like grip relaxed.

"We're alive?"

"Either that or Heaven has been misrepresented by its PR people. Are you hurt?"

Izzy took a moment to think about the question, mentally going through body parts in search of agony.

"I don't think I am," she said, quite astonished. "Result!"

"You're alright, Miss Grosvenor?"

"Boris!" Izzy squealed, giddy with relief. "You're okay."

"That may be overstating it."

Amelia looked back at Boris - a trickle of blood was running from the corner of his mouth, down his chin. His naturally dark complexion had become ashen.

"You need to get out of here," he said, his voice thick with effort. "The fuel..."

"We're not leaving without you," said Izzy, sharply. She panicked hard but she recovered fast, Amelia noted.

"That would be a mistake." Boris shook his head.

"Well why don't you try and stop us then?" suggested Amelia, as she and Izzy began to clear debris from around the Universal agent.

Boris continued to protest. "If we all die then..."

"Stop being so maudlin."

"I'm just saying..."

"Shut up or we'll leave you here!"

"That's what I'm telling you to do!"

As they managed to shift part of the console that had come loose and pinned Boris, Amelia let out an involuntary gasp. There was blood everywhere. His stomach had been badly torn and he had

125

been bleeding out for... Well, for longer than was ideal.

"We need to get you out of here quickly."

"I don't think I can walk," Boris admitted. His eyelids were drooping as he started to slip from consciousness.

"We'll find a way." For fraction of a second the thought did flash through Amelia's mind: *is this really worth it? He's going to die anyway.* But she suppressed it. Boris wouldn't have left her behind, no matter how futile it was.

In the body of the plane they found a seat that had been ripped from its place. This they turned into a makeshift stretcher, on which they could drag Boris free from the wreckage and out into the woodland in which they had crashed. As they did so, a movement made the women jump.

"It's that bloody cat!" snapped Amelia angrily, as Valerie, apparently unharmed, bounded from a tattered hole in the fuselage and scampered off into the undergrowth. "Sod's law, she would make it. You better run!"

"What now?" asked Izzy. She was looking at Boris with deep concern on her face. He was barely conscious now and had stopped talking.

"You stay here with him. I'll go for help."

"Amelia." Boris forced his bloodshot eyes open to look at her, and Amelia bent closer. "If I..."

"You're going to be fine."

"If something happens, it is imperative - it is *vital* - that you..." His eyes slipped from her into middle distance.

Amelia was silent for a moment then snapped. "You've got to be kidding! Don't you dare pass out now!" She grabbed him by the lapels and shook him. "Just a few more words! You can't leave it there, you bastard!"

"Heh-Low?"

The voice came from behind them, and Amelia and Izzy spun around to find a pair of men, built on a similar scale to the trees around them, observing this tableau in confusion.

"Hi," said Amelia.

"Our plane crashed," said Izzy, quite unnecessarily in the circumstances.

"Do you speak English?" asked Amelia hopefully. She didn't even know where they were.

126

The men looked at each other in incomprehension until one, adopting the international language of television said, "Bart Simpson?"

Fortunately, 'my friend is bleeding to death' is not a difficult message to get across when that friend is lying on the ground beside you. They might have landed in the middle of nowhere, but the people were as friendly and helpful as one could wish to meet. Amelia and Izzy slept in the truck that rushed them through endless woodland towards the nearest hospital. Every now and then Amelia woke and checked on Boris. His breathing was shallow, his pulse barely there, but he was alive. The locals, who all seemed to be lumberjacks, had done a good job of patching him up on the move - Amelia had hunch that this was a community in which anything short of cutting your own foot off was considered a flesh wound - but he had lost so much blood. He looked dead already.

When they arrived at the hospital, still with no idea what country they were in, Boris was rushed into surgery and the two women flopped down in the waiting room. The seats were the uncomfortable red plastic ones that are the standard of hospitals everywhere, guaranteeing that whatever condition you came in with, you would leave with a twisted spine. They stared at the posters on the wall opposite, trying to interpret them; they gazed into the glass-fronted snack machine and wondered why it seemed to have pine cones in it; they watched other patients and relatives come and go, each with their own little dramas. The world of Egyptological espionage and living mummies seemed suddenly very far away indeed.

"You know," said Izzy, finally, "this is exactly what my parents said would happen if I got in with the wrong crowd at university.

"Really?"

"Yeah. They're surprisingly prescient when it comes to this sort of thing. Where do you think we are? Did you recognise the language?"

"No."

"I thought you spoke a bunch of languages."

Amelia sighed. "I can read every hieroglyphic variation, ancient Sumerian, Linear B, Cuneiform, Latin, Demotic Greek..."

"Nothing anyone alive speaks then?"

127

"Enough Egyptian Arabic to get by. But basically, no. I studied French at GCSE but I was rubbish. You?"

"Same. Sucked out loud. But I don't think we're in France."

"No."

"Do you think any of them speak Middle English?"

"You're going to quote Beowulf at them?" wondered Amelia.

"Just having one of those moments of quiet clarity when you realise that the degree you've dedicated three years of your life to, really is worth shit in the real world."

There was a long pause before either spoke again.

"Amelia?"

"Yeah?"

"What are we going to do now?"

"Wait for the surgery to finish."

"Okay." A pause. "Amelia?"

"Yeah?"

"What do we do if...?"

"Let's just wait for it to finish."

In the antiseptic quiet of the hospital the minutes dragged by like days, but eventually someone came to update them. The building had been scoured and a doctor had been found who could speak more English than pop culture references.

"It is too early to say," he said.

"How long until we know something?" asked Amelia.

The doctor made a vague gesture. "A week? A month?"

"A day?"

"No." The man shook his head. "Your friend is lucky to be living. But it will be time before we know if his brain has cured. I am sorry."

And so there was a decision to be made, one that Amelia had desperately hoped would not become necessary.

"I guess we should call someone," said Izzy.

"Who?"

"Someone back home."

"Who?" Amelia repeated. "Call directory enquiries and ask to be put through to a secret organisation based somewhere in central London?"

A look of realisation passed across Izzy's face.

"We have no way of getting in touch with Universal," Amelia

continued. "Either we abandon the mission and head back for England by whatever means necessary or... we don't."

Izzy stared at her for a long time. "Do you know where we were supposed to be going?"

"Somewhere in southern Egypt called the Sarranekh. Boris mentioned the Western Desert and I saw the map at the library before the Priest took it."

"A four thousand year old map?"

"The desert doesn't change much."

It was nuts. Of course it was. She was an academic - a specialist in ancient languages - not Lara Croft. Even if they reached the tomb, she didn't know what she was supposed to do when she got there, or what to tell the excavation team there, or if she would be any use at all, or what the Mummy's plans might be - if it even had plans. She didn't know any of it. And if, by some fluke, she guessed the correct course of action, she would probably be useless at carrying it out. But she couldn't let it go. In a strange way, it felt as if this was always supposed to fall into her lap.

Izzy considered this. "Okay."

They left two messages: one for Boris for when he woke up, the other for anyone who might come looking for him - surely Universal would wonder what had happened to their man and would make inquiries? Then they set out. Fortunately, the hospital allowed them to go through Boris's belongings and these included a sum of money in a wide variety of currencies. Enough to make a start at least. He would understand that their need was greater than his at the present time.

They travelled by train, by bus, and on foot when they had to, conserving their money as carefully as they could, sleeping under the stars when they had no other option, heading in an erratic and wayward fashion, south-east.

It was far from a holiday. The language barrier was a constant problem and more than once they had to run from men whose intentions were specifically unclear but definitely malign. They had few clothes to change into and washed when and where they could.

Amelia never asked Izzy if she was sorry they had made this decision - they had made it and they would see it through - but she herself... She found it thrilling! It was quite unexpected. She had determined to take this course because it had seemed like the right thing to do and, for all she knew, she was saving the world from a marauding mummy and his wicked Queen. But now... It would be too much to say that she was enjoying it, a lot of the time she was hungry and miserable and she would have killed for a decent cup of tea. But it was different! It was exciting! It felt as if she was *doing* something after years of reading about doing things. Which was not to knock reading - reading was life's greatest joy - but this was... She couldn't put any of it into words, but Amelia Evans had found a version of herself that she had never known existed. And it was a version she rather liked.

When she had been little, or at least littler, her father had read The Lord of the Rings to her as a bedtime story. It should be noted that The Lord of the Rings is entirely unsuitable as a bedtime story for a child of the age that Amelia had been at the time, but she had loved it. Possibly she had loved it because, while she was too young to appreciate it, she was also too young to fully understand it, she just liked the sound of her father's voice and the world into which the story drew her. Amelia had always had a fascination with other worlds, historical or fictional. When she was older she had of course re-read the book and still liked it, but it was that early exposure that remained the most cherished, and there were certain lines she still heard in her father's voice when she read the book to herself. Now she felt strange parallels with the book. She was on a quest to a distant land; she and her closest friend had been separated from the rest of the group who, to be honest, were the ones better suited to completing that quest. They were making their own way, doing the best they could in bad circumstances, regardless of hardship and danger. She was Frodo Baggins and Izzy her faithful Samwise Gamgee, if you could imagine Samwise Gamgee as a stunning redhead who made traffic stop just by walking past. The road went ever on and on.

But as they travelled, there had emerged another less pleasing comparison with the book. Amelia tried to recall the specific line which, for some reason, was one of those that had resonated and so stayed with her, spoken in her father's familiar tones, '*As soon as the shadows had fallen about them and the road behind was dim he had heard again the quick patter of feet*'.

Someone was following them. More specifically, some*thing*. Amelia had noticed the sound footsteps on the road behind them in

Bulgaria and had instantly spun around to see, but nothing had been there. She had done the same thing twice more and then given up because she obviously wasn't going to catch a glimpse of it and Izzy was starting to think there was something wrong with her. As long as Izzy had not noticed, Amelia decided not to bring it up; there was no sense in giving the girl something else to worry about. It was not the Mummy. Even if the footsteps had sounded like the Mummy, Amelia had to think that she, or someone else, would have noticed a Mummy plodding along the roads of central Europe, let alone catching a train. It was something small and unobtrusive, something quick, something that could go anywhere without question and vanish at a moment's notice. She was pretty sure she knew exactly what it was. But if she was right, then it raised a very obvious question; why were they still alive? It was not a question to which she was sure she wanted to know the answer.

After many days of travel, they hit the Mediterranean having passed through Greece (which surprised Amelia who had thought they were entering Turkey), and camped out that night, prior to finding a way to cross the following day. How far had the Mummy come in this time? Perhaps it was out there now on the water, heading for Alexandria or Port Said.

They lit a small fire, ate their small supper, and Izzy rolled over to go to sleep.

"Goodnight."

"Goodnight, Izzy."

Amelia waited up, sitting cross-legged by the fire. More so than ever she had felt it today, a feeling that prickled at the back of her neck like an itch she could not scratch.

As she sat, watching the flames spit and curl, a movement from the bushes caught her eye. Amelia sat very still as Valerie the cat emerged and padded up to sit on the opposite side of the fire.

"I knew it was you. How long have you been following us?"

She wouldn't have been surprised if Valerie had answered, but the cat sat, licking its paws as if butter wouldn't melt in its mouth.

"So they know we're coming? Right?" Amelia pressed. She didn't exactly expect an answer, but talking her suspicions out with the cat actually helped, a strange echo of the times she had confided her theories on cryptoglyphics to Valerie, to see if they sounded as crazy out loud as they did in her head. "I have a theory about how they knew where the Universal Library was. Would you like to hear it?"

The cat stopped licking itself and paid attention.

"You were in my flat the night when Boris brought me back. You heard him ask me to the Library. You heard him tell me when and where to meet him. You told your friends so they could be there as well. They followed us. Am I right?"

Perhaps it was Amelia's imagination, but she would swear that the way the cat cocked its head to one side had a hint of, 'Very good, Mr Bond. But now I shall have to kill you'.

"You killed our pilot." No response. "His name was Mike, by the way. I didn't know him, but I'll always remember that his name was Mike. You also led to a friend of mine being close to death. Or worse. I don't know." Nothing. "It's pretty ballsy to just show up like this. What point are you trying to make?"

The cat scratched itself, which might have meant something or perhaps it just had an itch.

"Are you trying to let me know that I can't escape you? Or that I matter so little that I'm not even worth killing?" She dared to put voice to the question that had been bothering her since she had realised they were being followed. "Why haven't you killed us?"

Can a cat look smug?

"You could kill me if you wanted, couldn't you?"

Yes, a cat could definitely look smug.

"Or maybe you just think you could," suggested Amelia. "You took poor Mike by surprise. You've always got the advantage of surprise, haven't you? Because nobody ever suspects the cat. But in the end you are just a cat, aren't you? Maybe a bit smarter, but you haven't got any special powers, have you? Just vicious and unexpected. And you've lost that advantage with me. In fact, you never had it."

Now the cat's expression conveyed a clear sense of, 'Is that so?'.

"I'm a dog person," said Amelia, warming her hands by the fire. "I think you should know that about me. Other people might coo over you - oh, isn't it sweet - but not me. I've always found cats to be pointy, hissing, evil-minded bastards. All you've done is confirm what I've always suspected about your kind, and I have no qualms about hurling a rock at you." She looked up into the unblinking green eyes. "Do we understand each other?"

The cat meowed. Then it stood up and went back the way it had come.

Amelia sat up through the night. She thought that she had won this little battle of wills and that Valerie would not be back, but there was no sense in taking chances. The memory of what had happened to Mike played unpleasantly through her mind. She could sleep on the boat tomorrow. After the boat there would be a train, and then... Who knew?

Chapter 13 - By Sea and By Land

The novelty of a sea voyage wore off relatively quickly for Old Joe, not so much because of the cramped conditions - he was not exactly used to luxury - but because it was not very convivial. On the streets of Cambridge there was always someone to chat to, someone to pass the time with, to eat with, or even discuss tonal variations in the dialects of the New Kingdom. He didn't always get the most cogent argument back, but he enjoyed the conversations never the less. Here he was starved for company and intellectual stimulation. The majority of the boat's passengers and/or crew seemed to only communicate in whispers, and shot dark glances at him whenever he wanted to join in. He had never before come across people for whom secrecy was a way of life. Nobody wanted to talk for pleasure, nobody would eat with him, no one was interested in turning an essentially professional relationship into a friendship. The days dragged.

The only person he genuinely enjoyed talking to was the Mummy. It had taken Old Joe a little time to finally settle that the tall man who was in charge and yet incapable of giving orders, was indeed a mummy. The bandages were a giveaway, but he could have been hurt, or have an odd fashion sense - as ever, Joe did not judge. But when you combined the bandages, the language, the secret society atmosphere of his comrades and the fact that they referred to themselves - when they thought Joe wasn't listening - as the Brotherhood of Egypt, then mummy was a reasonable conclusion. Moreover, he had determined through logical deduction (location plus the language of the Lost Dynasty) that this was the Priest with Turquoise Eyes, who had priorly resided in the Fitzwilliam Museum and about whose robbery Joe had heard, via word on the street.

The prospect delighted Joe. His professional life had long since ended in ignominy, but he maintained a keen interest in his old subject that he was seldom able to indulge - the homeless find themselves distressingly unwelcome in most museums. The chance to talk to someone who had actually been there was one that he had never imagined would come his way, and he was eager to take full advantage of it. There were so many questions he wanted to ask. But Youssef and the rest of the Brotherhood kept Joe away from the Mummy unless they specifically needed him for translation, and then it was all business. So Joe took a risk.

Confident that Youssef would not notice, he began tacking his own questions onto the end of the sentences he was asked to translate. It had seemed a good idea, but the Mummy responded with confusion to inquiries about his homeland and his life four thousand years ago, so Joe reluctantly stopped. Perhaps it was understandable - Joe struggled with details of his life four decades ago, a man was bound to forget things over the millennia. And yet the experiment had made Old Joe wonder. It was not just that the Mummy seemed unable to remember, or that the questions confused him, Joe was sure that the Priest became actively distressed. Had Joe inadvertently touched on the subject of the Priest's death? It was possible.

It should be noted that, while he was delighted to discover his travelling companion's identity, Joe was not surprised. As has been previously noted, Joe had a somewhat transitory relationship with reality. He tended to accept what the world presented him without question. There was, onboard the ship on which he was travelling, a four thousand year old High Priest of Ancient Egypt who had served the legendary Queen Amunet. There seemed little reason to question it. Had he woken up the following morning back in his doorway in Cambridge then he would have accepted that just as readily. This sort of thing happened to Old Joe all the time.

The one thing he had been able to establish about the Mummy was that it did not seem to sleep. It was motionless for long periods, but whether it was resting or simply immobile was impossible to say. Onboard ship, while the Brotherhood slept, it would come up on deck and stalk up and down the length of the boat, its heavy footsteps thudding against the wood. Then it would come to a stop and stare out across the ocean, contemplating a watery vastness the like of which it could never have seen in life. Joe liked to watch it at moments like this. He tried to fathom what thoughts might be passing through its head.

When the ship finally docked, Joe would have appreciated the chance to do a little sight-seeing - it was years since he had been in Egypt. But that was not to be. Their arrival was as surreptitious as their departure had been, and they were met by men who bore a certain resemblance to those with whom Joe had travelled. They dressed similarly, but more importantly they were similarly conspiratorial. There were more whispers and more furtive glances at Joe. Clearly the Brotherhood of Egypt had branches in the homeland too.

"Him?" Joe heard one of these new men say, looking disdainfully at Joe.

Youssef nodded. "He used to be a Professor at Cambridge University."

"And now?"

"Now he is a transient."

Joe objected to that. The word 'transient' implied movement, and Joe was very settled in his doorway. True he moved into the shelter during the colder months but that was barely a twenty minute walk from his summer home. He hadn't left Cambridge for years. How was that 'transient'?

"Fallen on hard times?" the new man asked, curiously interested in Joe's history.

"Disgraced," replied Youssef, with unpleasant emphasis. "And now his mind is gone."

Again Joe objected to this. He was aware that his mind wandered from time to time but it always came back, and generally he liked to travel with it. Maybe he was mentally transient?

"There was no one else?" The new man clearly disapproved of Joe.

"There was a woman, but she could only read the high language, Also she was very excitable. Would have been hard to control. She went over to Universal."

"Where is she now?"

"Approaching. The spirit of Bast watches her."

"Let her come. She might be useful."

"It was through her that we learnt of Joe," Youssef continued, "who is much more suitable. He accepts everything without question and does as he is asked."

Was that a failing? It was not in Joe's nature - or at least not any more - to ask questions, but he found himself increasingly curious about what was going on. For so long he had simply accepted life on a moment by moment basis, now long-disused areas of his mind were starting to flicker back into reluctant activity. His life had once been defined by his curiosity, his eagerness to question, to learn, to expand on the sum of his knowledge. That impulse was returning. Was it because of the intriguing situation in which he found himself? Or was it because, away from Cambridge, he no longer had access to certain small vices which had ended his career all those years ago. He had suffered some withdrawal symptoms on the trip here, but was finding that curiosity was a natural antidote to the DTs.

Whatever the case, the more he thought about it, the more he realised that something was going on. The fantasy world in which he, if not lived then at least took regular holidays, made him more accepting of the strange, but there was a difference between the strange and the suspicious. Joe had no difficulty accepting a resurrected mummy returning to Egypt (why wouldn't he want to go home after so long?), but he now found himself wondering about the motives of those who accompanied it.

This increasing curiosity, Joe chose to keep to himself. If the conversation between Youssef and the new man (whose name proved to be Ali) was anything to go by, then his safety was at least partly dependant on his disengagement. The fact that they would discuss such things willingly in front of him showed how little they considered him a threat. Joe decided that it would be good to retain that status. They seemed to need him, but it did not do to rock the boat. Besides, if nothing else, it was good to be back in Egypt.

The day after they got off the boat they were travelling again in a convoy of decrepit vans. It was a long journey, and also a less pleasant one. The heat was close to unbearable, the noise of the van's elderly engine was deafening, and the rough terrain, over which they travelled as fast as their vehicles would allow, shook their bones and bounced them around the van's interior.

"Where are we going?" asked Joe, keeping his voice at that level of mild interest that had served him well thus far.

He got no answer. But that might, at least partly, be because the Brotherhood themselves were not sure. On the first day of travel, Joe had acted as translator as the Mummy - referring to an extraordinary papyrus which Joe would have loved to get his hands on - explained where they were heading. Somewhere called the Sarranekh.

"Surely he knows where her tomb is without a map?" Joe overheard Youssef and Ali talking.

"It's been a long time. Egypt has changed."

As the heat increased they took to travelling by night, sleeping as best they could through the blazing sun of the day. They were now out in the desert, not a sign of life for miles around. Joe took it for granted that they knew where they were going, never pausing to wonder if he might die out here in an overcrowded, oven-like van. It was one of the advantages of being Joe.

After a few more nights of travel, they saw a shape on the horizon; an embattled range of jagged rocks, rising out of the desert like a volcanic island in an ocean of sand.

"Tomorrow we will make camp," said Ali, and Youssef nodded gratefully. They were enjoying this journey no more than Joe.

The party bedded down for the day in the shadows cast by the vans. In the afternoon, Joe woke - the moving sun had found him, making sleep near impossible. Most people slept under the vans where there was permanent shade but Joe found it too claustrophobic. He got up to move back into the shade and then stopped as he saw the Mummy, standing some distance away, staring at the distant rocks.

As ever, it did not sleep. The turquoise eyes were always visible, but then it had no eyelids to close over them. Joe idly wondered how it saw. Were there human eyes beneath the inlaid mineral? Or did the turquoise somehow serve as eyes? How much of the Mummy remained human? Its organs had been removed after all. Did it retain any semblance of the man it had been? Or was it just a walking husk of skin? Interesting questions on which to muse.

Despite the heat, Joe went over to where the Mummy stood. The expression on its age-stiffened face was hard to read, but Joe thought he saw concentration in the way its jaw was working constantly.

"Nice view," he commented, slipping automatically into the tongue of the Lost Dynasty.

"I know it," came the Mummy's cracked reply, ancient words that sounded as if they had been cut from rock.

Joe looked out at the miniature mountain range that rose from the desert. A lot changes in four thousand years, but that would have been there when the Priest was alive.

"You come from round here?" suggested Joe. It was nice to finally be able to talk history, and for the first time the Priest was the one volunteering information.

"There was a great battle here."

Joe nodded. He did not know where 'here' was, but it was certainly not impossible. We complacently refer to 'Ancient Egypt' as if it is one specific period of time, like the Renaissance, but the term covers thousands of years, many of them turbulent. There probably had been a battle here; all trace of it long since vanished, bones eroded by the sweeping sands.

Joe was not sure what to say now. He had a sense that this was an opportunity - a sharp needle of curiosity piercing the fluffy cloud of his mind. Whatever he said next would determine whether the conversation continued, and whether other such conversations might take place in the future. It might also have some effect on the Mummy's ability, and desire, to recall events from his life.

"Who won?"

The turquoise eyes searched the pitiless landscape before the harsh answer rasped out. "They did."

"Joe!"

Joe turned to find Ali approaching briskly. He wore a smile, but it was painted on. It was not the sort of thing Joe would have noticed a few weeks back, but he was seeing more clearly now.

"What are you doing?" asked the leader of the Brotherhood.

"Just having a chat."

"About what?"

Youssef played this game better - the game of seeming a friend. Ali was ill-equipped by nature for such deception.

"History," said Joe, honestly. "I used to be a professor you know."

"I know."

"Rare opportunity to talk to someone who was there."

"Unique, I should think," agreed Ali. "Nothing strikes you as odd about it?"

"No. Should it?"

"Do you know why we're out here, Joe?"

"No. Should I?"

Ali's sharp eyes sought for some guile hidden in Joe's honest face, but found none.

"Is he alright?"

It quite surprised Joe to hear the genuine concern in Ali's voice. Whatever the specific relationship between the Mummy and

139

the men was, there was no denying that they were very protective of it.

"I think he knows where we are. Remembers it."

The answer seemed to please Ali. "Would you... Could you tell him that we are bringing him back to Her, to fulfil the prophecy?"

Joe opened his mouth to translate but Ali jumped in again.

"Please! Tell him, we are - that is - it is our *honour* - our deepest honour, to escort his Holiness back to Her Majesty, to fulfil the prophecy. And his destiny," Ali hastily added the last sentence, then thought better of it. "No; just the prophecy. I should not comment on his destiny. He knows that better than I."

As he translated, Joe wondered if that were true. As the only one who could speak to the Priest directly, he was also the only one to notice his increasing uncertainty. The longer the Mummy was awake after his long sleep of death, and the closer they got to his home, the greater his confusion seemed to be. Even when he was recognising things, it all seemed to be accompanied by an uncertainty of what it meant. If Joe was any judge, there was an internal war in the Mummy.

That said, his response to Ali's fawning words seemed pretty standard. "And you will be rewarded for your devotion. When she is risen."

Ali was pleased to hear that.

The following day there seemed to be some sort of problem. One of the men had scouted ahead and returned quickly.

"He's sure these are not the archaeologists?" Youssef asked.

Ali shook his head firmly. "Tomb robbers."

"Desecrators!"

"No worse than the 'archaeologists'."

Youssef acknowledged this. "But they at least serve a purpose. Without them we might never have found Her."

"What do we do?" asked the scout.

"We find somewhere else to camp," replied Ali. "And we wait. And we watch."

But waiting did not seem to be on the agenda for one of the party. They made camp to the west of where they had originally intended, to avoid the notice of the tomb-robbing party (which was in turn camped to the north of the Sarranekh to avoid the attention of the archaeological expedition). On the first night after they pitched

140

camp, the Mummy tried to leave, setting off into the Sarranekh.

"You! Joe! Translate!" Youssef called for help as he tried to balance deference with panic. "I would not presume to tell your Holiness what to do, but if we are discovered then all may be for nothing."

Joe dutifully translated, but it did not seem to change the Priest's mind, and he stalked off through the rocks into the night. No one dared to stop him once his mind was made up.

"He is drawn to her," said Ali, with quiet reverence.

"Should we follow him?" asked Youssef.

"That would be sacrilege," said Ali, no less concerned, but certain in his belief.

"But if he is spotted."

"I believe he knows that he cannot allow himself to be seen. He will be cautious. He lived here once, he knows the caves and tunnels that run through these hills."

Despite this apparent confidence, everyone seemed much relieved when the Mummy returned in the early hours of the morning. Joe could only guess at where it had been and why it might have gone there, but on its return it came straight to him, Youssef and Ali hurrying after.

"I cannot pass the threshold."

Joe translated.

"The inscriptions prevent it," said Ali. "While she remains within, no one who does not wish eternal damnation may enter. Only an unbeliever."

"Ironic," muttered Youssef. "If they have not yet removed Her royal body...?"

"Then we must wait until they do. Though I doubt the tomb robbers will wait."

"Don't be so sure," mused Youssef. "It will save them the trouble of removing her themselves - let the archaeologists do the work."

"Perhaps," admitted Ali, a man who did not like to be wrong. "Either way; we must watch them both."

In the next few days, two expeditions were made by Youssef, Ali and a few of the others. When they came back from the first the mood was not exactly downcast, but there was some uncertainty.

"Hardly ideal," Youssef observed, snappishly. "You should

have planned for this. Rather than just assuming that the desecrators would..."

"She will do until someone more appropriate can be found." Ali defended himself. "We only need one."

"You should have brought a woman along."

"And what would we have told her?"

"There are villages, less than a day's drive away. We still have time to..."

"We don't know how much time we have. Kidnap can easily go wrong and we don't want to draw attention to ourselves. Besides," Ali drew himself up, "if you recall, I *did* make provision for this eventuality. The spirit of Bast may yet provide."

"Let's hope so." Youssef gave a wry smile. "They'll wish they died in the crash."

The next expedition took an entire day. From what Joe could glean from half heard conversations, they were looking for something out in the Sarranekh. All he could say on their return was that they seemed to have found it.

Chapter 14 - The City of the Dead

"A cat?"

Amelia was not sure that she liked the young man, Arthur. It was probably too early to be making judgements - she was at the end of a long, hot and unpleasant journey through the desert, and a still longer one from England, so was naturally irritable and not in the mood to be well-disposed towards people. But the aura of disbelief that he had radiated during certain sections of her story, and his dismissal of Valerie as a threat, did not sit well with her.

"Yes," she said, her words etched in acid. "A cat."

"I've always rather liked cats," admitted Arthur, dooming him still further in Amelia's estimations.

"I used to," put in Izzy. "I've had a change of heart."

"Cats are bastards," said Maggie, an attitude that endeared her to Amelia, even if their meeting - characterised by Maggie pointing a gun at her - had been less than perfect.

"This one is more than normally a bastard."

Maggie shook her head. "I don't know what to believe any more. What happened here last night was tomb robbers. But what I saw on the way back and what you're telling me now... I've seen some strange shit in this world, but this is beyond strange shit."

Amelia was still making up her mind what she thought of Maggie. The excavation's site manager was pragmatic and down to earth, but still willing to accept that they had passed beyond the bounds of the natural when evidence was presented to her. She did not know what to make of Amelia's story but was not questioning it. On the flip-side, Amelia did not generally like people who handled guns so easily or pointed them at her so casually.

After a frustratingly slow boat trip across the Mediterranean, Amelia and Izzy had boarded a train that took them almost the length of Egypt, a journey that severely tested Amelia's romantic notions of long train journeys. On arrival, they hired a car and set out into the desert with directions on how to reach the Sarranekh - directions along the lines of; keep going that way, you can't miss it. During the journey south, Amelia had not developed any real idea of what they might find when they reached the tomb site. This was partly because she was so focused on getting there that everything else paled to insignificance, but also because she had not really thought that there

143

would be anything to find beyond an archaeological excavation. Despite all that had happened, she had not been expecting anything untoward. On the face of it, that seemed pretty optimistic; they had been attacked and delayed specifically so that the Mummy could overtake them, common sense dictated that the Brotherhood would have made its move before Amelia and Izzy arrived. But, truth be told, Amelia's brain was still rebelling against any of this being real, waiting for the logical explanation that surely had to come. However ridiculous it might seem, part of her expected to arrive at the excavation to find everything normal and that the whole thing had been an elaborate practical joke. Instead she had found a irritatingly sceptical man, barely older than Izzy, and a gun-toting woman covered in her own blood. It was not the worst case scenario, but nor was what she had hoped.

"Look, all this is beside the point." Amelia took the initiative - you had to live with the situation that life gave you. "What matters now is your friends."

Maggie nodded. "You're right. We've wasted enough time already."

"But..." Arthur stammered. "Now we've got the car we can go for help."

"From whom?" asked Amelia.

"The police?"

"You're going to go to the nearest town and tell the police that your friends have been kidnapped by tomb robbers pursued by a mummy and an evil cat?"

"I think we can keep some details on a need to know basis," Arthur acknowledged. "They take a hard-line on tomb-robbing here. If we..."

"That'd take a day at least." added Maggie. "What happens to Prof and the others while we're doing that? Before we didn't have a choice. You and me against all those people would've been suicide. Now there's a four of us."

"Not seeing a big distinction," muttered Arthur.

"And now we know what we're dealing with," Maggie went on. "Bunch of cultists and a mummy. We can take 'em."

There was something about Maggie, Amelia found; her confidence was infectious. Suddenly the whole thing seemed wonderfully possible. "Can you tell us which way to go?"

"I can show you," said Maggie, standing.

"You can walk that far?"

"Watch me."

"Obviously I am coming," put in Arthur, a little concerned that he was now pegged as the coward who wouldn't save his friends. "I was just putting forward an alternative course of action."

"Noted," said Amelia, more sharply than she would have a month ago.

"He's alright, once you get to know him," said Maggie. She stood to open a chest from which she drew out a pair of substantial hand guns. These she pressed into the hands of Amelia and Izzy. "Either of you ever killed a man before?"

"She's alright once you get to know her," said Arthur, perhaps a little smugly, seeing the shocked looks on the faces of the newcomers.

The trek through the Sarranekh was evidently hard-going for Maggie but she didn't let that slow her down, and the shade afforded by the rocks helped her keep going. At times Amelia found herself struggling to keep up. Which, she reflected, was the difference between a woman who had spent her life out in the open, climbing over rocks and hiking through deserts and jungles, and one who curled up by the fire with a nice cup of tea and a good book. There was no question that she would rather be the latter, had been designed by nature to be the latter, and couldn't wait to get back to it, but Amelia made a mental note that if she got out of this she would take better care of herself in the future. Perhaps take the odd spin class or a session of pilates.

As they hiked on, she took the time to wonder at the way in which she had taken charge earlier. Even within her own field, in which she was an acknowledged expert, Amelia would never have characterised herself as a leader, and yet there she had been, practically giving orders. She had changed. And she had done so without even noticing, since Izzy always looked to her to take the lead, anyway. Was the change for the better? Hard to say. But it was a useful change in the immediate situation. It had not been an overnight thing, but a consequence of meeting each fresh challenge. She never stopped to wonder if she should just lay down and quit, she simply made the decision and moved on, and so had become accustomed to it. It was interesting to meet this new version of herself, but Amelia also wondered if she would be able to make the transition back afterwards. Much as she liked, decisive, adventurous Amelia, forging a path through the wilderness, she still pined after cosy, quiet, Cambridge Amelia, and looked forward to the day she could slip back into her. Would that day come? It rather depended how this one went. Thus far, Amelia had made a conscious effort not to look too far ahead, dealing with each situation as it came up. But that was becoming less and less possible. What was at the end of all this? There was no question that the danger they were facing, and would face, was real. It seemed too much to hope that, when they found the Mummy, they could sit down to talk about things and discover it had all been a terrible misunderstanding. At the end of this, someone was going to die. Who that might be was still up for grabs.

As the morning wore on and they forged further north through the rocks, something else became visible up ahead of them.

"Is that smoke?" asked Izzy, staring at the black column, climbing into the sky, shifting with the desert winds.

Maggie nodded curtly, not slowing her pace.

"Who'd start a fire out here?" wondered Arthur. "In the middle of the day."

"Maggie?" Amelia had a bad feeling about where this was going. "Would I be right in thinking that plume of smoke is kind of in the direction we're heading?"

"Yep."

"Just thought I'd check."

An hour later, as they began to descend from the Sarranekh back to the desert sand, they got their first glimpse of where the smoke was coming from. The camp had been quite well hidden using military camouflage nets. Those, and the expensive, all-terrain vehicles, suggested that this had been a high-tech operation.

"Tomb robbers' camp," said Maggie, as they walked down the path. "Or what's left of it."

The vehicles were on fire, black smoke pouring from them. The tents had been burnt too and were now just smouldering. The place had been completely turned over. But it was inevitably the bodies that drew the eye.

"Arthur," said Maggie, her voice like flint, "see if any of them are our people."

146

Arthur nodded tremulously, and Amelia felt a pang of compassion for him. It was a task she wouldn't have wished on her worst enemy - checking the dead for anyone you knew.

Maggie rolled over a corpse. "Damn it."

Even in the heat, Amelia felt a cold chill shiver over her skin. "One of your team?"

"No," said Maggie. "It's the leader of the tomb robbers. Jago, his name was."

Amelia looked down at a face that, even devoid of life, remained a sharply cruel one. A brutal scar ran across one side of it and, much fresher, the neck was mutilated with dark, ugly bruises.

"That's the man who looked into my tent, my first night here!" exclaimed Arthur, joining them.

Maggie nodded. "Someone strangled him. Someone strong. Broke every bone in his neck." She stooped closer to examine the corpse. "One-handed too from those marks."

Amelia shivered again. She fancied she could guess the killer.

"Damn it, damn it, damn it." Maggie shook her head, clearly upset. "I wanted to beat the shit out of him myself. Now he's dead." She stood and kicked the corpse hard. "Selfish bastard."

Amelia watched the other woman closely; for all the bravado she was demonstrating, the walk here had clearly been hard on Maggie. Her whole body was starting to droop, her footsteps becoming heavier, and there was a just noticeable slur in her speech. Though Amelia had not known her long, it was obvious that Maggie was not a woman who easily admitted weakness, let alone defeat, but her body was speaking for her now.

"So, none of these people were on the dig?" asked Izzy. She had been strangely quiet today, struggling to find her place on this expedition.

"No," Arthur shook his head. "Looks like our guys made it."

Izzy nodded, but without much enthusiasm. "I don't want to be a downer - and; obviously great they didn't get killed - but is anyone else wondering why?"

Maggie and Amelia looked at each other.

"Their hands were tied," said Maggie.

"So they weren't a threat," agreed Amelia.

"Still, once you've killed the dangerous people," Maggie went on, "why not kill everyone else?"

147

"They might have run?" suggested Arthur, hopefully.

"All of them? And not one got picked off when he ran?" Maggie shook her head.

"So, if whoever killed the robbers didn't kill your team," Amelia reasoned her way through the thought, "then either they let them go, or they took them prisoner."

"Can't see them letting anyone go," said Maggie, grimly surveying the carnage in which they stood. It did not speak of merciful people.

"Agreed. And if they took them with them..."

"Then they had a reason. And that reason..."

"Is unlikely to be a good one," concluded Amelia. "We're talking about the Mummy here - the Priest - and his devotees. The Brotherhood."

Maggie nodded slowly. "I am willing to accept that." She looked at Arthur. "You know the stories. Why might High Priest Ramona - or whatever his name is - want all those people?"

Arthur looked uneasy. "We think he's trying to resurrect Queen Amunet?"

Maggie looked to Amelia for confirmation. Amelia nodded.

Arthur swallowed uncomfortably. "Obviously I've never read any texts from the Lost Dynasty, but there are spells written for the resurrection of the dead in later dynasties. Pretty much all of those spells - all of them really - call for a blood sacrifice. Usually human. In fact... always human - I don't know why I said 'usually', like it would make things better."

"A life for a life," said Izzy. She looked queasy.

"Not exactly," Arthur continued. He seemed happier when quoting facts - back on familiar ground rather than playing the adventurer. Amelia could identify. "One normal person's blood could resurrect many slaves. But it might take several people to resurrect one Queen. Depending on the spell. Varies a lot. And there may have been different rituals during the Lost Dynasty, we simply don't know. It's a fascinating area of research," he finished lamely.

"Here!"

While Arthur had been talking, Maggie had wandered off, searching the fringes of the camp. Now she seemed to have found something. Amelia hurried over with Arthur and Izzy behind. Maggie pointed at the ground.

"Tracks. They went that way." She pointed towards a narrow split in the rock wall, wide enough to admit two abreast.

Amelia stared. There had been a few of these moments since this whole affair had started, moments when she could theoretically go one way or the other, and in none of them had she felt there was actually a choice. It was in these moments that where she was and what was happening rushed in upon her. When you were active - simply reacting to what was happening - you never questioned the situation. When there was a decision to make then you tended to go back over the other ones and wonder at what had led you here. Nothing in Amelia's life had ever suggested that she might end up with the lives of fifteen or so innocent people depending on her. In an odd way, mummies and cats and ancient magic seemed the least of the strangeness to her - they were strange full stop, and would be strange to anyone. But for her, Amelia Evans, linguist, bookworm, tea enthusiast and avoider of the great outdoors, to find herself in a situation in which people were counting on her to save their lives - that was *really* strange.

"Let's go," she said.

Maggie had sunk to her knees to examine the tracks and now rose again. But not without difficulty. Amelia sighed - why did it have to be the one person who might actually be of some use?

"I think you'd better stay."

She had expected some resistance, but Maggie just pulled a face and nodded. "Yeah. Probably. I'm more of a liability than a help right now."

"Get some rest," suggested Izzy.

"Might see if I can get a radio working," mused Maggie, looking around the camp. "Gotta be one here somewhere."

"Get some rest," Amelia emphasised Izzy's words, once again hearing the unfamiliar note of command in her voice.

"I'll follow when I've got my strength back," Maggie said, and there was no doubting from her tone that this was *going* to happen.

Leaving Maggie to hunt through the remains of the burning camp for some way of contacting the outside world, the other three headed towards the rocks, and Amelia found herself leading the way once again. It wasn't that she would have characterised herself as a follower; more a buzzer around the periphery asking if anyone wanted anything. Which wasn't a bad thing to be. Being a leader, by

149

contrast, sucked. At least as far as she could see. You had to tell people what to do and if it turned out that you had no idea what you were talking about then the consequences were on you. Amelia was happy to be the leader of her own life, and she shouldered the consequences without complaint. Enter a long-term relationship with a cheat? That was obviously her poor judgement. Let your love of books get the better of you so you accept an invitation to a secret library that leads you onto a quest, the precise ramifications of which still remained frustratingly unclear? That too was on her. But people's lives? She didn't need that.

"Arthur?"

The younger man hurried to her side.

"Sounds like you know these stories better than me..."

"Good memory," interrupted Arthur. "Plus I have no life beyond reading."

"Okay." More than anything Arthur had so far said, that made Amelia warm to him. "There are stories about Queen Amunet planning to come back from the dead, aren't there?"

Arthur nodded. "A few. Again, all the ones I've read have been passed down and may have changed in the re-telling."

"Any of them touch on *why* she wanted to come back? I've heard the whole 'save Egypt' thing but - you know - anything a bit less vague?"

Arthur made uncertain noises. "Vague is kind of a running theme, but the overall message seems to be that when Egypt has forgotten its old ways and its old gods then she'll return to rule again."

"And Egypt will be a great Empire once more."

Arthur nodded. "Maybe a greater one."

"Greater?"

Arthur shrugged. "One thing about the stories that changes over time is the scale of their ambition. When Queen Amunet died, Egypt was the whole world. Over the years the world grows, as Egyptians become aware of other continents and cultures. But the stories they tell about Queen Amunet still have her coming back and ruling the world, with Egypt at its centre. "

"So," Amelia said slowly, "it's not so much about *saving* Egypt, as it is about restoring its imperial glory."

"As far as the stories are concerned," Arthur explained, "the two are interchangeable. In this context, 'saving' Egypt means Egypt ruling the world under the old gods."

"Like it should have been all this time?"

"Exactly."

"The Brotherhood really think the Queen can do this?" put in Izzy. "That she can conquer the world?"

"I guess."

"I'm just saying; the last time she was alive, the bow and arrow was at the cutting edge of weapons' technology. How big a threat can she be?"

"Weeell," Arthur made more uncertain noises, "if she can come back from the dead, then she at least knows *some* stuff we don't."

It was an argument that Amelia had played out in her head a lot since they lost Boris; was any of this worth doing? How dangerous could a resurrected Queen and her Mummy sidekick be? Now, of course, it didn't actually matter. It was strange how a potential threat to the entire world paled when put against the immediacy of a handful of lives in danger. They had to rescue Professor Andoheb's team. The fate of the world could be someone else's problem.

The party that had gone this way before them had done nothing to hide their tracks. Why should they? They did not expect to be followed. In other circumstances it would have been a pleasant journey, the path was mostly flat, and the high rock walls afforded them shade from the blazing sun. Although there was nothing archaeological to be seen, Amelia felt that weight of history she always felt when in Egypt, a country that carried its magnificent past before it like a medal around its neck, or possibly a millstone. Then, up ahead, buried deep in the heart of the rocks, the mouth of a tunnel appeared.

"There's still so much to find in this country," Arthur murmured to himself.

Amelia said nothing. He was right; Egypt was a land of secrets and many of them were still waiting to be discovered. Even now, in these less than ideal circumstances, there was something tantalising about a long forgotten cave in Egypt. Who knew what might lie inside?

They approached cautiously.

"No guards," whispered Izzy, shivering in a sudden chill that the cave seemed to exhale.

"Guess they weren't expecting anyone," Amelia hoped.

They entered the cave.

"What's that?" Arthur pointed up ahead to where the darkness of the tunnel gave way to a flickering light. Nervously they moved towards the light, the floor tending downwards as they walked, taking them deeper into the rock.

The light came from a pair of torches mounted on the wall - evidence that they were on the right track, though they still saw no one.

Or at least, no one living.

"Oh my..." Words failed Amelia as she stared down the tunnel, illuminated at regular intervals by torches on both sides. It had now broadened out into a wide avenue, stretching as far as she could see, decorated with enough wall paintings and cryptoglyphics to keep a university full of archaeologists in PhDs for the rest of their natural lives. But the main feature was that it was lined with the dead. Alcoves had been cut into the walls from floor to ceiling, each one housing a body. The flesh had long since shrivelled but the dry, cool conditions in the cave had done an extraordinary job of preservation, so sandpaper skin still clung to ancient bone millennia after death.

"There's a whole damn city's worth of people down here," breathed Arthur.

"No." Amelia was poring over the cryptoglyphics by the light of a torch. "A whole damn army."

"What?"

"Look at the dates." She pointed at the glyphs beside one corpse, then another, then another and another, before realising she was the only one there who could actually read them. "All the same. And here, and here. These people all died on the same day."

"All of them?" Izzy's eyes widened, "But there must be hundreds." She shivered.

"Cold?" asked Amelia.

"No."

"It is not the cold that makes me shiver," murmured Arthur.

"What?"

"Sherlock Holmes. The Speckled Band. Sorry. It calms me down."

Amelia indicated the dented skull of a well-preserved specimen beside her. "Look at his head. That's what killed him. Someone stove his head in."

"This one's missing an arm," said Arthur, looking elsewhere.

Everywhere there were catastrophic injuries, and the same date repeated over and over.

"They died in battle," said Amelia.

"There are stories about a battle that supposedly happened around here," said Arthur. "The diggers at the site used to tell old ghost stories about the spirits of a massacred army that haunts the Sarranekh."

"I'm guessing these guys lost," added Izzy. "Is this normal? This sort of... mausoleum?"

Arthur shook his head. "I've never read about anything like this in Ancient Egypt. And even if they buried their war dead like this during the Lost Dynasty, why would you go to all this trouble for the losers? Your friends you might bury - the victorious dead - but not this."

"Doesn't look like a tomb, does it?" Horrible thoughts had started to writhe around in Amelia's mind. She gazed up and down the rows of neatly shelved bodies. "Looks more like a store room."

Chapter 15 - Revolution

Local legend said that Ramose's personal guard were carried by the desert wind. Some whispered that they were not human at all, but summoned up from another realm to do the High Priest's bidding. Setka said that all such rumours were started by the Priest himself as a way of keeping everyone living in fear. It worked. Every time someone went missing, even if they were later discovered crushed by a block of masonry (the speed with which they were forced to work led to many such accidents) the gossips insisted it was the work of Ramose.

"Only a few days ago I heard him talking about the High Priest, and now he's dead. Now is *that* a coincidence?"

And Setka would point out that, on any given day, everyone in the workers' village probably said something about the High Priest that was less than complimentary. But it didn't matter, people preferred to believe in the legend.

For himself, Mahu was not sure what to believe. Obviously he agreed with Setka, and believed everything that he said. But when he heard the wind at night, whistling harshly across the building site and through the workers' village, that belief seemed a lot less certain. Who would it carry away this time? People seemed to be vanishing all the time, although Setka said that they were just runaways, men sick of the conditions in which they had to live and work. Some of them turned up again, dumped in the village as a reminder of what happened to those who disobeyed the Pharaoh's wishes, or discovered weeks later out in the desert, barely recognisable after the jackals had been at them. Either way it was considered the work of Ramose. There was no running away from here. There was nowhere to run away to, and if you were found by the High Priest's guards then being savaged to death by jackals would suddenly seem like a luxury.

Today, Ramose's guards were not carried by the wind but by chariots. Mahu watched them arrive. It was a more prosaic means of travel, but their presence was none the less calculated to strike fear into the hearts of all in the workers' village.

"Work has fallen behind schedule."

Nebamun, who had become an overseer after Djhutmose's death, stepped up querulously. "No. No, I don't think so. If you would consult the schedule..."

"The High Priest wishes the work completed faster." Although he could clearly see the soldier's face, Mahu would have been at a loss to describe it, or that of any of his comrades. Soldiers all looked the same to him, as if they were wearing masks.

"Then we will work faster." Nebamun was not about to argue.

"Your previous spokesmen have said that you could not work faster."

"We will find a way."

"So you were not previously working as hard as you could?" suggested the guard.

Nebamun floundered, his Adam's apple bobbing up and down in his throat.

"The High Priest feels that you will 'find a way' more quickly if properly motivated."

Nebamun swallowed awkwardly. "I assure you..."

The Captain snapped to his subordinates. "Gather up ten of them. Doesn't matter which."

"No!"

Nebamun started at the voice from behind him. Setka stepped forward, and Mahu held his breath.

"You know who I am?"

The Captain nodded. "The High Priest said you might interfere with the orders of the Pharaoh."

"Did he?"

"He said to tell you that it's time to pick a side."

Setka walked forward till he was face to face with the Captain. "Tell him, I picked a long time ago. Go back and tell him now."

The Captain shifted uneasily. "The building of this palace is the will of the gods. I was sent here..."

"There are a lot of us and very few of you," said Setka. "I've given you a message to deliver to the High Priest. An urgent one. It seems to me that that might be a legitimate excuse for leaving before your mission is complete."

The Captain still looked uneasy.

"No one is dying here today," said Setka, evenly. "Or at least no one who lives in this village."

The workers watched the guards leave with grim faces. No blow had been struck, no arrow fired, but something had started, and had already moved beyond stopping.

"Should we try to work faster?" asked Nebamun. "I'm not sure we can. Already we're cutting corners we shouldn't and losing men for it. I don't think people can work any more hours."

"If we don't then they'll find a way to make us," said Setka.

If you believed the stories then, before the workers' village, before stone mason and labourer were decent professions for a man, the buildings and monuments of Egypt had been built by slaves. Probably pretty shoddily - what did slaves know about architecture? - but very quickly. However hard you worked, however much you thought you could not work any harder, you could be taught different when the whip hand hovered above you. Everyone had heard the rumours, though for once they were being dismissed as idle gossip. Which was odd because rumour in the workers' village was usually given the status of hard fact. But these were rumours that nobody wanted to believe and so chose not to, rumours too terrible to believe. The rumour was that the workers were to be re-designated as slaves, their homes taken from them, their wages replaced by a roof over their head and three meals a day.

What difference would it make? Their contract already said they could not leave; their wages were invariably spent on home and food. But it made a difference. It made a difference to be able to say you were free, to be able to say you were an Egyptian citizen, and to know that, even if you could not choose the path your life took, at least that life was your own.

Mahu sat by the wall, listening as the conversation between the two most important men in the village continued. It was now joined by Bek, the sculptor and overseer of sculptors.

"The question is; is there anything that we can do now that will stop them from coming for us again in the future? You saw what was going to happen today. If you hadn't stepped in they were going to kill ten workers (or maybe their families), there in front of us, just to make a point. Not because we weren't working hard enough, but because they thought we probably wouldn't. Pre-emptive execution." He sucked at his teeth. "Is there anything we can do, any distance back that we can bend, any indignity we can voluntarily heap upon ourselves that is going to stop them from coming again and asking for more? The more we accept, the harder they push. If we concede without argument, they know they can push us further. When does it end?"

"Why are you asking me?" Setka snapped.

"Because you stood up to them."

Setka shook his head. "I won't be able to do that again. Any 'special treatment' I might have got is gone now."

Bek smiled. "But you *will* do it again. You won't be able to help yourself. And everyone here knows it."

"What are you saying?"

"I'm not saying anything."

"Then what are you suggesting we do?" Setka got up and paced. Mahu had never seen him so frustrated. "You sit there and say; when does it end? How much more will we take? Well what's your solution? Tell me that, Bek!"

"We say no."

"To the Pharaoh?"

Bek shook his head. "Everyone knows that she - he - is just a puppet of the High Priest. We swear loyalty to the Pharaoh, but say no to Ramose."

Setka shook his head again. "I'm not sure that is an option."

Bek nodded. "Perhaps not. And if we do nothing then the sun will still rise tomorrow. But who knows what else the day will bring? Who knows who will be next to go missing? Whose body will show up in a sheet like poor Djhutmose? Whose wife will be taken? Whose children will be killed in front of him just to gain a few days on their precious schedule? Our lives are worthless to them."

Setka sagged. It had never really occurred to Mahu how it might feel to be Setka. He had always envied his friend (a word he was proud to use) for his confidence in all company, high and low, but now he wondered if that came at a price of never feeling at home anywhere. Behind his back, Mahu knew, people said how easy it was for Setka to take a stand - nothing was going to happen to him. Why should he make decisions for the workers when he wasn't really one of them?

"Why me?" asked Setka.

"Because there's no one else," said Bek.

"No one will want me to lead," Setka insisted. "They'll think I have some personal stake in it - the way Djhutmose did. There are still some who blame me for his death. They won't want me."

"I'm not sure that's true," said Nebamun. His eyes had drifted

157

over to the open door.

Mahu followed the overseer's gaze, his mouth opening at what he saw. He looked back to Setka.

The architect stood up and walked across the room to the door. Outside were people, the whole of the workers' village from the looks of it. As Setka came to the door, they cheered.

The volume of the cheer was enough to disturb the cat that had been lying peacefully in the corner throughout their discussions. To a casual observer it might have seemed asleep, but if they had looked more closely they would have seen the narrow green slits of its eyes, taking everything in, hearing every word.

The plan of the revolution was based on speed. If they moved fast then they could strike before the Pharaoh arrived to take up residence at her new palace, and so before there was any major military presence there. With only the High Priest's personal guard and a detachment of other soldiers to protect the site, the workers would have the overwhelming weight of numbers. Also, soldiers were bound to switch sides once they realised the Priest could not win - it was only fear that kept them loyal. Builders, sculptors and labourers fighting professional soldiers was never going to be a fair fight, it was never going to be a foregone conclusion, and people would die. But with the element of surprise on their side, there was a spirit of optimism amongst the workers. Once the battle was over and the workers were in residence then they would send a message to the Pharaoh, respectfully inviting her, explaining the situation ,and making it clear that their loyalty to her was total and that they would be happy to get back to work under a less oppressive regime than that inflicted upon them, and upon the whole of Egypt, by Ramose, who by then would hopefully be 'the late' Ramose.

"She might even thank us for it," said Bek. "She'll be able to pick her own High Priest now, one who'll do as she says rather than the other way around."

They all knew that it might not pan out that way, but the alternative was to do nothing and so nothing would change. They were ready.

The attack started well. They used the caves that riddled the Sarranekh - which they knew as well as anyone - to sneak up unseen. They knew the best spot to attack the palace as they had built it.

158

They knew where to find the guards. They were past the perimeter wall in no time, storming on to the palace itself, with Setka at their head. Mahu tried hard to stay close to Setka, but it wasn't easy as the whole of the workers' village was trying to do the same. People felt safer beside Setka, as if the aura of invincibility he carried with him might extend to them.

But as the revolutionaries approached the palace, the sky suddenly seemed to darken. Few of those charging stopped to look up, too caught up in what they were doing. Those who did were those who feared the wrath of Ramose, and were looking to the sky for thickening clouds and bolts of lightning jutting down at them. What they saw was arrows.

Mahu dived for cover, and saw the man beside him fall, an arrow in his chest, dead before he hit the ground. Suddenly what had seemed like a glorious revolution was consumed by blood and screaming. Though he was not a thinker by nature, Mahu found his mind racing; surely this was wrong somehow? The number of arrows was far too great for the number of soldiers they knew to be stationed here. He peered out from his hiding place, and saw more soldiers pouring out of the palace - more and more.

An ambush.

The Priest had known they were coming. Of course he had known. How had they been so blind or so arrogant as to assume that they could hide anything from Ramose?

Mahu looked out again, scanning the fleeing workers and pursuing soldiers for Setka. It should have been a futile task in such chaos, but Mahu's eyes picked him out. He wasn't on the run - of course he wasn't - he was fighting up near the palace itself.

Then something else caught Mahu's eye. Coming out of the palace, more lavishly attired than anyone he had ever seen, was the most beautiful woman he had ever laid eyes on. It was more than beauty, she seemed to hypnotise with her attractiveness, projecting it before her as if casting a spell over any who dared look in her direction. It was the Pharaoh. Her hair was jet black, her skin so smooth that it reflected the sun, her eyes so deep that a man might fall into them. Around her elegant neck hung a jewel on a golden chain. It flashed as it caught the sunlight but also seemed to be lit from within with a ruddy glow - a trick of the light perhaps. She was a magnificent sight, spectacular to the point of unreality, and Mahu drank in her beauty.

But at the same time he knew that they had been wrong about her. However sunk in her beauty he was, however much he knew that if she but asked he would die for her, however much he would have given his life just to brush his lips against hers, Mahu knew that they had been so very wrong about Ramose controlling her. As he stood beside her now, the High Priest seemed diminished, almost small. He might be the face of terror for the people of Egypt, but the mind behind it was that of his mistress. Queen Amunet carried with her an aura of control and of power. She stretched out her hand like a puppeteer and her soldiers responded, hurrying to help those fighting with Setka.

Mahu willed his legs into motion, but they refused to respond. Where was the use anyway? All he would do was die beside his friend.

As Mahu watched, Setka was overpowered. A soldier held a sword to his throat. But the Pharaoh shook her magnificent head, and she laughed - a sharp, crystalline sound on which you could have cut yourself.

Though every fibre of his being told him it was worthless, Mahu ran. Not away from the battlefield as he should, but towards his friend.

The shock of being unable to breath woke Mahu. He choked awake, finding himself smothered. He tried to scream but had not the breath for it. He kicked out, thrashing with arms and legs. Was he being buried alive?! The thing that had covered his face rolled free and Mahu realised it was a dead body. Another pinned his torso, two more were across his legs. They were beneath him as well, fleshily cold but still sticky with blood.

A sharp scream of terror made Mahu look up and he saw a man running away as fast as his legs would carry him. The man had been clearing the corpses from the spent battlefield, and witnessing one of those 'corpses' come back to life had been something of a shock to him.

With a grunt of effort, Mahu struggled free and looked about him. So many dead. The whole of the revolution it seemed to him. What now?

With nothing else to do, Mahu set out for home.

When he arrived it was to a home in mourning. Every family had lost at least one member, usually more. And for what? What had changed?

The following morning another corpse was added. The body of Setka appeared in the village as if dropped there by the desert wind, as had so many before. His eyes had been put out. As Mahu stared, the sound of the Queen's laughter rang in his head. Had that laughter been the last thing Setka had heard?

Chapter 16 - The Brotherhood of Egypt

"These walls tell the whole story," said Amelia, her eyes moving across the cryptoglyphs, almost glazed in an academic trance. She had thought the Priest's sarcophagus was a research opportunity, but this... She could spend the rest of her life down here.

"Maybe not the time, babe?" Izzy's voice cut into Amelia's study, reminding her why they were here.

"Sorry. This is like hardcore porn for Ancient Egyptian linguists. Which is why we're all single," she added.

Izzy looked away at that last sentence. It was funny, Amelia reflected, how the human brain worked. Here they were in an ancient tomb trying to save the lives of innocent archaeologists from a resurrected Mummy and a soon to be resurrected witch Queen, and relationship awkwardness could still be a factor. Amazing really.

It was something she might perhaps have pondered over for longer, had a sound not brought her horribly back to the present.

"Did you hear that?!" Izzy hissed, her voice high with terror.

Amelia nodded, too scared to speak.

"Sounded like a cat," wondered Arthur. Then Amelia's story came back to him. "Oh."

"Torches," whispered Amelia.

They each took a lighted torch from the wall and continued into the tunnel, torch in one hand, gun in the other. As they walked, Amelia tried not to think about the fact that they were three people whose combined experience of firing a weapon probably added up to watching a John Woo film, then turning it off halfway through because it was too violent. If the cat, or anyone else, attacked, then what might happen next was difficult to say. In Amelia's opinion there was a very good chance that they would end up shooting each other.

The next meow sounded nearer or louder or both. It echoed around the tunnel, making its position impossible to pinpoint and bringing them all to a sharp stop. Flashes of Mike the pilot's face shot through Amelia's mind, now accentuated in her imagination, so she could almost see that tattered and bloody visage before her now, illuminated by the flickering torchlight. Her breathing was coming shallow and rapid, her heart pattering quickly in her chest. The gun felt unwieldy and unnatural in her grip. As long as she had the thing she felt obligated to hold it, but she wished it wasn't there.

"Come on," she hissed.

"It might be up ahead!" Amelia could hear the fear in Izzy's voice.

"Or behind. We do what we came here to do." As it had before, Izzy's distress forced Amelia to be certain, and that certainty in turn gave Izzy confidence.

They moved slowly down the corridor as it descended further beneath the hills towering above. Amelia led the way, Izzy a step behind, glancing side to side, Arthur bringing up the rear, casting long looks at the way they had come, holding his torch out like a shield at their back.

"Oh hell..." Amelia muttered irritably. They had come to a crossroads in the tunnel. "How big is this damn place?"

She was about to flip a coin to pick a route, but a noise from the shadows made her twitch. Something had moved. There was the patter of fast moving paws, the rustle of movement, and then, just for an instant, beside the empty eye sockets of a long dead soldier, two green eyes appeared, unblinkingly reflecting the light of the torch in her hand.

Amelia's hand tightened sweatily on her gun, but the eyes vanished as soon as she saw them, and the pattering paws were on the move again. From somewhere in the darkness, a long yowl issued, echoing up and down the cavern. Amelia could hear Izzy's rapid, panicked breathing, could almost feel her fear in the air. The yowl sounded again, longer and louder, a far larger noise than should have come from so small an animal, amplified by the cave. It had sounded threatening to Amelia at first - a prelude to attack. But now she feared it for a different reason.

"Come on!"

"Which way?"

"Doesn't matter!"

And it didn't. From out of the right-hand tunnel figures appeared, summoned by the yowling of the cat. That was why there had been no guards on the entrance; they had an effective early warning system of their own. Even by the flickering torchlight, Amelia recognised the distinctive clothing of the men who had abducted her back in Cambridge.

"Run!" she yelled.

Arthur took off down the left-hand passageway, but Izzy seemed frozen to the spot. Amelia wheeled about to face their attackers. She pointed the gun.

And did nothing.

All she had to do was pull the trigger but the action refused to come. The men had started back a beat at the sight of the weapon, but now charged forward again, grabbing and disarming the two women.

A dank self-loathing curdled in Amelia's stomach. What had she done? Nothing; that was what. She had had her chance. She could have stopped them there. Even just the sound of a gunshot might have been enough to scare them off and perhaps rouse Izzy into flight. But she had not even had the courage for that. She was pathetic. If Maggie had been here she would have gunned them down without a qualm. But Amelia had let herself down and let her friend down. She did not know what price they were going to pay for it, but it would not be a pleasant one.

At least Arthur had got away - her stint as leader had not been a total failure. But when trying to picture how Arthur might rescue Izzy and her and the rest of the captured party, Amelia found her imagination unequal to the task.

One of the Brotherhood barked an instruction in Egyptian, addressing it to the shadows, and Amelia watched as Valerie sprang lightly out and hurried off down the left-hand tunnel in pursuit of Arthur. So much for rescue. She hoped that, if Arthur was found, then it was by the men and not the cat.

"Come on!"

As she and Izzy were marched through the ongoing tunnels of the dead, Amelia tried to say 'Where are you taking us?', 'Where are our friends?', 'You'll never get away with this!', or any one of a hundred other things that people are supposed to say in this situation. But the words all died in her throat, choked by fear. She wasn't a leader, she wasn't an action hero. Right now she didn't even feel like an archaeologist or linguist, she was just a scared little girl who was struggling not to cry.

They turned into narrow side tunnel and reached a heavy door - a recent addition from the look of it. The two men tossed Amelia and Izzy into the room and closed the door behind them. A single torch burnt on the wall, illuminating a small room, lined with paintings and cryptoglyphics.

"Why are you doing this?!" Izzy screamed at the retreating men.

One of them actually turned back to answer. "She has promised us eternal life." The door slammed.

Rubbing a bruised knee, Amelia got up and began to examine the walls.

"What are you doing?" asked Izzy. There was an almost manic hope in her voice, as if she thought her friend might have some plan. Perhaps the cryptoglyphics talked about a secret passage or a hidden key or something, anything!

"Reading the walls," Amelia replied simply.

"Why?"

Because there was nothing else to do and it stopped her from thinking about blood sacrifice.

"Because all this comes from history. Whatever the hell is going on here began millennia ago, and the more we learn about it the better informed we are about what they're planning. Maybe if we know that, then we can do something to stop it."

Izzy nodded, seeming comforted by this. She needed to believe that there was something that could still be done to save them, and Amelia was not about to take that away from her.

"What does it say?" Izzy asked, after a while.

"There was a revolution against the Pharaoh, Queen Amunet," Amelia said, piecing together what she had seen in the corridor with what she could read here.

"Who won?"

"The Queen."

"Ah."

"Those are all the revolutionaries we saw out there," Amelia said sombrely. "A dead army. It was a bloodbath. The leader of the revolutionaries was captured." She deciphered the name. "Setka."

"Do I want to know what they did to him?"

Amelia traced along the glyphs with her finger, and swallowed. "They put out his eyes, then killed him."

"For future reference," said Izzy, her voice unnaturally controlled, "the answer to my previous question was 'no'. I did not wish to know what they did to him."

"There's something more here." Amelia frowned at the wall. "It's been painted and then someone has scratched over it. But the scratches are cryptoglyphs."

"Ancient Egyptian graffiti?"

"I guess."

"What does it say?"

Amelia peered but then shook her head. "The scratches are too eroded."

"Does any of it mention the Priest?"

Amelia nodded, turning back to an unscratched portion of wall. "Lots. He led the Queen's army. Oversaw the executions of any left alive."

Izzy stared at the wall. "You know what I like about literature over history? None of the bastards are real."

"He died many years later," Amelia continued.

"Why do bad people always have long lives?"

"And was laid to rest in a sarcophagus covered in spells. Spells that would," she strained for the words, wishing she had her notebooks with her. "That would bring him back to life when his Queen's tomb was... Huh."

"What?"

Amelia pointed. "This word. If I'm translating right - and I'm not an expert."

"I thought you were?"

"No one's an expert, I'm just as good as there's been for the last few millennia. Anyway, if I'm right it means violated - 'when his Queen's tomb is violated'."

"Makes sense."

"But," Amelia went on, "if you were more accustomed to reading regular hieroglyphics, then you might mistake it for 'when his Queen rises from her tomb'."

Izzy frowned. "One sounds good, one sounds bad."

"One is a promise, the other's a threat," Amelia mused. "If I'm right, then all those legends about her coming back... It doesn't sound like she wanted to come back to life at all. Which would make sense - Ancient Egyptians looked forward to the afterlife."

"But all these people have been waiting for her."

"Yeah."

"Thinking she's going to reward them with eternal life."

166

Amelia pulled a face. "Never trust an Ancient Egyptian offering you eternal life, they may not mean what you think they mean."

She continued to trace the words with her finger. Inevitably many were unfamiliar but the great thing about a pictographic language was that you could always make an educated guess.

"She will return when Egypt has forgotten its traditions, its old gods and its one true Queen."

"Like King Arthur," piped up Izzy, delighted that her own degree could prove in some way relevant. "He's meant to sleep in Avalon until England is in crisis and needs him. Frankly I think he's long overdue, but still."

"Similar," allowed Amelia. "This seems to be a little more self-obsessed. The criteria for Egypt forgetting its old ways would seem to be if anyone dares to dig her up. Basically, when people have stopped being scared of Amunet enough to violate her tomb, then she'll come back and remind them why they ought to have stayed scared."

"That's not very King Arthur."

"But it could have been read that way." Amelia's mind was racing. "The King Arthur way. Especially if you kind of *really* wanted it to say that." Was she over-interpreting? Was she making too big of a jump? On the other hand it did all make sense. "Languages don't just vanish overnight." She was ostensibly talking to Izzy but really just thinking out loud, talking out the problem as she had to Valerie so many times in her flat when deciphering the cryptoglyphs, or dealing with Frank's betrayal. "The people who speak or read them diminish over time and the specifics get blended, watered-down. Then the stories that were written in those languages are passed on by word of mouth. No one can read the original anymore. So what the Brotherhood believe is a prophecy has been progressively diluted by misinterpretation and repetition over the last four thousand years."

"Like a really long game of Chinese whispers."

"Exactly!" Against the grain of the situation, Amelia was getting excited by the thrill of discovery. "You know, it never made sense. If the Queen was *planning* to come back - if she *wanted* to come back to life - then why would the trigger be someone entering her tomb? And why make the tomb so hard to find? If she wanted it to happen then she could have asked someone to knock on the door the day after she died! She didn't *want* anyone to disturb her eternal rest."

"But if they did, then she'd have something to say about it?" suggested Izzy.

"Imagine the Egyptians at the time of the Roman invasion..."

"Cleopatra?" Izzy groped for a common frame of reference.

"That's it. Their whole culture - already diluted by the Macedonians..."

"Alexander the Great."

"Right. Their whole culture is being eradicated." Amelia raced on, her lips struggling to keep pace with her brain. "They need something to cling to. What could be better than a monarch who said she would come back when the old ways had been forgotten? I'll bet you anything you like that's when the Brotherhood started! A cult based around the return of the Queen - a Queen who's already been dead a few thousand years - and relying on a pretty basic mistranslation of this story. They thought she would come back to reward the faithful. And in fact she's coming to punish the forgetful."

"Why now?" asked Izzy, captivated despite herself. "If the Brotherhood wanted to bring her back..."

"They didn't know where the tomb was." Amelia knew she was making it up as she went, but it all felt so right. "It was well-hidden. Deliberately well-hidden. And Egypt is big. They needed archaeologists. They've probably been monitoring every dig since Napoleon came here. Plus," her mind kept moving, jumping ahead in stages like an internet download, "they needed someone else to actually go in. Even if you think a powerful witch Queen *wants* to come back from the dead, you don't want to be the one to go busting into her tomb. It's like giving your boss an early morning wake-up call - they told you to do it but they'll still be pissed when you wake them up."

"You have a gift for apt analogies."

"Thanks."

"Why here with all the corpses?"

Amelia deflated. "That I don't know. Maybe because this was the scene of her greatest triumph."

"The slaughter of hundreds of people?" said Izzy dourly. "Maybe she wanted company in the afterlife?"

Another piece fell into place in the historical Tetris game currently playing in Amelia's head. "Maybe she did! Egyptian tombs are full of grave goods - stuff their owners would need in the next world. What if she needed an army?"

"Like the Terracotta Warriors in China."

Amelia nodded. "Only with real people. Think about how close this is to her tomb. And we don't even know how big it is - it could stretch all the way. Maybe her tomb is bigger than we think - a whole complex!"

Izzy shook her head. "That doesn't explain why she needs to be resurrected here."

"Well maybe it's just convenient."

"What about the Priest?"

"My guess is she can't be resurrected without him. When her tomb was opened it woke him up and he came to find her. That's how it was set up to work via the incantations on his sarcophagus. Of course he didn't expect to be in a different country, but he had the Brotherhood to help and here he is."

Izzy waited a beat before speaking, letting it all settle in her mind. "Are you sure about all this?"

"No," admitted Amelia. "But you've got to admit, it does make sense. More sense than the Brotherhood's version."

Izzy sighed. "I can't remember the last time anything made sense. Does any of this help us?"

She sounded desperate, and Amelia wished that she had something more positive to say.

"Well, it could mean that the people who brought us here are in as much trouble as we are. Only they don't know it. So there may come a point when guarding us ceases to be a priority. I guess it all depends on what the Queen is going to do once she's back."

"A cranky monarch dragged back from the afterlife out of a four thousand year doze?" Izzy shook her head. "The word 'wrath' is the one that keeps rattling around my head."

"Does fit the bill," Amelia admitted. "The question is: will her wrath be limited to the Brotherhood, or will she want to make the whole world pay?"

"We're assuming she *can* be resurrected."

Amelia shrugged. "I wouldn't have said so a month ago, but based on the evidence of the four thousand year old Priest walking

169

about, I'm guessing, yeah."

"Can't help thinking," murmured Izzy, staring towards the door, "that all those dead people out there have some part to play in this."

Nothing she had read on the wall suggested that, but Amelia had been thinking the same thing. And the imagination did not have to stretch too far to concoct a role that the dead revolutionaries might play in the wrathful return of Queen Amunet.

The hollow was narrow, dark and dank, and the other occupant kept staring at Arthur in the most disconcerting way. The empty eye sockets of his bunk mate were starting to make Arthur twitch nervously. The dead revolutionary seemed to be staring straight at him accusingly.

"It's not my fault. I needed somewhere to hide."

The revolutionary said nothing. Which was at least some relief.

"I only moved you over a bit. I could have just chucked you out onto the floor," Arthur pointed out.

The revolutionary stared on.

"Okay, you're right; I would have chucked you out onto the floor but I thought it would draw the attention of anyone passing," admitted Arthur, adding, "As will me talking to myself."

When Amelia had yelled for them to run it had seemed to Arthur like very good advice indeed, and he had followed the instruction with gusto. It was only when he had been going a while that he realised he was alone. Somewhere along the line - and he did not even know where - he had lost the two women.

"I couldn't go back for them," he said to his silent companion. "I mean, I could but... where would be the point? It's not like I could help them."

A brief pause.

"Yes, I know I have a gun! There's no need to go on about it."

So what now? Was he planning to spend the rest of his life here? He thought that he could probably find his way back out again. He would have to explain to Maggie where Amelia and Izzy were, but he could come up with something. And then, having decided that there really was nothing they could do, they could both just get on with their lives.

None of that appealed to him.

Arthur's quandary was that he was not a selfish man. He badly wanted to help his friends. He also did not think that he was a coward, although he was experiencing some difficulty making his legs understand that - they steadfastly refused to walk in the direction of danger. Fine; maybe he was a coward, but maybe there was something to be scared of! He was not prepared for this, not trained for this, and not keen on this.

He had a hunch that this was exactly the sort of thing that Helen had hoped he would encounter when she sent him out here. She would be very proud of him if he could save all his friends and stop the Mummy. She would be all over him, telling him that she had always known he had it in him and that now, finally, he was a man she could be with. And all he could think right now was; screw her! What the hell was wrong with being a bookish research archaeologist?

His mind turned to those women with whom he had come here, all of whom had more guts than he did. But more than that; three women who were simply themselves. It was impossible to imagine Maggie changing who she was or doing something she did not want to do, to please anyone. Though he had just met Amelia and Izzy, neither of them seemed to feel obligated by any outside pressure to be here or to do what they were doing; they just followed their own best judgement. None of them wanted to be in this situation, but it was their own decisions that had brought them to it and their own decisions that would see them through. Arthur, by contrast, was only here because his girlfriend had told him to be. He would have been far happier staying at home in pure research. That was where his heart lay, and if you did not follow your heart then what did you do? You couldn't live your life on someone else's approval. You had to be your own person.

Arthur sat up in the hollow in which he was crouched. He *would* find Amelia and Izzy, and Andoheb, and the rest. He *would* save the day. Not because it would please Helen, but because it was what he, Arthur, wanted to do.

He looked up at the dead revolutionary with a new sense of purpose, and his gaze was met by another pair of eyes, belonging to the largest rat he had ever seen, perched on the man's shoulder. It stopped nibbling the wasted skin for a moment to stare at Arthur.

Suppressing the shriek that welled up from within him, Arthur leapt athletically from the revolutionary's final resting place and raced down the corridor. It was not the bold exit that he would have liked to make on his way to saving his friends, but it would have to do. And it was very Arthur.

Chapter 17 - The Witch Queen

Was it worthwhile, Amelia wondered as she and Izzy were marched through the dark cave, trying to tell the Brotherhood that they had misread their prophecy? Probably not. Cultists tend to get a bit miffed if people (especially people from other cultures, and *especially* women from other cultures) start correcting their beliefs. That was the sort of plan that ended with someone yelling 'Sacrilege!' and killing her on the spot. Besides, she could not be certain that she was right. That was the thing about archaeology and history in general; there were few absolutes, it was all about interpretation. She had always considered that to be a good thing when viewing history from a pleasant distance, but when history rose up and got in your face then it could be a pain in the arse.

A flickering light issued from the entrance-way ahead of them and, as they passed through the doors, Amelia drew in breath, her eyes widening. They were now in an immense cavern, its roof supported by bulbous pillars, lit by a host of torches, the smoke from which curled up towards a hole in ceiling, which presumably led out somewhere in the middle of the Sarranekh. There were bodies of the dead here too, laid out on carved biers. Were these the leaders of the revolution? Or had they just run out of space elsewhere?

At the far end of the room was a broad dais, roughly three feet high, carved from the rock. At its centre stood something that looked chillingly like a sacrificial altar. Amelia glanced at Izzy, and the look on the younger woman's face was enough to confirm that she had come to the same conclusion. On the bright side, the altar was currently occupied, by what could only be the mummy of Queen Amunet. It was in a startling good state of preservation - which pleased the archaeological side of Amelia's mind. Behind the altar stood the Priest, and a chill ran through Amelia's bones at the sight of him. Back in his case at the Fitzwilliam Museum she had seen him on a daily basis, had even come to view him as a friend. He had not changed that much really; his shrivelled face allowing for only minimal movement. But any movement at all in something that had been immobile for millennia was unnerving. Then there were those eyes. The turquoise seemed to glow from within as he watched their approach. He turned and spoke to someone behind him.

Amelia frowned; someone could understand him? Even she

had needed him to write everything down. None of the Brotherhood had been able to understand the Priest, that was why they had kidnapped her. And it seemed inconceivable that the Mummy itself had picked up a second language - if you couldn't teach an old dog new tricks, then an ancient mummy was definitely a non-starter.

The figure to whom the Mummy spoke was a man wearing a bemused expression and extremely 'lived-in' clothes. He looked to be in his seventies, although lifestyle might have added a few years to his appearance. His face was immediately familiar to Amelia but it took a few moments for her to work out why.

"Professor Muller..." she breathed.

"What? What?" Izzy was still frantically hoping that Amelia was concocting some brilliant plan.

"I know that man."

"What a small world."

Though he had changed a lot, there was no mistaking the man whose face Amelia had seen, virtually every day, on the dust-jacket of the book that had been her Bible while deciphering the Priest's sarcophagus. Joseph Mulller's notes had been written up by a third party into an excellent treatise on the language of the Lost Dynasty, but he had been 'relieved of his duties' before completing his work.

Or had he? He was talking with the Mummy now.

Even given the exigencies of her current situation, Amelia still found brain space for a pang of annoyance. Bugger. She had thought she had got there first and it turned out that her antecessor had already done it and had gone further.

"Wait, I know him too," said Izzy.

"You do?"

"That's Old Joe. He's a homeless guy. Talks nonsense most of the time but he's harmless."

There were a lot of questions raised by all this but none of them really warranted pursuing right at this moment. The leader of the Brotherhood, dressed in a ceremonial robe, pointed towards the towering stone pillars on the left-hand side of the dais, and Amelia and Izzy were led towards them. They were each placed with their back to a pillar, and their hands tied around the stone column.

The leader of the Brotherhood strode over to them, a gloating smile on his face. "Thank you for coming. We thought we would be forced to go and look for you. You have made our ritual possible."

"Where are the rest of the excavation team?!" With things as bad as they could get, Amelia found the courage to speak slightly easier to come by.

"Their time will come." With that, the man swept away to continue preparations for the upcoming ceremony.

"Why just us?" asked Izzy.

Amelia shook her head; she did not know. But a potential reason hovered at the edge of her mind.

"Let me go, so I can kick your ass!"

The sound of Maggie's voice echoing around the hall as she was dragged in, pulled Amelia out of her troubling contemplation. Though they had left her only a matter of hours ago she seemed to have recovered much of her strength, and was currently using it to make the lives of the Brotherhood as awkward, and briefly painful, as possible. A few steps behind her, Valerie followed at the sedate but somehow quick pace that cats use when they want to look casual. She seated herself by the door.

"I am remembering the faces of everyone who touches me," said Maggie, as she was secured to the pillar next to Amelia, "and am planning appropriate retribution for each of you."

She then repeated this threat in Egyptian, just in case there was any misunderstanding, before turning to Amelia and Izzy.

"You seen any of the others?"

Amelia shook her head.

"Just us girls, huh?"

Which was the thought that had been percolating unpleasantly in Amelia's mind.

"Were there any other women on the team?"

Maggie shook her head. "Andoheb's funny like that. Old fashioned. Or sexist. One or the other."

There could be all sorts of reasons, Amelia considered, that the Brotherhood had only brought the women out for their ritual, but they all seemed to exist somewhere on a sliding scale from bad to horrifying. No sense in dwelling on it now.

"How did they get you?"

Maggie pulled a face. "Couldn't get the radio working. I wasn't going to just sit around doing nothing."

"You came in after us?!" wondered Izzy.

"I'm feeling much better now. Had some food in the camp.

Then I had a run in with some damn cat and these bastards jumped me."

Although Maggie being here seemed to suggest that their last hope of rescue had gone, Amelia could not help being glad to hear her voice again. Danger seemed somehow less dangerous with Maggie narrating it.

There was also some slim comfort to be had from activity elsewhere in the room. Perhaps it was absurd optimism on Amelia's part but there seemed to be some confusion between the Priest and the leader of the Brotherhood as Professor Muller translated between them. It almost seemed as if no one knew who was supposed to be doing what. The leader of the Brotherhood looked perplexed, almost irritated. He recovered quickly however and spoke.

"Seal the doors!"

The Brotherhood hurried to close and bar the door to the chamber.

"And now, the great Queen Amunet shall rise from her four thousand year rest, to rid the world of unbelievers and establish a new empire of Egypt!"

Now the Mummy itself spoke, its voice harsh and serrated, filling the room with the ease of a natural orator. Amelia, ever the Egyptologist, could not help wondering at the effect that voice must have had on people four thousand years ago. They were the first to hear it give a speech since then. Joseph Muller hurried forward to translate into Egyptian and English - it apparently being important that the sacrificial victims were kept in the loop.

"In blood she ruled, and in blood she will return!"

"It is my honour," said the leader of the Brotherhood, "as the last Priest of Amunet, standing here beside her first Priest, to perform the sacrifice that will restore our glorious Pharaoh to life. Bring her to me."

He pointed at Amelia.

But whatever shock Amelia felt at being selected for sacrifice was instantly blown away as the Mummy swung a knife out from the folds of his cloak, and in one swift stroke, slit the throat of the Brotherhood's leader. A feeling like a tidal wave of ice hit Amelia. She had never seen a man die before, certainly not like that. Her surprise however, was nothing to that of the man himself, who died with an undignified WTF expression on his face.

Before the man had even hit the ground, the Priest had spun around, with a speed he had not previously demonstrated, his knife gleaming, and two more of the devoted Brotherhood were dead. For a moment, the remainder of the Brotherhood stood frozen with shock, then, as one man, they panicked, rushing for the barred doors.

A roared instruction burst from the Priest's ragged throat, and Valerie sprang to her paws to meet them.

Amelia closed her eyes tight until the screaming had stopped, then gradually peeled them open. None of the Brotherhood had escaped the wrath of Queen Amunet. Eternal life was not all it was cracked up to be.

"Yikes," said Maggie.

One thought was now uppermost in the minds of all three women: if that's what he does to the people on his side, what will he do to us?

The Priest stalked back up through the chamber, wiping the knife on his forearm. Where the blood touched, his skin seemed to revivify for a moment, regaining its natural colour, fullness and elasticity before lapsing back into shrivelled emaciation. Reaching the altar he spoke again.

"The Queen shall rise!" Muller translated.

The Mummy paused and, for a brief second, its face seemed even more creased than usual. When it spoke again, the dramatic timbre and theatrical projection was absent.

"The Queen *must* rise." Muller tried to replicate the tone in his translation.

The knife descended again and again into the corpses of the Brotherhood as the Priest cut their bodies open. Izzy shut her eyes against the sight, even Maggie winced. Amelia wanted to look away but found she could not. It was not as bad this time. These were just bodies. As an Egyptologist she worked with the dead virtually every day - the only difference was how much time had passed. Although that *did* make a difference.

Turning to his Queen, and working with a deal more reverence, the Mummy Priest slit the linen wrappings that enclosed her. Against her better judgement, Amelia strained to see. It was not every day you got to see a mummy unwrapped. She had hoped for a remarkable state of preservation, assuming that the Witch Queen would cheat death by retaining her beauty. She had not. The only beautiful thing revealed was a bright jewel, that hung around the Queen's neck.

With clawed hands, the Priest scooped out the entrails of his late devotees and used them to anoint his Queen, painting her in the gory viscera of her fallen followers. The Priest lowered his head and murmured grating syllables in prayer.

Amelia looked to Professor Muller, but Old Joe could only shrug. Not even he could translate what was being said now.

The Priest laid his hand on Queen Amunet's forehead and...

Amelia jumped, pulling hard at her bonds, as the Queen moved, her corpse jerking into unsteady life. With broken, staccato movements like a puppet, or a badly animated model, the Queen sat up on the altar. A strange tide of vivacity waxed and waned across her body. As it had with the Priest, the blood of the Brotherhood seemed to restore youth to her long dead flesh, but could not sustain it. Her cheek swelled to fullness for an instant only to shrink back into concavity; her lips became red before shrivelling to wasted black; her breasts rose and fell; for a moment, an eye peered out before being swallowed once more by an empty socket. As the Priest applied a second gory coat, the fluctuations continued, the bloody corpse fading in and out of youth in an ever-shifting pattern of gore-fuelled vitality.

When the Queen spoke, her voice, like her body, fluxed from clear, almost musical tones to the cracked, genderless, croak of the grave.

"Well done, faithful Ramose." Muller seemed largely unaffected by all that was going on around him, continuing to simply act as a translator. Amelia wondered at his mental resilience; was that the result of years spent living on the street? Or the truly heroic intake of hallucinogens that rumour said he had consumed during his last few years at the university? Either way, it had worked out well for him.

The Queen's head turned slowly, still relearning the basics of movement, and her gaze lit on the women tied to the pillars. Her eyes (or eye sockets - changing every moment) roved up and down the row. Then she raised a thin arm to point directly at Izzy.

"Her. The beautiful one," Muller translated.

The vagaries of the human brain under pressure were brought home once again to Amelia, as her first thought was *'Sure, Izzy's the beautiful one. Same as always.'* Which was, at best, an idiotic thought in the circumstances.

Izzy shrieked hysterically as the Priest strode towards her, then reached behind the pillar to undo her ropes. Beside Amelia, Maggie was yanking at her own ropes, hurling herself this way and that, trying to get free. For herself... Amelia had no idea what to do. She couldn't get free, she couldn't help her friend. Her only skill was ancient languages, which had afforded her a better understanding of what was happening, but that did not seem to be helping. She was useless.

Holding Izzy's wrist in a grip of steel, the Priest dragged the screaming girl over to the altar. The Queen took Izzy's head between bloody hands, holding it tight, turning it left and right to examine the features, which apparently met with approval. By now, Izzy was beyond fear and out the other side. She had stopped screaming, her face a rictus mask of unblinking terror. Small gulping sounds issued from her throat as her body reminded her to breathe. She still struggled, but could not escape the Mummy's grip.

"What the hell's going on?!" asked Maggie, as furious at her own incomprehension as she was at her inability to do anything. "Is he going to kill her too?"

"I think she needs a body," said Amelia, hollowly.

"She's got one."

"The Priest can't make her young again, he can only make her like him - a walking corpse. The blood only lasts so long. But I think... I don't know, but I think he can put her in Izzy's body." As ever she couldn't be sure, but it all added up horribly well. This was why that damn cat had let them live. Its mistress needed the body of a young woman, and preferred to have some choice.

The Queen released Izzy and clasped the jewel around her neck with both hands. Then she dropped back to the altar, lifeless and inert.

"She's dead?" asked Maggie hopefully.

Amelia said nothing, but did not hold out much hope.

Still holding Izzy with one hand, the Priest used the other to remove the jewel from around the neck of the lifeless Queen, and hung it around Izzy's neck. Instantly, Izzy stopped struggling. Though she remained the same in every physical way, she seemed suddenly to grow. She held herself differently, moved more

179

elegantly. Izzy had never struck Amelia as someone who lacked confidence, but now she seemed to exude it - more than confidence, an assurance of her own self and her place in the world; at its top.

"Well done." The words seemed to astonish Izzy as she spoke them - she had not been expecting to speak in English. She went cross-eyed trying to look at her own mouth and then laughed at the phenomenon. There are few things more personal than a laugh. This was not Izzy's laugh. It was a peal of cut glass, somehow arrogant and mocking.

"She's the Queen," murmured Amelia.

"I got that," Maggie replied. "What now?"

"Ask her."

Whether she had heard this brief exchange or not, the Queen now answered it.

"Kill them."

But Amelia's attention had turned back to the Priest. Something was wrong. When the Queen laughed it seemed to awake something in him, some memory perhaps. Whatever the case, he seemed suddenly not the same. He seemed confused. Lost, even. He looked at Queen Amunet, and touched his turquoise eyes.

Chapter 18 - The Army of the Dead

Once he was done running Arthur began to retrace his steps the way he had come, but this was proving more difficult than he had at first imagined. The problem was that one torch-lit corridor lined with the bodies of the long dead looked pretty much like another torch-lit corridor lined with the bodies of the long dead. There were no sign posts in the City of the Dead; and had there been, Arthur would not have been able to read them. Amelia could have read them, he reminded himself, forced to ponder once again on his own inadequacies.

How big was this place? How long could he wander down here? How long would it be before that cat found him?

As he walked, wondering at the scale of the mass tomb, a thought occurred; how many entrances did it have? He remembered the first time he had heard the Mummy in the camp by night - he had gone out to look for it but it had vanished. Then, a few days later, when he and Maggie had seen it outside the tomb, it had been heading back towards the camp and had again vanished somewhere before they could cut it off. What if one of these tunnels led all the way to the southern side of the Sarranekh? That would also explain how the Brotherhood had got behind Maggie when she was following the tomb robbers after the attack on the camp.

The idea that there might be another way out - maybe even more than one - was a tantalising one, but he put it from his mind. He was not looking for the way out, he was looking for his friends.

Up ahead now, he could see a line of heavy, wooden doors in the wall. It was nice to see something different - something that practically qualified as a landmark down here - but he was sure that he had not passed doors before, which meant he was still going the wrong way. That said, it might be an idea to have a look inside. He was sure that was what Maggie would do.

None of the doors was anywhere near as old as the tomb itself, in fact they all seemed to have been installed recently - probably in the last month. The first one Arthur came to had a small barred window in it, through which he peered nervously.

A single torch lit the interior, and by its light Arthur saw something that made his heart nearly jump from his chest.

"Professor!"

Andoheb rolled over and sat up, staring in astonishment towards the door. "Arthur?"

"It's me!"

"Arthur, my boy!" The Professor leapt up (or struggled to his feet as quickly as was feasible for a man of his girth) and hurried to the door. "You escaped?"

"I was never captured. I was taking a walk when they attacked. What about you? Are you alright? Maggie said you were unconscious."

Andoheb rubbed the back of his head. "One of those swine hit me over the head before I knew what was happening. I'm afraid I was no use whatsoever. But you've spoken to Maggie? She's alright?"

"She was hurt. She's outside waiting for us."

"So... *you're* the one doing the rescuing?" Andoheb did his best to keep the uncertainty out of his voice.

"Not alone," Arthur explained. "Well... maybe alone now. It's a long story and I'm not sure this is the best time. Do you know where the key is?"

"How would I know a thing like that? The guards have one, that's all I know."

"I haven't seen any guards for a while," said Arthur. That was strange, wasn't it? It was a big place to patrol, but surely he should have at least heard them? Not that he was complaining. "I'll have to break the door down."

"It is fairly solid," said Andoheb, again trying not to hurt Arthur's feelings.

On reflection, Arthur had to admit that the door was more 'solid' than he was. Maggie probably would have kicked it in, but he wasn't Maggie. He was just Arthur.

"Maybe I can find something to crowbar the lock off!"

"Good plan!" Andoheb responded with almost too much enthusiasm.

Arthur hurried away.

"Arthur!"

Arthur hurried back. Andoheb was still at the window, staring at him in a little perplexity.

"Arthur, are you holding a gun?"

"Oh, yes. Maggie gave it to me."

182

Andoheb nodded. "Perhaps you might shoot the lock off?"

There were no two ways about it, Arthur was not cut out for heroism. On the other hand, he was here and he was trying. Ninety percent of heroism is showing up.

He levelled the gun at the lock and Andoheb stepped back from the door.

Arthur paused. "Can you hear something?"

From out of the surrounding shadows a noise was creeping. A noise of movement, soft and susurrating. It ought to have made Arthur run away, as it surely heralded the approach of the guards, but the noise seemed to be coming from every direction. It was not a trick of the echoes, whatever the noise was it was coming from all around him. Which meant it could not be the guards, and that there was nowhere to run.

The jewel around Izzy's neck (Queen Amunet's neck? Amelia did not know what to think any more) began to glow, and she turned her attention to the rest of the chamber. She stretched out her hands, fingers spread wide, then clasped them into tight fists.

"Not that I'm complaining," Maggie hissed to Amelia, "but why isn't he killing us?" She nodded towards the Priest.

"I don't think she was talking to him," replied Amelia. The Priest still seemed to be struggling with issues of his own. Strange to think that a mummy might have personal problems, but there was no other way Amelia could interpret his behaviour. There was some sort of internal battle going on.

"Then who's she talking to?" Maggie pressed. "There's no one else... Oh you've got to be shitting me!" Her eyes slowly turned to the ranks of the dead arrayed in the main chamber before the dais. "That lot?"

"Maybe not just them," said Amelia, thinking of the army of dead men they had seen on their way in. How many were there? Hundreds? More? What would the Queen do with an undead army? What were her plans? Not that it would matter to Amelia herself - her part in this story, and any other story, would be over in the next few minutes.

"Doesn't anyone stay dead around here?" growled Maggie.

"I think we might."

Maggie shot an angry look at Amelia. "What sort of a way to

talk is that?!"

Amelia felt as if she was being scolded by a teacher. "I'm being a realist."

"Well you can damn well stop!" Maggie rolled her eyes in exasperation. "We've just watched a Mummy bring a four thousand year old Egyptian Queen back to life to possess the body of a classics student. This is the last situation to which 'realism' should be applied!"

None of which was of any help, but it did make Amelia feel better. Maggie wasn't giving up and so nor would she. She looked out into the chamber.

There! One of the corpses had moved. Now another. And another. They were coming back to life, called by the power of the witch Queen and nourished by the spilling of blood. The Brotherhood had intended the excavation team to be the sacrifice that would bring back the dead revolutionaries - in the event, they themselves had become that sacrifice. It was as Arthur had said; it took the blood of many to resurrect a Queen, but the same amount of blood could bring back many more commoners. Maybe even a whole army.

"Is someone there?" Perhaps it was a dumb thing to say, but if there *was* someone out there then they could already see Arthur, who was well lit by his own torch, so there seemed no harm in asking.

"What's going on?" asked Andoheb. "Why haven't you shot the lock off?"

"I think you might be better off where you are," murmured Arthur. He could not see anything yet but was overwhelmed by a sense of foreboding. Something was about to happen. Something was already happening.

The noises were louder now and had changed in character. There was a cracking like someone walking on dry twigs, a scraping of something dragged along the ground, all underscored by that whispering sound he had heard earlier.

A shadow moved and Arthur flattened his back against the wall, trying to see everywhere at once. Now they were all moving, shadows closing in on him from all around, indistinct shapes getting nearer, now passing into the light and revealing the hideous decomposed faces of the revolutionaries. The Army of the Dead had risen.

Amelia managed to tear her gaze away from the reanimating corpses of the revolutionary army to look back at the Priest. He was touching his eyes again.

A thought wheedled its way into Amelia's mind, joined up with another and together they suggested a plausible translation for that scratched cryptoglyphic graffito she had seen earlier. Was it possible? She could only guess at how it might have happened, but...

As she wondered, treasuring the brief glimmer of hope that the thought had dared to kindle in her, she saw the Priest look up towards his Queen. The facial expressions of the Priest were always slow to form and hard to interpret - his face partly hidden by bandages, the expressions hampered by atrophied muscles and wasted skin. But there was no mistaking the look that he now directed at the Amunet/Izzy creature standing at the front of the dais, laughing - it was a look of pure hatred.

Chapter 19 - The Burial

The sharp rapping of the staff that accompanied High Priest Ramose wherever he went was magnified by the hard rock of the floor and re-echoed down the long corridors of the vast tomb, hacked from the mountain to house the revolutionary dead, who would serve Queen Amunet in the next life, when the time came. It was an honour, it was also the ultimate punishment for their disloyalty - they had been workers in this world, they would be slaves in the next. It had taken time to properly decorate and extend the natural cave complex in which the corpses had been preserved all this time, but that was no matter; the Queen would not be needing it any time soon.

The guards shifted nervously as the High Priest approached. They had not done anything wrong - that they could think of - but people did not need a reason to be nervous of Ramose's approach, they just were. It saved time.

"Where?" asked the High Priest as he reached the guards.

One of the guards pointed at the wall, all three of them finding their tongues temporarily useless. Ramose turned his bright eyes to see the hieroglyphics scrawled over the official decoration: 'Setka Lives'. He regarded it dispassionately.

"When?"

"Sometime last night, High Priest." One of the guards found his voice enough to stammer a response.

"It's such a large tomb. We can't cover all of it," another said, immediately wishing that he hadn't. The Priest hadn't asked for any explanation, making excuses just made it sound as if he was... making excuses.

But Ramose seemed unconcerned. He focussed on the wall. It had been years since the brief workers' revolution and yet this slogan continued; Setka Lives. The mass slaughter would have been easily forgotten, but the death of one man had somehow galvanised the murmurings of dissatisfaction that had already existed but lacked focus. Setka had given them focus. He had become a martyr, a hero, a symbol into which all the hopes and dreams of the downtrodden had been poured, like some Gestalt entity, waiting to be called back into existence. Word had it that the workers had not buried Setka, but that the whole village had pooled their meagre earnings to pay for him to be mummified, as befitted someone of his ancestry. As befitted their hero.

'Setka Lives'. Ramose wondered if people would be scrawling his name so long after his death. Would they even remember it? Yes, of course they would. He would make sure of that.

"Clean it off."

The High Priest did not wait for a response but stalked back up the tunnel the way he had come. In a way it was futile; there would be more such scrawlings, they could not find them all. Some were painted, some scratched on the rock or into the decorative paintwork, some had been quite elaborately carved. A condemned prisoner had written it on the floor of his cell in his own blood. It should not have troubled Ramose, but it did. He was an expert in reading the signs of nature that portended the future and they told of a future for him in which Setka figured. The man's death had achieved nothing, and yet in it he seemed to have accomplished what he could not in life. When the building of the new capital faltered - thwarted by labour shortages and threats from outside - people claimed it as a triumph for Setka. When the floods failed to come, when invasion threatened, when any of the Queen's grandiose plans for empire-building fell apart, there hovered the unseen hand of Setka, reaching from the beyond. And when people believe something passionately enough, it becomes true. Setka Lives.

Night was falling as Ramose left the Sarranekh. Up ahead of him was the latest Workers' Village - a makeshift town housing those working on the mass grave. The fires were lit at its outskirts and around them the people sat and drank and laughed and told their stories. Ramose knew that many of those stories would be about him, about Setka, and about the ghosts of the Sarranekh. The stories would change in the telling through the years, but they would last as long as the desert itself.

Travelling back from the Sarranekh to the capital took several days, and Ramose would not have made the journey out there simply to check on the mass grave of the traitorous revolutionaries. There was another project in that area, a far more important one and a far more secret one, though one that he hoped was not urgent. Pharaohs had always constructed their tombs long before their deaths so they could have their say on the style in which they were to spend eternity. It had been Ramose's idea that Queen Amunet's should be in the Sarranekh, partly because of its seclusion, partly because the revolutionary tomb provided a useful smokescreen. He could claim that any workers and craftsmen being shipped out west were going to work on the mass grave. And when the Pharaoh's tomb was finished then those who worked on it could be quietly killed. A very neat plan.

Arriving back in the capital and at the palace, Ramose was met by one of the Queen's attendants. "The Pharaoh welcomes you back, High Priest, and invites you to an audience in her chamber."

Ramose stalked off towards the Queen's private apartments. Though he tried to suppress the feeling, whenever he walked through the palace, Ramose could not help thinking how much better the new one would have been. People were so short-sighted, so unable to see what would be best for them, for everyone, in the long-term. There was no denying that the empire of Pharaoh Amunet had failed to materialise as she and Ramose had planned it. There had been a time when she could drive her people towards her vision of the future by fear alone. Somehow that time had passed. The people had become stubborn, wilful and uncooperative. Again, it was the spectre of Setka.

"Enter!"

The Queen wore a mask when Ramose entered her private chamber, in deference to the pretty young slave girl who was pouring wine for her. Ramose bowed low to his Pharaoh, who very slightly inclined her head in reply - a show of respect she would not have given anyone else living.

"Welcome back, High Priest."

"Thank you, my Queen. It is an honour to be in your presence once again."

"Your return is well timed. There are pressing matters to attend to."

Ramose followed the subtle trend of his Pharaoh's eye-line to observe the slave girl. She was perhaps sixteen or seventeen, with wide, doe-like eyes and an appealing bow-shaped mouth set in a desperately pretty face. She was small in stature, slimly built, and extremely shapely in the revealing costume she wore, showing off her smooth skin and youthful flesh. In all this she was typical of the palace slave girls the Queen sought out. They never lasted long - there was always someone better.

Ramose looked back to the Pharaoh, nodding his agreement. "When, my Queen?"

"Now."

"Girl!"

As the slave looked around at Ramose, the High Priest cracked his staff upon the floor and her pretty eyes widened still further. She tottered on her feet like a sleepwalker, staring dumbly at the Priest. He beckoned her and she came.

Queen Amunet removed her mask and laid it to one side, then clasped the jewel around her neck.

When Ramose left the Queen's apartment an hour or so later he spoke to the guards who stood outside.

"The Queen's slave has died. Remove her body."

The guards did as they were told. Perhaps they even noticed that the slave girl who they took out, did not look much like the one who had gone in. Ramose headed back to his own apartments by the temple.

As the years had passed and the frustrations of failure mounted, the Queen's focus had shifted from empire-building to a new obsession. At first she wore a mask to hide the passage of time, but then more drastic measures were needed, measures she did not hesitate to take. People had begun to whisper about the number of pretty young girls who vanished by night, never to be seen again. The jewel she wore around her neck at all times was said to have been a gift from her great aunt, a woman sentenced to death for witchcraft. Even Ramose did not know if that was true, but he knew that the jewel could have told many stories, and that the mask now hid a greater secret than wrinkles.

But if the Queen could live forever, then perhaps the great empire was still a possibility. The thought cheered Ramose - while the Queen lived he was safe in her protection. But they had both made many enemies. Setka Lives.

Years passed. The unfinished temple-palace by the Sarranekh was scavenged for building materials and its foundations reclaimed by the desert, as if it had never existed.

The death of Pharaoh Amunet came as a shock to all, perhaps because she had never seemed to get older. Perhaps because people like that never seem to die. Popular rumour had it that she was

189

strangled by a slave girl, whose sister had gone missing from the Pharaoh's service the previous year. It was a rumour angrily suppressed by the authorities. Pharaohs could not be killed by slaves, the Queen had simply tired of this world and decided to continue her dominion in the next.

Her funeral was a day of national mourning but, to protect the sanctity of her tomb, its location was a closely guarded secret. Ramose might be able to pretend that everyone was in mourning, but he was wise enough not to believe it himself. Setka Lives.

On the day she was laid to rest, the High Priest, old himself now though still with an aura of power surrounding him, made a great speech, the content of which was sent to every town and village in the country.

"The Pharaoh has not left us forever. She will return." It was the first time in any public address that Amunet had been acknowledged as 'she', as if in death she had earned the right to her gender. "I have seen the future," the High Priest continued, "there will be a world that stretches further than the mind can conceive. A world beyond the seas. This is the world which fate has decreed the Pharaoh should rule. She was too great to be confined to this one, and so she will return. I myself shall guide her back to this world from the next. She will rule again, and this time forever. When the world has forgotten her, when they have forgotten our gods and our traditions, Pharaoh Queen Amunet will return to set them back upon the true path." Ramose had plans for his Queen that she knew nothing about.

It was a speech about a heroic quest to make the empire of Egypt live forever, and yet it was delivered like a threat.

"And," Ramose concluded, "she will have an army to do it."

Mahu, standing in the crowd, heard that last sentence, and felt his skin crawl.

Some said that High Priest Ramose had gone to join his mistress in the next life. Some said he was removed by the gods for a higher purpose. Some said that, like Queen Amunet, he had chosen the time of his own passing. Some said he had been poisoned by the new Pharaoh, who was as afraid of the old priest as everyone else. A few said that he had died because he had been alive for so long, but no one listened to them. The important thing was that he was dead, and he was buried with all ceremony due to someone who had served the empire so well and so diligently. Great care was taken to ensure that it was a magnificent funeral, more befitting a Pharaoh than a priest - even in death there was a general feeling that it was best to keep Ramose happy. He was also buried out in the desert, as far from the capital as was possible without it being 'disrespectful'. The new King did not like the idea of Ramose's ghost looking over his shoulder.

The night after the High Priest was buried, a small party moved through the dark sands, carrying a long box between them. The moon was irritatingly bright and illuminated their furtive journey to the tomb. It was a long job to re-open it - again, the King had not taken any chances and had specified a big, heavy door, though even the most fearless of tomb robbers was not entering the tomb of Ramose. You had to have a very good reason to do that. People knew the stories.

While the tomb's location had been determined only recently, The High Priest had made preparations for his death. He had personally overseen the decoration of his sarcophagus and had placed certain incantations upon it. To have those incantations depicted he had hired the best artists and scribes Egypt could provide. A lesser man might have been concerned that such information would get into the hands of his enemies, but Ramose wanted people to know his plans, knowing that fear would protect him.

If Ramose had a flaw, then it was his arrogance.

Mahu peered into the darkness of the tomb, lit by the flickering torch he held. He hoped that the flickering would disguise the shaking of his hand - it would not do for his companions to see his fear, they were risking enough in this venture.

"Come on," he whispered. There was no one to hear them out here in the desert, miles from anywhere and with the whistling wind swallowing all sound, but the thought that someone might be listening from within the tomb pricked at each of them.

The little party crept into the tomb, the long box held between them. Mahu had been in many tombs in his life - they all had, building them was their business - but this was the first time he had been in an occupied one. It felt different; colder somehow. Though it had only been sealed that day, it seemed haunted by old ghosts, the air stale and still, as if it had not been disturbed for centuries.

"This way." Mahu felt he needed to keep speaking, if only in these short interjections, to keep morale up, to prove that he was not frightened to do so, and to bring some sound to the silence that lay like a lead blanket on the tomb.

As might be expected with the grave of someone like High Priest Ramose, there were booby traps along the way, but Mahu and his companions side-stepped and bypassed them with practised ease. Ranofer was considered an expert in such traps, one of the finest in Egypt. If Ramose had been expecting trespassers at all - and he had counted on fear keeping most away - then it had not been trespassers like this. Artisans were commoners, and such people were too superstitious to enter the tomb of the dreaded Ramose.

Gradually they picked their way closer to the centre of the tomb, arriving at the door to the burial chamber itself.

"Never seen a seal like that," commented Ranofer. He spoke without inflection - just saying - but there was a sense of foreboding in his words that they all felt.

"I heard he made it himself," said Khuy, the most nervous of the party. "From a secret mixture of bees wax, ground bone and human blood."

"If it's a secret mixture then how did the person who told you that find out?" asked Mahu. He was not letting these fears in now, it was just a seal.

To prove the point he broke it with a mallet and the shards clattered noisily to the floor.

Without any member intending to, the group stood still a moment, listening for whatever curse Ramose had placed upon the seal coming to annihilate them.

Nothing came.

"There," said Mahu, with finality tempered by relief. "Now we'll have no more of this nonsense."

They began to attack the heavy stone door.

The slab of granite had been built to keep people out (and possibly in), but to a group of men who had spent their lives working with rock, it was the work of barely half an hour to remove it. A thin breath of cold air whispered out though the jagged hole, making the hairs stand up on the back of Mahu's neck. He stepped through into the burial chamber of High Priest Ramose. It occurred to Mahu that,

192

although the man had dominated most of his adult life, this was the closest he had stood to the High Priest since the day that he and Setka had gone to meet with him. How long ago that had been.

"Setka Lives," he murmured under his breath, a little mantra to give him strength.

Iumeri edged as close as he dared to the great sarcophagus that dominated the middle of the room and held his torch closer to illuminate the hieroglyphics.

"Well?" asked Mahu impatiently.

"It's like he said," Iumeri confirmed. "He will rise when the sleep of his Queen is disturbed. He will bring her back to life and back to power. It is a powerful spell."

"Let's obliterate it!" hissed Ranofer.

"No!" Khuy held his friend back. "You cannot scratch out words of power. Remove the words but the incantation remains."

Mahu nodded. For once Khuy had a point. Besides, that was not why they were here. They were here to ensure that the evil of Queen Amunet never troubled the world again. And for revenge. They did not know where she had been laid to rest - years of searching had proved dangerous and fruitless - but perhaps they could still stop her, when they themselves were no more than dust in the desert wind. Then the revolutionary dead would have their vengeance.

"Let's get this thing open."

There was not a lot of enthusiasm amongst the group as they laid down the box they had been carrying and moved to the stone sarcophagus. They lined up wooden wedges with the fine gap where the lid met the base.

"1, 2, 3!"

With a loud thunk, mallet hit wedge. Slowly the wedges forced the lid up until levers could be inserted to move the heavy stone lid to one side.

"Don't push it off," Mahu warned. "It might break. And anyway, we'd never get it back on." And it had to go back on. The whole plan hinged on everything being as it was. He wondered briefly if the plan was good, if it would work. He would never know.

With the lid now half off, the workers were able to peer inside at the wooden coffin of Ramose.

"Nothing like him," judged Iumeri. The painted face on the

coffin had certainly failed to capture the likeness of the late High Priest, it looked kind, almost benevolent. Presumably this had been intentional, as Ramose always got what he wanted.

"There is something about the eyes," suggested Ranofer. The eyes might be kind but they were hard, and had that turquoise brilliance that Ramose's had had in life.

"Let's get the bastard out of there," said Mahu.

Together they lifted the wooden coffin lid and placed it to one side. Mahu looked back in. There was the mummy of Ramose, freshly wrapped, arms folded neatly across his chest, his staff laid beside him. Mahu jumped a little as the shifting shadows cast by the torch made it look as if the mummy had moved.

He grinned at his comrades. "For a moment there I thought he..."

Ramose's arm shot out like a striking snake, grabbing Mahu and dragging him down into the sarcophagus. The other men, panic-stricken, backed away, while Khuy ran screaming for the door.

As he was dragged closer, Mahu saw the mouth beneath the bandages open and a long rasp of angry breath was sucked in, as if all the demons in the world were being drawn into that dry corpse to fill it and give it life and strength enough to kill one more time. Another hand snaked out, gripping Mahu behind the head. The hand felt thin and fragile but the grip was solid as stone and the strength beyond anything Mahu could have imagined. He was powerless to resist. The mummy growled and Mahu was sure he heard an evil satisfaction - it longed to kill. As his head drew closer it blocked out the torchlight, but with the last of it Mahu saw a glint of turquoise iris flaring into life through the linen of the bandages.

With his free hand, Mahu grabbed the side of the sarcophagus, pulling with all his strength in a useless attempt to fight against the mummy. It was laughing now, a rattling, sepulchral echo beating against the inside of its ribs. As he adjusted his grip to pull back again, Mahu's hand touched something that moved. It was the mallet he had used to hammer in the wedge. He gripped it, raised it, and brought it down with all his might.

The mummy howled in anger, as its arm snapped, forcing it to let go of Mahu's head. Mahu brought the mallet down again, now on the Priest's chest. Then on its head. Then again and again and again. He screamed as he pounded the mallet into the skull of Ramose till

194

nothing was left but a pulp of skin, bone and the straw with which his skull had been stuffed.

"Mahu...?" Ranofer edged forward; guilty of his own fear but still terrified.

Mahu stared into the coffin of the man who had haunted his nightmares for so many years, the man who had robbed him of friends, of freedom, of his very life. The revenge had come all too late, but it had come.

"I'd do that to your Queen too if I knew where to find her," he growled down at the broken mummy. "But that pleasure belong to Setka."

He turned back to his friends. This was no time for recriminations - when something like that happens you never know how you might react, and he certainly wasn't blaming them for their fear.

"Let's try this again."

They took the body of Ramose out of the tomb, quartered it, and buried the pieces in the sand, far apart. If his mummy had somehow been able to survive what Mahu had already done to it, then it would not survive that.

Back in the tomb they opened the long box to reveal the mummy of Setka. Iumeri placed slivers of turquoise over the revolutionary leader's empty eye sockets, tucking them into the bandages, 'So he will be able to see'. The spells placed on the stones had cost them all the money they could raise. Reverently, they lifted Setka into the coffin of the High Priest.

"I'm sorry," whispered Mahu. "I know it's not where you would want to lie, but I think it's the only way."

They could have just left the tomb empty, but who knew what incantations the Priest had placed on the tomb of the Queen? Perhaps she would rise without his help. This was the only way - the only way Mahu could think of - to be sure.

They placed the lid back on the coffin and closed up the sarcophagus.

"Will he remember who he is when he wakes?" asked Ranofer.

Iumeri shook his head. "Not at first. He will be entirely animated by the High Priest's incantations, and there is nothing I can do to stop that. He will do as the Priest would have done. He will seek out the Queen, he will bring her back to life, he will not let anything or anyone stand in his way. He may well do terrible things. But the longer he is alive, the more of Setka will return."

"He will stop her," said Mahu, with confidence. "He is Setka. He will find a way."

They sealed up the tomb as best they could. No doubt tomb robbers would find it and would plunder the grave goods within. But they would leave the sarcophagus untouched.

After all, this was the tomb of Ramose.

Chapter 20 - The Hero of the Revolution

"SETKA LIVES!" Amelia screamed the words at the top of her lungs. Who knew how much of the Mummy's brain remained working? How much was personality, how much driven by the spells that had empowered it this far? But if there was one sliver of the man he once had been remaining alive within him, then Amelia was determined to awaken that spark.

At the sound of the name, Queen Amunet spun on her heel to look at Amelia with an imperious expression. Never had Izzy's red hair flowed with such majesty, seeming to billow about the haughty face which was imposed onto Izzy's as if it had been forced into a mould.

But she was not the only one who reacted. The Mummy straightened. Amelia realised she had not seen it stand tall before, it had always been an angular creature, stooped and bent like a bow. Now, despite its still horrific aspect, it suddenly seemed... Heroic. She had been right. How he had got into the Priest's sarcophagus she could not imagine - a mix up or the work of some unsung hero whose name was lost to history - but this was not the mummy of High Priest Ramose, but of the revolutionary leader, Setka.

"Professor Muller!"

Old Joe looked somewhat taken aback to hear his old title, almost ready to look behind him as if to say, 'Who, me?'.

"Tell him that they are his people!" yelled Amelia, indicating the dead men who were struggling back to life.

Muller, caught up in the moment - even if he was not exactly sure what that moment was - delivered Amelia's words to the Mummy in the tongue of the Lost Dynasty.

Amelia could almost see the confidence flowing into the Mummy, his body seeming to swell within its linen wrappings as he remembered who and what he was. He moved more fluidly and more purposefully, as if up to now every movement had been a battle with himself. Suddenly the knife was in Setka's hand and he was striding towards the Queen.

"Don't hurt her!" Amelia suddenly realised the deficiency in this particular plan. The Mummy could not see this creature before him as anything but Queen Amunet, but if he killed her then Izzy died as well. Muller translated immediately but the Mummy of Setka did not stop.

The Queen, however, was not about to go down so easily. The undead revolutionaries, now the soldiers of Amunet, flowed forwards, putting themselves between Setka and their Queen.

Either the soldiers did not like the light, or perhaps they simply did not need it. As they closed in on Arthur, cowering against the wall, they put out each torch they came to, closing a skin and bone hand over the flame and squeezing till it was extinguished. It was not a sight that gave Arthur much hope for his chances, but he had a gun and he would damn well use it! He fired wildly into the approaching soldiers, and with so many of them, even someone with Arthur's level of firearms experience could not help hitting something. The ancient soldier stopped for a moment to stare down at the hole in his chest. He managed to raise his bony shoulders in an emaciated shrug, and resumed walking.

"Shoot the lock off and get in here!" Andoheb yelled from within the cell.

"They'll just push the door open! You're safer like this!"

"But you..."

"There's no sense in both of us dying!"

Andoheb looked almost broken. "This is a very brave thing you're doing, Arthur."

"I think I'm about to wet myself."

"Even so," Andoheb reached through the bars, "I shall ever regard you as the best and wisest man whom I have ever known."

To a Sherlock Holmes fan, there was no higher tribute.

The last of the wall torches was crushed out of existence, so the only light came from the one Arthur was carrying. He swung it around him, creating a semi-circle of fire against the wall. Andoheb thrust his own torch out through the bars of his cell, waving it about as best he could. Arthur wondered how long could he hold out like this? Probably not long, but maybe quicker would be better.

It occurred to him that, when you added it up, this was all Helen's fault.

The men who had once been his friends and comrades attacked Setka, hurling the Mummy off the dais, knocking over a burning torch as he went.

Amelia gazed in horror. Izzy's body was now safe, but the Mummy had been their only chance. Perhaps they would have been better off if Setka had killed her - who knew where Izzy's mind even was now, or if it could be restored to her? But the Mummy was not done fighting yet, it battled back against the soldiers. Was it stronger because it had been resurrected longer and had more time to get used to being alive again? Or because resurrected mummies are naturally stronger than the more run of the mill resurrected dead? (Amelia resisted using the 'z' word - you had to draw the line somewhere or you were just giving up on reality as you knew it.) Or perhaps Setka was stronger because he was a man fighting for something, not simply a walking corpse with no mind or will of its own. Amelia hoped it was that last one. Perhaps that might make the difference.

A movement and a cry beside her caught Amelia's attention. Maggie flung herself flat along the floor, stretching out one leg as far as it would go, the ropes that bound her to the pillar stretched tight, her arms almost pulled from their sockets as she clawed with out-stretched foot for the torch which the Mummy had knocked down. Amelia watched with baited breath as Maggie got a toe hold. She gasped in pain as the flame caught her ankle but still managed to drag it closer and closer, until finally it was at the base of the pillar, allowing Maggie to hold her rope against the flame.

"Come on, you son of a bitch!"

Amelia glanced back to the fight. The Queen (how swiftly Amelia had ceased to think of her as Izzy) watched as the soldiers overwhelmed the Mummy with weight of numbers. She laughed that sharp, cruel laugh.

"A shame we cannot blind you again, but we will think of some other way to punish you for what you have done to my faithful Ramose."

"Get in!" Maggie had the good sense to whisper rather than shout as her rope snapped.

"Untie me!" Amelia hissed, and Maggie quickly complied.

"See if you can get your friend back," said Maggie, as Amelia's ropes dropped.

"What are you going to do?"

But Maggie was already moving, running to the edge of the dais and hurling herself onto the soldiers attacking Setka. None of them were armed (you didn't bury your enemies with weapons if you believed in an afterlife - that would be asking for trouble), and they still had the unsteadiness of the newly alive. They were also, if Maggie's vicious punch to the skull was anything to go by, somewhat fragile. On the negative side, a busted skull did not seem to stop them from moving. The revolutionary dead had not been brought back to life as Amunet had, nor even as Setka had, they were simply animated corpses, no trace remaining of the men they had been.

Tearing herself away from the compelling spectacle of Maggie battling the undead, Amelia looked towards Queen Amunet. It was a strange sensation - physically this was Izzy, not a feature out of place, and yet somehow it looked nothing like her. Amelia had to hold onto that thought.

The sudden arrival of Maggie into the fight made Amunet turn to see where she had come from. There she saw Amelia, running towards her. And she laughed.

When she had started to run, Amelia had not had any plan of what she might do when she reached her target. She had a vague idea that by knocking Amunet over she might sort of dislodge the Queen from her friend's head. If she could knock her unconscious then maybe Izzy would come back. Then there was the jewel, which clearly had something to do with the possession - if she could get her hands on that then surely it was game over? Any of these options was worth trying and they all started with knocking an ancient Egyptian monarch on her smug backside.

In the event, running into Amunet was like running into a wall. Amelia rebounded, stunned and fell back on her own backside. The Queen stooped, grabbed her by the throat and picked her up as if she weighed no more than a rag doll. The world turned blood red as Amelia fought for breath, suspended in the air by her neck. The Queen looked at her with detached interest.

"I know you, don't I?" So Izzy was still in there somewhere, her brain still accessible to the woman currently in control of her body. "I feel a strange compulsion not to kill you." The Queen casually threw Amelia across the dais. "I believe I can overcome it."

Amelia lay on the ground tasting blood and dirt. The world spun unhappily around her and the various pains in her body all clamoured for attention. Why was an ancient linguist, who was happiest in front of the fire with a good book and a properly made cup of tea, lying on the floor of an underground mausoleum doing battle with a supernaturally powerful queen inhabiting the body of her friend? Admittedly, that was not 'all in a day's work' for anybody, but there were people who would be far better suited to it. Adventure had never been part of Amelia's life plan and she had never really worried about its absence. Then again, that life plan had already taken a few detours from the ideal. She had to admit that, when all this started, she had found herself unexpectedly thrilled by it. Maybe there was a world beyond tea and literature - not better, but perhaps equal. She had even wondered if, since her life plan had already been diverted, maybe it could be expanded to include adventure.

She was not thinking that now. If she had been a proper 'adventurer' - if such things existed outside of Hollywood - then she would have been worrying about what her abject failure would mean to the rest of the world. Was Amunet a threat to the globe? To the security of the human race? Or would she be defeated by modern weaponry in one absurdly mismatched battle? After which, everyone would laugh at the idea that anyone would have died to stop her. What fools those people were. Perhaps it was just as well such things were not on her mind. All Amelia could think about was herself; how she had got here, why she had taken such stupid risks, what could have possessed her. None of it mattered now. She had two choices: lie here and die, or stand up and die.

Painfully, Amelia clambered back to her feet.

The Queen watched her, smiling, and tapped her temple. "She knew you would do that."

Aiming low this time, Amelia ran at the Queen again, more out of anger than expectation that it might do any good. It didn't. Moving like lighting the Queen side-stepped so Amelia thundered past awkwardly. She turned, skidding on the dusty floor, but the Queen was instantly behind her. The fingers closed on her throat again. The red descended over her eyes, and beyond it, beckoning in the distance, darkness.

A dead hand closed over the head of his torch, and the last light went out, plunging Arthur into darkness.

"Arthur!" Andoheb cried uselessly.

Arthur lashed out. He fired into the dead soldiers, that he could no longer see but which he knew closed in all around him. It didn't do any good. With the light gone, the noises suddenly seemed much worse, much louder, much more threatening, pushing in on him. Hands clawed at him, tugging at his arms and legs. Bony fingers scored deep scratches across his face and he cried out in pain. He tried to fight back. They weren't strong, but nor was Arthur, and there were so many of them. The tearing sound of his shirt ripping was followed by the feel of cold, skinny fingers scratching across his chest - the dead skin like chilled sandpaper against him. Now they were clawing at his throat, their grip seeming to get stronger.

Arthur yelled at the ceiling of the cave - a wordless, meaningless howl. It was all he had left to do.

Across the room, Amelia was vaguely aware that Maggie had been knocked to the ground by one of the soldiers and was struggling to defend herself, while the Mummy was pinned against the wall. There was no help coming from anywhere.

The void closed in around Amelia's vision. A blackness that consumed her every sense, numbing everything but the pain. The Queen watched her like a child burning ants with a magnifying glass, dispassionately fascinated by the pain she could cause. In life she must have killed so many, must have so many times watched that moment when the last spark of life was snuffed out. But that had been a long time ago. It was something with which she was keen to reacquaint herself and Amelia would be her first victim in this, her second life.

"Would you like to say goodbye?" There was a matter of fact cruelty to everything the Queen did or said.

Amelia goggled at the Queen's face, blurred before her failing vision.

"I'll take that as a 'yes'."

The grip loosened incrementally, just enough for Amelia to cadge a few more seconds of consciousness and see more clearly. She managed to focus on the Queen's face and, for a moment, it was Izzy again. Nothing changed, and yet everything changed, and there was no mistaking the student who had turned up on Amelia's doorstep in tears all those months ago.

"Amelia?" said Izzy.

That was all she was allowed to say. The face shifted again, morphing back into that of the Queen - the same face and yet so very different in every respect.

"That should do."

The grip tightened once more, but Izzy's face remained sharp in Amelia's vision, and this time she saw red for a different reason. That was why she was here. That was why her life had taken the turn it had taken, away from what it should have been. Because of Izzy. Beautiful, sexy Izzy who Frank had been unable to resist. Izzy who had slept with Amelia's partner and who Amelia had then comforted. Amelia had never yelled at her, had never slapped her, she had never called her any of the names you were supposed to call women who did that sort of thing. Instead she had befriended the girl! She had become close friends with the woman who had stolen the man with whom she had planned to spend the rest of her life, and Amelia had never even mentioned it. They had never talked about it after that first night. The demons had never been exorcised, the wound had never healed, the anger had been repressed and left to fester, boiling away, held tightly under ferocious pressure as it grew more concentrated, more heated, screaming for release.

Until now.

Amelia was powerless against Queen Amunet, but right now all she could see was Izzy, and the strength poured into her. Amelia had never kicked another woman in her life, but she now kicked as hard as she could, with every last shred of strength she possessed, fired by an anger that she should have released a long time ago. Contained in that kick was the wrath of a betrayed woman, every bit of hate she had felt for Izzy and forced down because, to be honest, it hadn't been Izzy's fault. Well screw that! So what if it hadn't been Izzy's fault?! Life isn't fair! What happened to Amelia hadn't been fair so why should Izzy get all the fairness that had been denied to her? In that situation a person is not supposed to be rational, they are supposed to be angry. They are supposed to lash out wildly at whoever is there, not make the other party a cup of tea and let her cry on your shoulder. Contained in that kick was the rage that Amelia had held back and persuaded herself not to feel; at Izzy, at Frank, and at herself for letting it happen and being too stupid to notice. It was a kick that set her free. And in more ways than one.

No Witch Queen, be she ever so supernaturally magical, is immune to a good strong kick in the gut. Amunet doubled up, clutching her stomach, dropping Amelia as she went. It was unlikely that, in her former life, anyone had ever dared kick the Queen. Well, times had changed.

As Amelia hit the ground, her legs started to buckle beneath her, oxygen deprived limbs all screaming out for nourishment, blood pounding through her, trying to get everywhere at once. But she forced weakness and pain from her mind. She had a narrow window - she could not waste it. Even as Amelia moved, the Queen was straightening up again, quickly recovering from her shock. Amelia's hand shot out, grabbing the chain around Amunet's neck and pulling it over her head. As it went, the Queen screamed and reached forward, clawing the air, grasping for the jewel. But Amelia lurched aside as quickly as her leaden limbs would allow. She brought the jewel around in a wide, wind-milling arc and, with whatever strength she had left, smashed it to the ground.

She followed it down, dropping to hands and knees, coughing and choking whilst still trying to force air into her lungs. Had they won? Had she won?

Arthur gasped.

They had stopped. Everything had stopped. It was so quiet and still now that he could actually hear the blood trickling down his cheek beneath his own strained breathing.

"Arthur?" Andoheb's voice emerged out of the darkness.

"Still here." Arthur was almost afraid to speak, as if his voice might bring the soldiers out of whatever resting state they had slipped back into.

"What's happening?"

"I don't know."

He stayed where he was, hemmed in by darkness; relief and fear doing battle in his belly.

"Amelia?"

She must have blacked out for a second. Maybe longer. Maybe the whole thing was just a dream.

Amelia opened her eyes and squinted into the face of Maggie Moran. Blood was smeared across one side of her face, plastering her hair to her forehead.

"Still with us?" she asked.

"Are you alright?" Amelia asked weakly - her throat hurt horribly.

"Time will tell. You kicked some ass there."

"Izzy?!" There was panic in Amelia's voice. She had turned on her friend - what had the result of that been?

"Amelia." Izzy loomed into Amelia's vision, hugging her close and tight. "Thank you."

"For what?"

Izzy pulled back. "What do you mean; for what? You saved my life."

"Yeah. Yeah, I guess I did." There was no need for her to know how. At least not the details. "Sorry about..."

Izzy rubbed her stomach. "You've got a kick on you. But I know you did it to help me."

"Yeah." It was out of her system now, and there was no reason that Amelia and Izzy could not continue as friends. They made good friends. "Now, where's that bloody cat?"

"Made a dash for it," said Maggie.

"Typical."

"So what now?" asked Izzy.

Amelia was about to respond, but something had claimed Maggie's attention, and from the look on her face it was nothing good.

"Maggie?"

"I don't think he's done yet."

Amelia followed the direction of Maggie's gaze to where the Mummy stood amongst the now still soldiers who had at one time, four thousand years ago, fought alongside him as comrades in revolution. As ever it was hard to read the Mummy's face, but there was something in Setka's now that made Amelia instantly understand why Maggie was worried.

There was the sound of a match striking, the flare of light sudden and intrusive after the total darkness. Andoheb reached the match through the bars and Arthur suppressed a squeal as he saw the soldiers still arrayed around him. They stood like statues, perfectly motionless.

"Any thoughts?" wondered Andoheb.

"None that spring to mind."

"No bullets left in the gun I suppose?"

Arthur checked, and against all the odds found there was one. "I'll get you out. Before..." He hesitated, not wanting to tempt fate. "Before anything else happens."

"What do you think is wrong with them?" asked Andoheb.

Arthur did not answer. He was trying not to think about it. The soldiers were as still as stone, and yet he could not get over the feeling that they were not merely standing, they were waiting.

The Mummy's bandages were tattered now, damaged in the fight to reveal the shrivelled skin beneath. But he stood with more authority than ever as he turned to survey the room, filled with the men whom he had led in life. And he spoke.

"Comrades!" Professor Muller's voice coming from behind them made all three women jump. "Sorry," he added.

"This isn't the time," said Amelia, hastily, "but I'm a big fan of your work."

"Thank you."

"He's talking again," Maggie cut in sharply.

"Time has passed, my friends." Muller picked up the translation. "The world has changed. When we last breathed we faced an insurmountable foe to fight for our rights. Now that foe is gone. We have outlived her. Our reward - our justice! - has been slow in coming, but there is a world out there that is ours for the taking! A larger one than we ever knew. They have no power that can stop us. The world is a fair price for what we have been through. What we have suffered. We shall not stop till we have what we deserve!"

If you had asked him beforehand, Arthur would have said unhesitatingly, that shooting off a lock is something that only works in the movies. And yet it did work!

"We have to find the others," said Andoheb, wrapping Arthur in a bear hug as he came out of his cell.

Arthur nodded. "Any idea where they were taken?"

"No. Is there much to search?"

Arthur was about to answer when a sound caught his attention. Immediately he looked back to the soldiers, but they remained like statues - imminent but unmoving. He listened again. There was no doubt about it; someone was coming.

It was only when she was about six feet from the mummy of Setka that Amelia realised she was walking towards him. Her feet had started moving of their own accord, apparently assuming that her brain would come up with some sort of a plan by the time they arrived.

She reached out and touched the Mummy's arm, trying not shrink from the feel of dead skin beneath her fingers.

Setka turned to look at her. One of his turquoise eyes had been cracked in the fight, but he still seemed able to see through them. How much did he recall of what he had been through back then? What Queen Amunet had put him through? Based on his words and attitude, he remembered all of it. It was tough to go against him. In a way, he was right; his people had been treated abominably and if anyone deserved the chance to go conquer the world, then it was them.

But that's not how history works. You can't study history without gaining some sort of shell of objectivity. You can't wonder at the Forbidden City in China *and* despise it as a monument to all those who died in its construction. You can't marvel at the unique civilisations of South America *and* abhor them for blood sacrifices some practiced. You can't judge history; you can't take sides; above all, you can't change it. You can only look at it for what it is - immutable and unchangeable - and understand that, for all its tremendous cruelties, we are a product of it. If it hadn't been for each event, terrible or banal, then you might not even be here to wish it hadn't happened. Look at it, learn from it. Don't try to fix it.

Of course, those are easy things to say when it's all theoretical. Very few historians (one might almost say none) have to stand face to face with the living dead and explain to them why, despite the horrors of their own existence, they don't get a second chance, that their time is passed. The dead stay dead.

"Hi," said Amelia. Probably the least impressive beginning to a speech designed to save the world that has ever been spoken.

Setka's ancient face knotted into a frown and Professor Muller once again popped up to translate.

"You are a leader here?" the Mummy asked.

"No."

"A warrior?"

"No."

"I thought not."

"Hey, I think I did pretty well!" Amelia objected.

"You will not do so well against me."

There was no denying that. As Setka's mind had returned to him, so it seemed had his strength. With a vast army of undead soldiers who could not be killed, perhaps he could conquer the world. Certainly he could kill a lot of people in the attempt.

On the tip of Amelia's tongue hovered a speech about the rights of man; about how wrong it was to kill; about how Setka ran the risk of becoming as bad as Amunet if he went down this road, and that he was too good a man to do that; about how he had already killed innocent men under the influence of the Priest's spell and why would he want to kill more? But those words did not come, instead she said simply. "She's dead. It's over."

The Mummy glanced to the bloody remains of Amunet on the altar. They were empty now. The destruction of the jewel had ended her.

Amelia looked at the revolutionaries. "All your friends want now is to rest."

The Mummy reached up to his face and, with difficulty, extracted the turquoise insets that had served as eyes, revealing the ragged, hollow sockets beneath.

"I am myself again," Muller translated, a catch in his voice.

A shiver passed through Amelia as she looked into the empty eyes and saw a single tear force its way from a long dead duct, and trickle down the dry skin of the Mummy's cheek.

Setka stiffened, his body becoming rigid, life abandoning it as if it had never even been there. He fell to the floor. And then they all followed him - the revolutionaries tumbled to the ground, shattering as they went into dust and bones. Whatever sort of rest there was in the Field of Rushes, they deserved it.

"Miss Evans?"

The sad sight had so hypnotised Amelia that she had not heard the people come in. There was Arthur and Professor Andoheb, there was the remainder of the excavation team, there were some other people whom Amelia did not know, and there at the head of all of them, was Boris.

He flashed a small smile at Amelia. "I seem to have arrived late."

Epilogue

The body of Queen Amunet was burnt. Her ashes were sealed in a jar, which was locked in a box, which was placed back in her tomb. The tomb was sealed, and the warnings inscribed on its door in the language of the Lost Dynasty were augmented by new ones in Egyptian, English and every other language for which there was space: 'Do Not Open. SERIOUSLY, Do Not Open.'

The Fitzwilliam Museum was not pleased by the news that it would not be getting its star Mummy back, but Professor Andoheb had some pull with senior archaeological bodies in Egypt and England, and the decision was final. The mummy of Setka would remain with his comrades in the city of the dead beneath the Sarranekh.

Investigations were carried out into who might have hired the American tomb robber, Jago, to steal the mummy of Amunet - a rare treasure for any serious collector. But this official investigation came to nothing, and in fact was abandoned surprisingly quickly.

"Money talks," Boris observed. "Universal will conduct our own investigation. We'll find him."

When the artefacts from the tomb of Queen Amunet became public knowledge they were hailed as the greatest archaeological discoveries since Tutankhamen. Andoheb invited Arthur to remain in Egypt to participate in further investigation into the items and into the area surrounding the tomb, which surely had some deeper connection to the Lost Dynasty. Arthur declined, politely. He felt that he had learned a great deal from his first field expedition, but the most important thing that he had learned was that it would also be his last. Some people are meant to be out in the heat and the danger, others are meant to sit in comfortable reading rooms in large university libraries, poring over pictures and providing vital context to discoveries made out there in the big, wide world. The most important thing a person can learn is who they are, and Arthur had a better idea of that than ever before, and was happy in the knowledge. It was with this newfound self-knowledge in mind that he ended his relationship with Helen on his return. Better to be single than to be with someone who insisted he try to be something he was not.

Izzy returned to her course in Cambridge with a new respect for what goes into the making of a legend. She began writing their story, fulfilling a long-held ambition to be an author. To fill in some of the blanks she was able to make regular visits to the office of Cambridge University's newest professor. With his work on the language of the Lost Dynasty now officially recognised, the University was happy to welcome Professor Muller back after his 'brief hiatus from employment'. As with all events in his life, Old Joe took it in his stride, and settled happily into his old job without missing a beat.

It did gall Amelia a little that the work, to which she had devoted much of her life, had already been completed by someone else some years previously, but she had other things on her mind. Before they left Egypt, Boris took her to one side.

"You did an incredible job here."

"Thanks."

"And I believe you saved my life."

Amelia shrugged. "Seemed like the thing to do."

"I've been authorised to make you an offer."

"Authorised by whom?"

"By Universal," Boris explained. "They want you. That is to say, I put in a recommendation and based on that, they want to hire you."

"To work for Universal Egyptology?"

Boris made a face. "Universal is a slightly larger concern than I may have let on. We do work in places other than Egypt."

"Keeping the dead, dead?"

"Among other things. I think your skills would translate well. You seem to have a knack for it. What do you say?"

Later that day, Amelia tracked down Maggie, who was packing all her worldly possessions into a single rucksack. It wasn't actually that difficult; a handful of clothes, a toothbrush, a gun and a Wham! T-shirt took up little space.

"Going somewhere?"

Maggie nodded. "Taking a break from Egypt."

"Really?" said Amelia, straight-faced. "Why?"

"I think the sun might be getting to me."

"Where are you headed?"

Maggie shrugged. "Not sure yet. I'm pretty employable. Looking at digs. Who's crewing up. Seeing what grabs me."

Amelia nodded, drawing casual patterns in the dust with her

foot. "Look, my area of study is about to get permanently closed down by Professor Muller - lovely guy, wish him all the best, but... I genuinely don't know what I'm going to do next. This has all been..." She sought for words. "Horrifying. I mean, genuinely horrifying. But also weirdly good. I don't want to give up what I do - I love what I do and I'm good at it - but I feel like maybe I need a new challenge and..."

"For the love of God," Maggie rolled her eyes, "if you want to come with, just say."

Amelia paused. Was that what she wanted? She genuinely hadn't been sure when she'd started this conversation. "Would I be in the way?"

"Yes. But no more than anyone else."

There was a very comfortable flat back in Cambridge waiting for her. "I'm not really sure how I can..."

"There's a dig in the Carpathian mountains," Maggie interrupted. "They've found something no one can explain, covered with inscriptions no one can translate. Weird shit and that. In or out?"

"In."

"Good."

And it was. As soon as the decision was made Amelia felt a weight lifted. Just as she had known that Boris's offer was not right for her, she knew that this one was. There was no reason you couldn't be a bookish tea-enthusiast and an archaeological adventurer at the same time. The two weren't mutually exclusive - you just had to budget your time carefully and follow what your heart wanted at any given time. Right now, hers wanted adventure. And if books and tea could be involved, so much the better.

"The Carpathian mountains?"

"In Romania," Maggie added. "The old Transylvanian region."

"When do we leave?"

The nearest village to the Sarranekh is still many miles distant from the tombs of Queen Amunet and the revolutionary army of Setka. It is one of the remotest spots imaginable, based around an old well that has been providing clean water for centuries, surrounded on all sides by empty, uncrossable desert.

Only a few of the inhabitants saw the cat, and none of them

were able to say why the animal, which seemed quite ordinary, made such an impression on them. What was most remarkable about it was that it had come from the desert, which ought not to have been possible. It stopped to drink at the well, then set off again into the desert, heading north, and seeming to have a very definite destination in mind.

The End

Made in the USA
Lexington, KY
20 October 2017